Murder — All Kinds

Murder — All Kinds

By William L. DeAndrea
Introduction by Jane Haddam

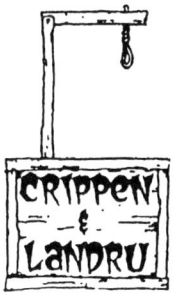

Crippen & Landru Publishers
Norfolk, Virginia
2003

Copyright © 2003 by Jane Haddam

Cover artwork by Juha Lindroos

"Lost Classics" cover design by Deborah Miller

Crippen & Landru logo by Eric Greene

ISBN (cloth edition): 1–932009–12–4
ISBN (trade edition): 1–932009–13–2

FIRST EDITION

Crippen & Landru Publishers
P.O. Box 9315
Norfolk, VA 23505
USA

www.crippenlandru.com
CrippenLandru@earthlink.net

Contents

Introduction	7

Matt Cobb, Special Projects

Snowy Reception	11
Killed Top to Bottom	19
Killed in Midstream	35
Killed in Good Company	62

Other Stories

Hero's Welcome	89
Sabotage	94
A Friend of Mine	119
The Adventure of the Cripple Parade	139
The Adventure of the Christmas Tree	153
Prince Charming	173
Murder at the End of the World	191
Bibliography	208

Introduction

Just about a week ago, I promised Doug Greene to deliver this essay in less than twenty four hours. I was not, I thought, exaggerating the ease with which I could write it. In the nearly six years since Bill died, I've written many essays on his life and work, and they've never caused me any trouble. It isn't as if my memory of him is fading. If anything, it has become stronger the longer he's been gone, helped along by the fact that our older son is so very much like him, in looks and attitude, that there are times when it almost seems I have him back again. The problem, I suppose, is that I don't have him back again, and never will. Some part of me that has never accepted that fact has become resistant to the writing of eulogies.

Still, a eulogy is required of me, and Bill certainly deserves one, another one, many more. It's Labor Day, 2002, as I write this, and it was on Labor Day, 1996, that Bill and I first realized that we'd lost the fight, and he was — inevitably — dying. That may sound strange, under the circumstances. By then, he'd been living for over a year with a rare form of cancer that we both knew was fatal more often than not. Still, up until that day, we'd had hope, and progress reports good enough to give us reason to think we were not being unrealistic. Six weeks later, a doctor who had treated Bill's cancer but hadn't seen him since the 15 of August would call the house and, being told that Bill *had* died, demand incredulously, "Of *what?*"

Bill died of a carcinoid tumor that had spread to his liver long before we ever caught it. If the tumor hadn't suddenly become virulently active and begun metastasizing to his lungs and his lymph nodes with the rapidity of kudzu in Arkansas, his life might have been saved by a liver transplant. He was just weeks away from being approved for the transplant list. The tumor had lain dormant and inert for months. It had stubbornly refused to shrink with chemo, but it hadn't been growing, either. Then, all of a sudden, it did grow, fast, and in a matter of days Bill was disoriented, weak, half–comatose, dying.

Some of the stories in this book were written during that long stretch that we lived with Bill's cancer — and, by the way, agreed with Crippen & Landru that there would be a book of short stories at all. Our sons were then nine and two. The younger one didn't understand what was going on. The older one did, and spent most of his time terrified. Bill produced a remarkable amount of work during that last year, including the second novel in his last mystery series (*Fatal Elixir*, published by Walker) and a long partial for a new Matt Cobb he would never get to finish. He wrote columns and reviews. He helped our older son work on *his* novel. Then there came a day when he couldn't sit up for more than a few minutes at a time, and couldn't remember what he'd meant to write in the next sentence, and lost the thread of a conversation in the middle of delivering his own lines.

If I had to say what was most remarkable about the stories in this volume, it would be the fact that it's impossible to tell which were written when he was sick and which when he was well. Bill DeAndrea had the strongest narrative voice I've ever heard. It was so distinct and so insistent, so utterly himself, that even now I can hear his voice in my head whenever I read what he wrote. And even when the author of a passage isn't identified, I know what he wrote just by the way he wrote it.

As a voice for mystery and suspense, it's surprising gentle, almost always opting for humor and understatement rather than graphic detail and intellectual harshness. Bill often found people both strange and funny, but he almost never found them contemptible. In his non-fiction essays and columns, he could lash out at stupidity and injustice. In his fiction, he looked on everyone — even murderers with the basest of motives — as deserving of understanding if not respect. Most of all, he found the world a very funny place.

I hope you enjoy the stories in this volume, and your acquaintance, or reacquaintance, with the man who wrote them. Bill loved to write and he loved to be read. He carried on correspondences with fans that spanned decades, arguing the finer points of humor in the mystery and the relative literary worth of Chandler and Westlake. His real voice, like his narrative one, was always full of laughter.

Maybe the truth is that Bill was a man who believed that fairy tales come true, and that we can live happily ever after — but his fairy tales were more like the fractured ones from the old *Rocky and Bullwinkle* show than anything that might have been written by brothers named Grimm. These stories are fairy tales in their way, and at the same time homage to the genre he spent his life immersed in.

Jane Haddam

Snowy Reception

I was tired of concrete, so I tried looking at the sky for a while. It was hard to tell the difference. The clouds and the Kennedy Airport runways were the same dark grey and both were threatening to bring trouble from over the horizon.

I turned my overcoat collar up against the late–winter wind and said, "We're standing out here freezing and the damned plane probably isn't even going to land."

"Why not?" Burke snarled. Burke was a Federal agent, second in command of the New York office.

"Because it's going to snow," I told him. "The sky looks exactly like it did before the last two blizzards."

"You really think so, Cobb?" Rogers put in. He was also a Federal agent, but he had a long way to go before he'd have a snarl perfected. He was a good young boy from Mobile who'd gone right from college into the Caracas office of the agency. This was his first trip north of the Mason–Dixon Line, and his enthusiasm at the prospect of seeing snow for the first time was a little more than he could filter from his voice.

Burke shot him a look that spoke badly for the agency's *esprit de corps*. "It'll land. Snow or no snow. Don't doubt that for a second." He lifted his walkie–talkie and asked the tower, for the fourth time in three minutes, if the special Mideast Airways flight was on schedule. It was.

The young woman standing beside him began to laugh. Her name was Laurel Magee. She was a petite twenty–year–old with a bright smile and yellow hair. In her prison uniform she looked like a cashiered Girl Scout, but Uncle Sam had bought her a cape for this little outing, to keep her warm and to hide the manacles. Laurel, a confirmed terrorist, had committed four murders the authorities had been able to prove. She kept laughing.

"Stop it," Burke snarled.

She didn't stop. "Wait, pig. Just wait till Leo gets back. The Revolution's not dead, you know — only dozing. Now that Leo's coming back, it's going to wake up. And all pigs like you will be executed."

Rogers was going to argue with her. I figured the cold must be affecting his brain. You might as well argue with a telephone pole as with a fanatic.

I sighed. I had come to the network to make game shows, and this was what I got for allowing myself to be put in charge of the Department of Special Projects instead. Special Projects deals with the unusual problems the network sometimes has — not strange, considering we're a giant corporation that's a very visible part of the daily lives of two hundred million Americans.

This was the second time Leo Calvin had become an unusual problem for us. Until about four years ago, Leo had been a healthy, normal middle–class boy from Buffalo, not especially troublesome or even noticeable. Then he somehow made simultaneous discoveries of radical politics and guns, and set himself up as Generalissimo of the League to End Oppression — modestly abbreviated as LEO. One of the first operations Leo planned for LEO was a way to bring the message to the people — by taking over the network.

Leo Calvin and a few followers, including Laurel, tried to shoot their way into the studio of the *Evening News* and hold the anchorman hostage while they had their say. They didn't make it, but they did manage to kill six network security men while losing four of their own people.

I was a witness at the trial. Fortunately for me, my testimony was two days finished when the rest of the LEO raided the courtroom. They left a few more bodies behind, but they did manage to spring their leader.

That was the last I'd heard of him until this morning when Burke and Rogers showed up at my office, dragging Laurel behind them and asking me if I was Matt Cobb.

I told them yes, I'd changed my name to match the sign on the desk. Then they started talking about Leo Calvin, and I no longer felt like making jokes.

The agency, it seemed, had never stopped trying to track him. Every once in a while, Leo would poke his nose up a bit from the international underground — first with the PLO, then with the Baader–Meinhof gang, the Italian Red Brigades, and back to the PLO.

"That's where we got a solid line on him," Burke said. "One of our overseas agents, who was on a totally different assignment, stumbled across him in one of the more militant Persian Gulf sheikhdoms." Actually, he used the name of the country, but the network has a couple of people there and the State Department wants the whole thing played down, so I'll leave it out.

Burke went on. "Rogers was receiving this agent's messages — that's the way the pipeline works."

"Used to work," Rogers drawled.

"Anyway," Burke continued, "our man told Rogers that Calvin's had plastic surgery and is planning to come back to the States."

I nodded. "He wants to put all his postgraduate education in bombing and maiming to work, I guess. But how am I involved? If he's had plastic surgery, I doubt if I'd recognize him."

"You might, though. That's what she's here for." He pointed at Laurel, who made a rude gesture.

"You promised to help, honey," Rogers reminded her.

"I lied. I wanted a change of scenery, that's all. What are you going to do — beat me?" I looked at her. Laurel was a living anachronism. For her, time had apparently stopped in 1969.

I was positive Rogers and Burke had never expected her to cooperate. The idea was to show her to Calvin and see how *he* reacted. It seemed like a very long shot. For the first time I realized just how desperate the agents must be.

"You still haven't told me what you want from me," I said.

Burke scratched his nose. "Our man in the Middle East told us Leo Calvin has wangled his way into the sheikhdom's delegation to that little clambake you're holding here."

Now *I* wanted to call him a pig. Damn, I thought fervently. This is what the network gets for trying to be nice.

You see, television is all over the world now, but in a lot of countries, particularly third-world nations, they're trying to make it from the Stone Age to the Video Age in one jump. Sometimes they ask the network for help.

Then, a little while ago, some genius in the public-relations department got the idea to have a bunch of foreign technicians come to New York for the network Third World International Broadcasting Seminar. In all fairness, I must admit I thought it was a great idea when I first heard about it. But now Leo Calvin was flying back, to blow us all up most likely, and the network was picking up the tab.

I looked blearily at Rogers. "I hope your contact told you what name our friend Leo is using."

"No, he didn't," the southerner drawled. "He was killed before he had the chance."

"Oh," I said, ignoring Laurel's smile. "Well, can't you —"

Bust everybody, fingerprint 'em, and weed Calvin out that way? No." He went on to explain, but I could already figure out why.

In going over the guest list for the conference, the network had discovered that none of the delegates had ever been in the U. S. before — most had never even left their native countries. Then they found out that one of the participants, a postage-stamp island in the Pacific, had been a country for so short a time they hadn't even had a chance to send us an ambassador yet — the delegation would be their first official visitors to the U.S. In their youthful exuberance, the government announced full diplomatic status for the three people they were sending. That was also fine — kind of cute, in fact.

But sometimes countries can be more infantile than little kids. When word got out that Tinynesia was going to be represented by diplomats, everybody else had to be represented by diplomats, all with diplomatic immunity. Including, of course, the delegation Leo Calvin had wormed his way into — the one that was landing in two hours.

"So if we can just spot Calvin —" Burke was saying.

"— we can nail him with no trouble at all," Rogers finished for him. "But if you happen to spot the wrong man —"

"All of a sudden it depends on me?" I said.

"You're all we have, Cobb — or all we have time to get."

"Gee," I said, not very happy, "just for the record, what happens if I finger the wrong man? Or if I honestly can't recognize anybody?"

"If you're wrong, the Arab countries all get mad," Burke said, "and the United States may never see another drop of oil. If you can't do anything, Leo Calvin's back in business."

Laurel was laughing again. I was getting sick of all three of them.

"Well, Cobb?" Rogers asked earnestly.

I sighed. "We'd better get out to the airport, or we'll miss the damn plane completely."

Something cold and gritty landed in my eye. I shook myself from my reverie enough to notice that the snow had started. About a second and a half later, Rogers started spinning around with his palms out, grinning like an idiot. Sometimes I wonder if the security of our country is in the right hands.

Burke looked as if he had a few doubts on the subject himself, and seemed about to say something when his radio squawked to tell him the plane was coming in. It must have been my imagination, of course, but the entire airport seemed to stop moving and tense up, just as I was doing.

We went in out of the snow and walked through the terminal toward the arrival gate. Laurel Magee was the only one who spoke, and she kept telling the world at large that we were just too stupid and too puny to thwart her leader. I would have argued with her, but I had a sickening feeling she was right.

Because, of course, Leo Calvin could look like anything now. They can do wonders with plastic surgery these days — ask half the actors you see on the network. The only thing they wouldn't have been able to do about Leo was make him shorter — and that was no help, since he was a nice, anonymous average height to begin with.

If he was supposed to pass for a native of the Middle East, it was a sure bet his skin color would be different, but what about his skin texture, facial features, voice, and walk? Any of those things could have been changed, surgically or otherwise.

The concrete didn't look any better up close than it had from the observation deck, and the 727 rolled up looking like a winged whale. We weren't the only ones out there on the runway — there were representatives from the sheikhdom and a minor-league flunky from the network, along with a photographer. If Rogers, Burke, and I were going to mess up, it wasn't going to be in private.

The ground crew rolled the stairway to the hatch and a stewardess took her position at the door.

"Here they come," Rogers said.

"Yeah," I said, "thanks for telling me."

There were about forty of them, and they all looked alike, right down to their identical grey western-style business suits and blue ties. Not one had an overcoat. Not one looked the slightest bit like Leo Calvin.

"Well, Cobb?" asked Burke.

"Leave me alone," I snapped.

There was a noise from the knot of passengers. Someone, obviously the man in charge, was ordering his companions to hurry up.

Laurel giggled. "Look," she said, pointing to them and nudging Rogers. "They're as bad as you are, redneck."

She was right. Those sons of the desert were delighting in the snow, something they'd never seen before, just as Rogers had earlier.

Then it came to me. "Thanks, Laurel," I said quietly.

She didn't know what I was talking about, but the two agents looked at me expectantly. "Wait a second," I said.

Burke didn't feel like waiting and was about to speak when another burst of impatience came from the head man in the delegation.

"That's Leo," I said. "The grumpy one."

"Are you sure?" Rogers demanded.

"Of course I'm sure, clown. And what would you do if I weren't?"

They didn't answer. Instead they walked toward the group, leaving me to guard Laurel, who was insulting me with verve and imagination. "Save it," I told her. "I could be wrong."

Grumpy was so calm at the approach of the two Federal men I decided I *was* wrong. For ten seconds, nothing happened. Then he ran. I figured Rogers or Burke had said a magic phrase, like "Hell or high water, we're getting your fingerprints." Whatever the provocation, I watched the chase with relief.

Leo started running away from the terminal, decided there was no future in that, circled around a landing gear, and headed back toward the door. It was a smart move — the agents couldn't shoot at him while he was running into a crowd of people.

I was going to stand aside and trip him as he ran past, but Laurel screamed at him to watch out for me. So I left her unguarded — she couldn't get too far in manacles, I figured — and joined the chase.

I may as well take the credit for catching him. When he saw me coming he changed course, around the corner of the building, and was run over by a luggage truck.

There's a hospital at the airport. They brought Leo there and set his broken bones. Then Burke and I went in to talk to him while Rogers reported back to Washington.

"Hello, Leo," I said. "Long time no see."

He spat on the hospital linen, then proved he knew as many obscenities as Laurel did. I couldn't stop looking at him.

"What are you looking at?" he demanded angrily.

"A loser," I said affably. "But it's amazing. You look totally different. I never would have recognized you."

Burke snorted. "What are you talking about, Cobb? How did you finger him if you didn't recognize him?"

"I *still* don't actually recognize him," I said to Burke.

Leo said, "Then how did you know? Even if you were told I'd be on that flight, I was sure you'd never spot me as the head man."

"That was the trouble. You spent too much effort acting like the boss and not enough acting like an Arab — especially one leaving his sheikhdom for the first time."

"What do you mean?" Burke asked.

"I mean there's something else besides your fingerprints that plastic surgery can't change — your past.

"I got my clues from Rogers and Laurel — she's going to love knowing she betrayed you in spite of herself. Rogers is from the South, and when the snow started he reacted to it like a schoolboy, in spite of the tense situation.

"You and Burke and I are New Yorkers, and snow has long since become just a nuisance to us. But for the people who got off that plane tonight, snow was as much a novelty as it was for Rogers. They wanted to stand around and enjoy it, but the head man kept trying to hurry them up. And for no good reason. All else being equal, he should have been enjoying the snow as much as the rest of them."

Burke was choking, and Leo had turned pale under his new skin. "You mean," Burke sputtered, *"that's all you had?"*

I looked sheepishly at him. "It seemed a lot more conclusive at the time. Besides, I'm not a cop — I'm a TV man. And in television you learn never to trust anyone who isn't smiling."

Killed Top to Bottom

Gunfire rang out, and everybody in the studio went down as if he'd been shot. One of us had been — K.L. Adkinsen, PhD., professor of linguistics, and chairman of the Whitten College Communications Council. Tonight though, he was the host of a show for local cable called *The Whitten College Channel Presents a Media Circus*. Adkinsen was the ringmaster, and the newly built studio had been decked out to look like a fairgrounds, with a painted backdrop and cardboard mock–ups of concession stands. There were balloons everywhere. A little sad–faced clown stood before three or four tanks of helium almost as tall as he was, filling balloons and handing them out to everyone who walked by.

Adkinsen was speaking at the Media Circus's podium when the shooting started. When I heard the first shot, I thought it was just a balloon popping. That had been happening from time to time all evening, and people had gotten used to it. This one was louder, but I wouldn't have given it another thought, except that Adkinsen's top hat flew off. He'd been saying something about "closer ties between the college and the larger community that supports and nurtures it …" but when the hat went west he turned with a puzzled look on his face to see where it went.

That's when the second shot went off. This one hit him in the side of his lofty brow, right where the smooth skin of his handsome face met his prematurely silver hair.

There were three more shots, and two of them hit him, but I didn't see it. I was too busy hugging the grey–painted concrete of the studio floor, trying to find a crack to crawl into. There was a lot of gasping and screaming and thumping as the other two hundred or so people in the room did the same. A lot of them were crawling behind the cardboard and canvas of the set, which struck me as fairly foolish. A bullet doesn't care much for one layer of cardboard or canvas, or even two or three.

It struck me as a sad commentary on our times that so many people should know what to do at the sound of gunfire. Either that, or unrest on college campuses was even worse than it had been when I'd gone to Whitten.

Not quite everybody, my brain said. It took me a second to catch up with it. Not everybody had hit the deck. One person was still standing, the sad little clown with the balloons. If I turned my head slightly I could see him standing as if in shock, with a forlorn bunch of 15 or 20 balloons rising with agonizing slowness to the ceiling above his head. He was looking at the body as if there were going to be a quiz on it later.

I could see that lone figure standing right near the helium tanks. What if the killer decided to drop the clown with a bullet, and the bullet pierced one of the tanks? Gas, under high pressure would rip the steel to shreds. The shreds would turn from a mess to a holocaust before you could blink.

"Get down," I said.

The clown kept staring at the podium. Tears glistened on white cheeks.

"Get *down*, dammit!" I said. The clown turned to me and scowled, as if I were spoiling his concentration at a concert.

"*Down!*" I said again.

The clown wrote me off as a bad job and returned to gazing at the stiff and crying.

I respect grief, but this was ridiculous. Not only was this clown (possibly) putting two hundred of us in deadly danger, he wasn't doing Adkinsen any good either. Maybe 15 seconds had gone by since the last shot. That was not long enough to assume our friend with the gun was finished.

I swore under my breath, gathered my legs under me, ran five steps in a crouch, and brought the clown down with a waist-high football tackle that ended with us lying on the ground as safe a distance as I could manage from the helium tanks.

"Get off me!" the clown said. The voice was somewhat strangled. I'm six–two and weigh 225 pounds, and gentleness had been low on my list of priorities when I'd launched the tackle.

White gloved hands beat feebly on my back. The voice yelling curses at me got stronger as it went along. It was high and clear. And this clown was pretty soft under the motley.

Oops. A Bozoette.

"Okay," I whispered urgently. "I'm sorry. But there's danger here; you go running around you'll make it worse. Try to calm down."

It didn't work. She started screaming.

"Adkinsen's dead," I said. Diplomacy was pretty low on my list by now, too. "The idea is not to join him, right?"

No luck. The screaming was getting worse. I was trying to figure out what to do when guys from campus security came in with guns. Good, I thought — let somebody else take some responsibility around here.

One of the security men came over to me and my friend. I was just about to roll off her and let her tell him her story when he smashed me in the side of the head with a six–battery flashlight, and I was gone.

I had driven from New York to Sewanka in the Southern Tier yesterday, by invitation. If I'd gotten the invitation privately, I might have skipped it, but while the envelope had been addressed to "Matthew Cobb," it had been sent through the network's PR Department, and they'd made me go.

My alma mater, Whitten College, in Sewanka, New York, after untold pain, travail, and fund–raising, was at last ready to open their newly built studio and launch their own cable TV channel on the local system, thereby bringing the benefits of faculty and student thinking to the culture–starved multitudes of the Southern Tier of New York state.

To mark the occasion, various alumni VIP's were being invited, of which I was one, by virtue of my exalted position at the network.

"Oh, give me a break," I said, but the powers above me were adamant.

The first thing on yesterday's agenda had been the welcoming reception. A graduate student named Katherine Streeter had been assigned to introduce me around. She was dark and pretty, and she managed to give an impression of shyness without ever doing anything that could legitimately be characterized as shy. She certainly didn't hesitate to bust up conversations to say I was "Matt Cobb, class of seventy–blah, a vice–president at the network in New York." I've never been introduced to so many people who didn't give a damn in my life.

Some people cared. Professor Harrison Billings of the Division of Performing Arts, for instance. Professor Billings was head of the drama department. Nothing ethereal about him though. He was bald and burly and looked like a plumber. He had a grip like one too.

He was trying hard to look academic. He wore a black turtleneck under a grey corduroy jacket with patched elbows. He smoked a pipe. He'd come to Whitten since my time, but I had heard of him from actors who worked for the network. He was well spoken of. I told him so.

"Nice to hear you say that, Mr. Cobb. It's always nice to know that *someone* holds a good opinion of you." Then he favored Ms. Streeter with a sardonic smile.

Oh great, campus politics.

"Have you come to offer advice on programming the cable service, Mr. Cobb?"

"Oh, no. Just an alumnus here for the festivities."

"Very wise of you. Chances are, you wouldn't be listened to. Adkinsen has very firm ideas about what's going to be broadcast. Rock hard you might say."

"Oh," Katherine Streeter said. "There's Dean Jamison." She pulled me away.

As we crossed the room, I made my voice low and said, "What was that all about?"

"Professor Billings is upset that *he* wasn't named to head up the cable channel. It got to be quite a power struggle."

"From the look he gave you, I take it you were on the other side."

"I don't count. I'm just Professor Adkinsen's grad assistant. I won't even be here past June. I'm going into the doctoral program at Farber."

I was duly impressed.

"Fellowship and everything." She looked at me earnestly. "Billings wanted to put on *experimental drama*."

"Well, I'm no big experimental drama fan, but what the hell, it is supposed to be a cultural service —"

"Every night. He wanted to put it on every night."

Then it was time to meet Adkinsen. Katherine Streeter showed me off like a prize fish. We shook hands.

Adkinsen's sharp blue eyes looked at me suspiciously. "Cobb," he said. "I remember you. You took a course of mine."

"For a while," I said.

"That's right," he said. "That's right. You dropped it. With some rancor, I recall. We had some sort of disagreement."

"Not at all, sir," I told him. "We had an agreement."

"I'm not sure I follow you."

You asked for it, I thought. "One day in class, you treated us to a rendition of a *New York Times* story about the latest casualty figures from Vietnam. According to you, the deaths were well deserved, and quite humorous. I tend to think young men getting killed for no goddamn good reason at all is not so funny. I raised my hand and asked you what any of it had to do with the linguistics I was supposed to be there to learn. You said there were some things more important than any academic regimen.

"And I agreed. I got up and left, walked to the administration building, and dropped your course. Like a hot brick."

"Ah," he said. He smiled expansively. "We were young and passionate then, weren't we? It was all so long ago."

"Yes," I said. "It was. But the boys are still dead. Good luck with the cable operation." I walked away.

I grabbed a few more *hor d'oeuvres* and a glass of champagne and put them where they belonged.

Katherine Streeter caught up with me. She was not happy. "You didn't tell me you knew him."

"It's not a favorite memory for both of us."

"Sometimes, I don't understand your generation at all."

Adkinsen's adventures weren't over for the evening. At one point, there was a party crasher, a tall skinny kid in white shirt and tie, wearing a tweed jacket he'd borrowed from someone a lot shorter than he was. People looked at him as he crossed the room, but they were invisible to him. He had a glare on his face, and he was bearing down on Professor Adkinsen like Michael Jordan heading for the hoop.

I was between mingles at the moment, so I watched. The kid had something that looked like a newspaper in his hand. When he caught up with Adkinsen, he was fuming, but he waited politely until there was a break in Adkinsen's conversation. Then he unrolled the paper and waved it in front of the professor's face. He smacked the paper with his hand, not gently, and said something. The professor looked angry, and sorely embarrassed.

Voices got loud.

"— damn well *better* find out what's going on!" the kid said.

"Please Mr. Johnson, I assure you ..." The kid showed signs of calming, and Adkinsen's voice fell into inaudibility. He took the kid by the elbow and walked him to the door, talking earnestly. The kid still looked upset, but he was nodding and agreeable by the time they got to the door. He shook Adkinsen's hand and left. The professor returned to his party.

Somebody groaned. Me, I think. Somebody said, "He's coming around." A third voice said, "Matt?" and I opened my eyes. That third voice belonged to E.R. Bowen, recently elected district attorney for Sewanka County, and an old friend of mine since college days.

"Aspirin," I said.

Eve laughed. "I thought you were going to ask where you were."

"I know where I am. In the Student Health Center. Why the hell did that guy clock me?"

The district attorney shook back her dark red hair. "He thought he was stopping a rape."

I tried to roll my eyes in disbelief, but it hurt. "Oh, brilliant," I said. "Yes, surrounded by two hundred people ducking gunfire and clawing for cover. The *perfect* circumstances to commit a rape."

Someone in a white suit handed me two pills and a little cup of water. I swallowed. While I did, he told me I was going to live. I'd been out about an hour.

"Feel up to coming along to headquarters?"

"Am I suspect or something?"

"Don't make jokes about it. You might be, if I didn't have a better one. You did have a fight with the victim at that reception last night."

"That was a *fight*? Come on, Eve."

"Well, a less than pleasant encounter."

"Who have you been talking to?"

"Everybody."

"Well, everybody is a jerk."

"I think so, too. That's why you're not a suspect. I asked you to come along in case you wanted to help out."

"I thought you had a suspect."

"I'm not sure everybody isn't wrong about him, either. Maybe you can help me find reasons not to arrest him that will keep the press off my back."

"Boy, it didn't take you long to become a politician."

I got up and followed her. Outside, Katherine Streeter was waiting on the sidewalk. Her face was recently scrubbed. She still wore the clown suit. She looked about 12 years old.

"It was you!" I said foolishly. "I didn't recognize your voice because you were screaming."

"I've been waiting, Mr. Cobb. I — I wanted to tell you I'm sorry. I shouldn't have panicked like that. My father was a cop. He told me all about people freezing in shooting situations, but after all the talk I heard about it growing up, I never thought I'd be one of them. Is your head all right?"

"They tell me I'll live."

She turned to Eve. "I've phoned a friend, Mrs. Bowen. I'll just get back to my apartment and change, then she'll drive me down to the Public Safety Building to give my formal statement."

Eve told her it could wait until morning, but Katherine said, "It's all right. I don't think I'll be able to sleep much, anyway."

The Public Safety Building was a pile of ugly grey limestone, courtesy of the WPA, circa 1933. Police headquarters was in the basement. Eve spoke to a young lieutenant. "Suspect ready?"

"Talking to his lawyer. Should be ready any minute." The lieutenant sounded just short of elated. The chief, it seemed, was in the Bahamas on vacation, and the lieutenant was feeling every ounce of the responsibility he'd assumed. They don't get many murders in Sewanka. He was delighted to have the D.A. take charge of things.

Eve led me to her office, told me to sit down. We made a little small talk. Then she told me the suspect's name was Alfie Johnson, and that he was a student at Whitten College.

The interrogation room was covered in off–white soundproof panels. The suspect sat looking at his fingers as they drummed the top of a cigarette–scarred table. His lawyer stood nearby. His name was Lou Weston. He was tall and bald and his face was fixed in a permanent look of mild regret, as if he rued eating that fourth taco.

Weston said his client was willing to answer questions about what had happened last night at the reception and tonight at the studio. Eve began, gently. She wanted to know what Johnson's crashing the reception had been all about.

"Somebody stole my paper. I wrote a paper for Dr. Adkinsen's class. He didn't have them back yet, but he told me I got an A–minus on it. I would have had a full A, but I lost points for grammar. Next thing I know, I pick up this week's *Native* —"

My God, I thought, is that thing still in business? It had started just about the time I'd arrived in Sewanka as the local "counterculture paper." It featured articles by undergraduates being pretentious about politics, films, and music, but it had nothing to do with the college. It was distributed free on campus, left in piles in dorm lobbies.

"— And I found my paper in it! Someone had done it as an article. This guy 'Daddy Cool,' he's in there every week. Fixed up my grammar, I guess, but everything else was the same. Changed the title. My paper was called 'Black English on a White Campus.' In the *Native* it was called 'Alma Mother.'

"I knew the Professor would be at that party, you know, so I dressed up and went to ask him what was going on. I wasn't causing any trouble. I just wanted to know."

"He said he didn't know what was going on, but that this wasn't the first weird thing that happened. He said someone had been messing around in his files."

Eve pursed her lips. "Did he say who it might be?"

"He didn't mention nobody — anybody, I mean — by name. He looked at somebody, though. Professor Billings. I knew him and Professor Billings have been feuding over this TV thing, but I didn't put too much store in just one look. Anyway, Dr. Adkinsen said he'd look at the *Native*, and call them and make sure they printed something about its being my work they published, and that he'd get to the bottom of things as soon as this TV thing was taken care of next day. Tonight. He'd give it his full attention."

"Did it ever cross your mind that Professor Adkinsen might have stolen your paper himself?"

"No, ma'am. Why would he?" Alfie Johnson's eyes showed a flash of anger. "Dr. Adkinsen was a full professor, and a main man in his field. Why's he need to steal some paper from a sophomore to make fifty bucks under a fake name in a little throw–away paper? Besides, he was my friend. Wasn't for him, I wouldn't be here." And Alfie Johnson told us how, as a freshman on the Whitten basketball team he'd struggled to meet academic standards, until he met the professor. Adkinsen had taken a real interest in him, arranged tutoring where he needed it, and cheered him up when he got discouraged.

"Why were you in the studio tonight?"

"It was open house. I wanted to see what was going on. Excuse me. I'd like to talk to my lawyer for a minute."

We left the room. Eve let go a breath that ruffled the hair over her brow. "What do you think?" she asked.

"If that's the best you can do for a suspect, you're hurting."

The lieutenant came up. "Any luck with Billings?" she asked.

"Not a bit. He won't admit anything except that he was there, and I don't think he'd have come across with that if it wasn't on videotape. He didn't know anything about Adkinsen's office being trashed. He says. What everybody else tells us was a blood feud over this cable TV thing, he describes as a difference of opinion, no animosity at all. Greatest respect for the man. Give me five more minutes, and I'll probably have him saying that Adkinsen isn't even dead, possibly not even wounded."

"Let him sit awhile," Eve said. "I'll talk to him later. Any luck on the gun?"

The lieutenant shook his head. "Not a trace of it. Sergeant Havers says they've searched that place top to bottom three times, and haven't found so much as a bean shooter."

My brain gave a little start, as though a bright idea had just passed through it. If it had, it had been moving too fast to recognize.

Eve was talking. "... want you to do now," she said, "is find the editor or publisher of the *Native* and find out who this 'Daddy Cool' is."

The lieutenant must have been at least my age, but he blushed. Actually looked at the ground and blushed. "I ... ahh ... I've already taken the liberty of starting on that, Ms. Bowen. Editor and publisher Roger Criss. I ... haven't been able to find him yet, to ask him who Daddy Cool is. He's not at his home or office or any of the places he usually hangs out."

Weston poked his head out of the interrogation room and said his client was ready for us.

"There was another reason I came to the TV thing tonight," Johnson said. "I wanted to tell Dr. Adkinsen something. I wanted to tell him I got impatient, and couldn't wait, and I went to see that Criss guy who puts out the *Native*. I didn't get any cooperation *at all* from that guy. He wouldn't tell me who 'Daddy Cool' was. Said it was confidential."

"When did you see Criss?" Eve said.

"I don't know. 'Bout eight–thirty. Just before I came to the studio."

"Did Criss mention anything about going anywhere?"

"Not to me."

Eve told Johnson and his lawyer to hang around. Outside she asked me what I thought.

"You keep asking me that. I think it would be nice if you found the gun."

"It'll turn up. It's got to be there. Nobody left that studio without being skin searched."

"Nobody?" I said. "Not even me?"

"Not even you," she grinned. "I supervised that one personally."

"I hope you had a good time. But I think the only way you're going to make a case here is to find that gun and tie it to somebody."

"Thank you for the penetrating analysis. We're doing what we can. As I said, it's got to be in the studio. My best men are searching for it."

"Yeah," I said. "Top to bottom." I scratched my head.

We went to another room and talked to Billings and his lawyer. By the end of the interview I was beginning to hope Billings had done it, just to see what a few years in Attica would do to the smug look on his face.

There was another session with Johnson, and another with Billings, and it still boiled down to nothing.

Eve summoned the lieutenant. "Let them go," she said. "Tell them to stay in town, but let them go. We can't do a damned thing until we find the gun."

I barely heard her. I was greeting Katherine Streeter, who had walked in, as promised, to give her formal statement. She was wearing faded jeans and a polo shirt under a V–necked Whitten College sweater. It took me a moment to recognize her. I'm usually pretty good at spotting people, even after years, but Katherine Streeter, going from gown to clown to child, was too much for me.

I turned to Eve. "No," I said, "Don't let anyone go. Let's move the party over to the studio."

"And what are we going to do at the studio?" she asked.

"We're going to search it," I said. "Top to bottom."

The whole gang rode over in three police cars. I told Eve what I had in mind. She said it was plausible, but it was by no means a sure thing.

"I know that," I said. "That's why I should be the one to do it. This way, if I'm wrong, everybody has a good horse laugh at the amateur's expense, and you press on."

The TV lights were off in the studio, and the house lights were up. There were two technicians on the scene — the lieutenant had radioed ahead and arranged for them. One stood in the middle of the vast concrete floor next to a small spotlight on a wheeled stand, the other stood at the lighting panel.

"The reason we're here now —" I began.

"I'd like to know it," Professor Billings huffed.

I ignored him. "— is to do in fact what people have been saying all night as a figure of speech. We are literally going to search this studio from top to bottom."

I looked at faces — no help there. Everyone was looking at me as if I were nuts. "The sergeant and his men have already done a thorough job on the bottom of the place. That means we can concentrate on the top. Look up," I suggested.

They did, and saw what I saw, the ceiling 50 feet above, spotted thickly with the colors of the helium balloons that had been released during the party. I turned to the technicians. "Gentlemen?" I said.

The spotlight came on. The colors of the balloons bloomed in the light.

"Sweep it slowly across the ceiling," I said. "What we're looking for, folks, is a gleam of metal, or a black dot, *in front* of the backdrop of balloons. There's plenty of metal up there, with the catwalk and the lights and the grid, but they won't be the right color or shape, and they won't be isolated in front of a field of color.

"The medical examiner," I went on, "says that Professor Adkinsen was shot with a .25–caliber automatic. That's a very small, very light gun. One balloon might not float it out of harm's way, but 10 might, and 20 definitely would."

Eyes were tracking the ceiling. "To hit a man three times with a pistol like that, at fairly distant range — no one, as I recall, was within 25 feet of the lectern — is pretty fancy shooting."

I'd spotted the gun by now, but I'd known where to look. I'd find it if I had to, but it would be better if someone else did.

"Of course, anyone could get a gun and practice, but it doesn't make a lot of sense. In the time it would have taken to become a good enough shot to do what was done here last night, there had to be plenty of opportunities to dispose of Adkinsen more easily. This setup smacked of a spur–of–a–moment deal. It's much more likely to have been someone who, we can presume, had been taught how to shoot —"

"There it is!" Alfie Johnson was pointing ceiling-ward. He had it all right. Eve told the lieutenant to get up to the catwalk and snag that bunch of balloons. I turned to Eve. "I think it's time to read some rights."

Eve said, "Sergeant?"

The sergeant was a big guy with a walrus moustache. "Yes, ma'am," he rumbled. "Who to?"

"To her," I said. "Katherine Streeter, otherwise known as 'Daddy Cool'."

It took a long time to get the rights read to her, because she wouldn't shut up denying her guilt long enough to listen to them. First she was amused, then she was hurt, then she was angry.

Eve said, "Hey! Shut up! There are two defense attorneys in this room, witnesses to this arrest, so you can bet we're going to do this right. Besides, we don't have a question to ask you, do we, Mr. Cobb?"

"No, just some things to tell her. If you don't mind."

"No, go right ahead." That took faith. I hoped I was worthy of it.

"Here's what I'm thinking, Katherine. District Attorney Bowen and the Sewanka police will check it all out, of course, but it hangs together, and it doesn't really matter anyway.

"You were the one that wrote the Daddy Cool column. It wasn't such a big deal at first, I supposed. A chance to make some spending money, a chance to sound off about things without having to face the consequences. Then you ran out of ideas, or you had a deadline coming, and you latched onto a paper you corrected as Adkinsen's grad assistant, rewrote it a little, and handed it in. You trashed Adkinsen's office to make it look as if someone might have stolen the paper from his files.

"You might even have thought no one would notice, or having noticed, that Mr. Johnson wouldn't know what to do about it. But he's proud of his work, and he goes directly to Professor Adkinsen. His friend and advisor. Adkinsen promises he'll get to the bottom of it. Maybe he has a suspicion already, but he doesn't want to make a fuss before the opening of the cable channel the following night.

"Adkinsen might have confronted you with it, demanded you apologize, in person and in print, for your plagiarism. Maybe he just dropped a few heavy hints. Whichever, you knew he'd find out if he didn't already know. You knew your fellowship at Farber was history; that any first-rate academic career for you was out the window.

"But you went through with your part in the cable show. That was your best chance — and only yours — to kill Adkinsen. You're the daughter of a policeman. You'd know how to go about getting a gun. The authorities can find out if your father taught you how to shoot. I know how *I'd* bet.

"And simplest of all, *you were the one handing out balloons.* You were the only one who could have enough balloons in one place to float the gun away without being conspicuous.

"Hell, I even saw it happen. I saw you standing there looking at Adkinsen's body with a bunch of balloons rising slowly behind you. It was the weight of the gun that made them rise so slowly, wasn't it?

"And the fact of your standing there. You were shocked, sure. But you also knew there would be no further shooting. And you were the only one who did. That's why everyone but you hit the floor. You must have realized how funny it could look — you called attention to yourself outside the Health Center this evening.

"Is that everything? Oh. Your hysteria when I tackled you. You must have thought I'd seen what you'd done and was arresting you."

Weston spoke. "That's a pretty circumstantial case, Mr. Cobb. Not ironclad by any means."

"Not until they run a paraffin test and a few more things on Ms. Streeter's hands. No matter how hard she's washed in the last 24 hours, the tests will show if she's fired a gun."

Katherine Streeter mumbled something.

Eve said, "Please say nothing, Ms. Streeter. Unless you give up the right to counsel and the right to remain silent."

"What's the use? What's the use?" She looked like someone who had three diffcrent fours in a row on her card when someone else shouts Bingo. "What's the use?"

Eve was stern. "Do you give up those rights?"

"Sure, yes. What the hell. But it was his fault, dammit! It was Adkinsen's own damn fault."

Back at headquarters, we found out why it was his own damn fault.

"His stupid party. That stupid launch of his cable TV channel. You know I was his grad assistant for a year, and I couldn't even get him to make a pass at me? He was so involved in the thing. And he kept me so busy the last week, I had no time to write my 'Daddy Cool' column. It was just the way Cobb said. I figured I could sneak into the studio after a few days, get the gun back, and heave it into the lake. Criss is in the lake too, so you couldn't find out I was 'Daddy Cool'. You must think I'm stupid or something."

Eve and I looked at each other, then back at her. Stupid, no. Or something, yes. I shuddered and walked out.

Professor Billings, of all people, was waiting outside for me.

"I wanted to congratulate you, Mr. Cobb. Such drama! I was quite taken away, even though I was a suspect myself. I imagine I'll be asked now to run the cable channel. What a TV play this will make!"

"Fine. My gift to the school." I tried to move on, but he grabbed my sleeve.

"But there's one thing I don't understand."

"Just one? You're way ahead of me."

"No, seriously. Why all the rigamarole at the studio at all? Why not simply have run the paraffin test on Ms. Streeter as soon as you suspected her?"

"Because we weren't sure it would have worked."

"I thought you said no matter how hard she'd washed —"

"She was dressed as a clown," I reminded him. "You saw her. She was wearing gloves."

Billings burst out laughing. "A bluff! A psychological manipulation! Brilliant."

"Listen," I said. "Do me a favor, okay?"

"If I'm able."

"You're able. When you've written your play, and cast it and rehearsed it, and mounted it, and are all set to give it its gala premiere …"

"Yes?"

"Do me a favor and don't invite me."

Killed in Midstream

"Where the hell are we?" she asked. The air conditioner was on full blast in the rented Chrysler, but the person on the sunny side of the car still caught a laser blast of heat in the lap or shoulder or the side of the head. It had been my turn all morning; now it was Mona Tarren's.

"I'm not sure," I said. "Where's the river?"

She showed me a look of total disgust. "You mean you're *lost?*"

"No, I am not lost. I am on Highway Six-oh-nine, heading south." As if to oblige me, a rusty white-shield-on-black sign popped up on the side of the road. "I thought you wanted to know what state we were in."

"I do."

"Okay. I was daydreaming and lost track of the river. We've been back and forth across it how many times today?"

"I forget. But it's off on your side of the car. Behind those trees somewhere."

"Then we're in Louisiana," I told her.

"Thanks," she said. She almost seemed to mean it, which would be the first civil word anybody'd gotten out of her since she'd broken a nail opening the car door this morning.

Not that she'd been sweetness and light before this, mind you. There'd been the nervous pulling of the blonde-streaked hair, the tightening of the square jaw, the narrowing in the blue eyes, and the snap in the voice since we'd left New York.

I knew what her problem was; she was desperate to protect her job. Mona had a left a secure but low-profile job in network news to become chief field producer for *Justice Quest,* our version of the TV wanted-poster genre that's popped up over the last few years. The networks love them. They're popular with the public, incredibly cheap to produce (compared to a drama or comedy show), and they sometimes actually do some good. Furthermore, although they deal with true events in a (more or less) nonfiction way, they're produced by the entertainment divisions of the networks, rather than by news, thereby freeing them from even the pretense of considerations of accuracy and ethics and exploitation and other things that get in the way of good viewing.

Unfortunately, *Justice Quest* had come late to a crowded field, and the glut was beginning to set in. It was too much like the others. Re-enact a crime, interview surviving victims, if any, discuss possible suspects, offer a reward and an 800 number to call in tips.

The trouble was, the more glamorous the case, the richer and better connected the people involved are, the less likely they are to want to trot out their misfortunes for our amusement. There may be, in these violent times, a lot of murders out there, but the pool of *interesting* middle-class on up murders (in television, poverty is uninteresting *ipso facto*) is too small to go around.

So *Justice Quest*, whose ratings were way below what they had to be to make even a cheap show viable, faced an ultimatum. Get some high-profile society murders to feature, complete with interviews, or say goodbye.

And now this was it. Somewhere on an island in the middle of a minor tributary of the Mississippi River lived a man who'd been at the center of one of the most gruesome murder cases in history. Him and his cat, who'd also figured in the case. Mona Tarren needed him, bad, or she was out of a job altogether. I was supposed to get him for her.

M y name is Matt Cobb. The sign on the door says Vice-President, Special Projects, but that sounds a lot more impressive than it is. *Special Projects* was the euphemism some forgotten genius came up with to describe what we do, which is namely everything too ticklish for Security, and everything too nasty for Public Relations.

This, however, was semi-personal. I'd been begged to do it by Jack Hansen, an old friend who had made the jump from local crime

Killed in Midstream 37

reporter to anchor of a network prime time show and didn't want to go back. "You can do it, Matt," Jack had told me. "You charmed this guy once, after all."

"Yeah," I said. "But I was a lot cuter then."

The name of the man on the island was Earl Rushton. Yes, *the* Earl Rushton. No, you can't just walk through a particularly heavy door just off Fifth Avenue in New York and see him whenever you feel like it. You never could do that, anyway. At Earl Rushton, as at Harry Winston and the other very tip-top jewelry establishments, one and one's bank account need to be accepted for an appointment before one gets to see the rocks. However, while Earl Rushton Limited is still in business at the same address, one will find it was sold shortly after the holocaust to a Belgian conglomerate.

"The holocaust" is what the tabloids, with typical class, called it. "THE GOLDEN HOLOCAUST," read the headline in question, probably because of the poison gas involved. If you asked me, it was still going a little far.

Not to say that the carnage wasn't plenty bad enough. Twenty-seven dead, four paralyzed, tens of millions of dollars worth of diamonds taken. The press finally settled on thirty-five million as the figure, although that was probably high.

And I knew Earl Rushton. At least, I'd met him and had a meal with him.

Not as a customer. I wear a Timex watch, and that's as far as any discussion of jewelry you ever have with me is likely to go. But Earl Rushton is a prominent alumnus of Whitten College, in upstate Sewanka, New York, which is also my alma mater.

It got to be my alma mater because I got the scholarship — the one athletic scholarship that little bastion of academic rectitude hands out each year. Part of the process was a meeting with a member of the scholarship committee. In my case, that was Earl Rushton. He took me to the Four Seasons for lunch. He probably wanted to see if the po' boy would be flustered by the place. The only thing that threw me was the fact that there were no prices on my menu. I later learned that there are special menus for the host which do have prices. The way it was, I figured first you ordered, then somebody gave you an estimate.

Anyway, I remembered to use my silverware from the outside in, and I didn't belch at the end of the meal, and Rushton seemed to be satisfied. Conversation was easy, since all he wanted to talk about was basketball, and I could talk basketball in my sleep in those days. If I'd been a little bigger (I'd topped out at six–two) I would have been looking for a more prominent school to play for, education or no education.

Rushton seemed like a nice–enough guy. I never formed any vivid memory of him. I never spoke to him again after that afternoon. He apparently approved of me, but he hadn't kept in touch.

I had tried to tell this to Mona, and to Jack Hansen, but desperate people don't listen well. There's the old proverb about a drowning man grasping at a straw. You're supposed to nod sadly and sympathize with the poor guy. Now I was having a look at things from the point of view of the straw, and that was no fun either.

It was about ten minutes later when we found the turnoff toward the landing. A kid of about seventeen wearing cutoffs, a work shirt, and battered deck shoes over bare feet was waiting for us.

He waved us to a stop. I rolled down the window. Hot, wet air poured into the car like dog breath.

"Are you Mr. Cobb?" he asked.

"That's me," I said.

He grinned. "And you must be Ms. Tarren. Pleased to meet you. I watch your show all the time. I'm Lew Rushton. You're a little early, but Granddad won't mind. He told me to bring you as soon as you came."

"That's nice of him."

"Don't be too sure of that. He said he just wants to get it over with as soon as possible."

Lew directed me to the only building near the landing, a six car garage made of no–nonsense concrete blocks, with tough metal doors and serious locks. I drove in; we got out of the car. It was no cooler in the darkness. When my eyes adjusted, I saw several expensive cars and wires for burglar alarms.

Lew saw me looking. "Rings at the sheriff's office about five miles down the road," he explained. "Grandmom sometimes throws a party for the local gentry, you know, and since the only way out to the island is by boat, the cars have to be well protected."

I found the kid interesting. With his sun–browned skin and tousled blond hair, he could have been Huckleberry Finn, until he opened his mouth. That was pure eastern prep school, en route to Hahvud. Or Whitten College. We had our share of accents at Whitten.

On the other hand, he was much too chatty to go with the accent. My experience with the crowd in question has been that they hand out personal details like hundred–dollar bills, but Lew Rushton seemed to like to talk just to hear himself.

It was the same in the launch heading toward the island, but now he was concentrating on Mona.

"Your show is the most popular thing going at school, Ms. Tarren," Lew said. "I recognized your name from the credits. Granddad just said you and Mr. Cobb were from the network." He looked at me. "I haven't seen your name in the credits."

"I take extra money instead," I told him.

Mona slapped my arm. "Don't listen to him. What do you like best about the show, Lew?"

"The phone number at the end," he said. "We use it to play Baffle. We do it with all the shows, but we like yours the best, because you've had some incredibly heinous crimes lately."

"Baffle?" Mona asked. "How do you play that?"

"Oh, we wait for you to do a story on something really good, like a child dismemberment or something. Then we think of somebody whose guts we hate who sort of fits the description, and we turn him in. We had one guy actually picked up for questioning by the FBI. It was fabulous!"

Mona looked sick. "That's Baffle? How — how often do you do this?"

"Oh, at least once a week. Remember, there's four shows on the air like this now, so there's usually at least one heinous crime we can hang around somebody's neck. Baffle stands for 'Bust a Fucker for Light Entertainment.' "

He sighed as if he couldn't wait to get back to school, and drove the launch with a smile on his face. Looking at Mona's face, I wanted to laugh; looking at Lew's, I wanted to knock his head off.

The boy spoke again before I could do either. "Hey, that was a pretty heinous crime at my Granddad's place ten years ago, wasn't it? Are you going to do that one? I hope so. I was only a kid when it happened, and nobody'll tell me the details. I looked up all the microfilm I could find in the library here, at school, and in town over there, but all I got out of that was that somebody put a gas bomb in the place, my Granddad would have bitten the big one if he hadn't slipped out the back door to chase the cat, they got away with a lot of goods, and that one of the people who got killed was my father's girlfriend."

I noticed that Mona had surreptitiously turned on her pocket tape recorder. I wasn't so sure Lew Rushton hadn't noticed it, too.

"That was no big deal," he said. "I mean, I met her, but I don't really remember her. My father had divorced my mother long before. She married somebody else. Lives in Hong Kong now, I think. I might see her again when the Red Chinese take over in 'ninety-seven and kick her butt out of there. That'll be weird."

He turned to Mona. "You probably know all this already, though, right?"

"I've done some research," she conceded.

"Then you know my dad ate a bullet about three months after Wanda — that was the girl friend — bought it. That was a bummer." He grinned. "As your generation used to say."

We were close enough now to the island to make out details. The main house was a rectangular white wedding cake, loaded with curves and columns, sitting in the middle of a spectacularly lush, green lawn. White gravel paths curved gracefully through the green. It occurred to me that island would be a frustrating place for anybody who like to walk in straight lines.

Lew said, "Uh–oh."

"What's the matter?" I asked.

"The boat's not there?"

"Of course not," I said. "It's here."

Lew looked at me quizzically, then gave me the benefit of the doubt, deciding I couldn't possibly be that stupid and must be kidding.

"Not this boat," he said. "The oyster boat."

"Oyster boat?" Mona echoed.

"Hey, I think I've given you a scoop, after all. It's not a crime, exactly, but it's something nobody back East knows. Granddad couldn't get the jewelry business out of his blood, no matter how disgusted he got with the whole New York scene after the holocaust thing and my father's suicide. So he's trying to grow pearls."

"Here in the river?" I asked.

"Round the back of the island. Says one of the reasons he bought this place years ago was that he always had it in the back of his mind to give it a try. He's been studying everything about how the Japanese do things for years. Finally got hold of the right kind of oysters just before the trouble back in New York. So he was ready for the big move, you know"

"Sure," I said, although I hadn't even known there were oysters that could live in fresh water. "Any success?"

"Nah. But the old boy keeps trying. What the hell, he's old and rich, this keeps him in shape."

"Where shall we wait for Mr. Rushton?" Mona asked.

"No need to wait. I'll swing around the island and bring you out to the oyster boat. You'll probably get more time with him that way."

"Oh," Mona said. "But I wanted to get a picture of the cat, too."

"The cat'll be there. Wherever Granddad goes, Phluphy goes. That's P–H–L–U–P–H–Y. Grandmom got the cat and wanted me to name it, so I did. I had no imagination as a kid. Grandmom was horrified I wanted to call such a fancy cat Fluffy, so my dad came up with the spelling to make everybody happy. Funny, the way he turned out to be Granddad's pet. He never gave a damn for animals until about three weeks before the attack, when he started taking Phluphy to the office."

"And the cat wound up saving his life!" Mona said. She was showing signs of excitement — if she could land this story, she'd get the crime freaks, *and* the cat lovers, who were legion. And the Baffle players, too.

The oyster boat was a low, flat job with a railing around the deck, a control center with a canopy over it, and a tiny outboard motor. Earl Rushton was aboard. He wore a maroon Izod Lacoste alligator shirt, crisp yellow bermuda shorts, immaculately white deck shoes, and white cotton socks with maroon and yellow stripes at the top. How he managed to keep all that dry and do what he was doing was beyond me.

What he was doing was dredging the river bottom, the way the clam diggers in Long Island sound do it, with a dustpan–like thing on the end of a long pole. He would pull the thing onto the deck, avoiding the drips of water, dump the oysters into a pink plastic bucket, then lower the dredge back over the side, its handle resting neatly in a little chain–and–clip contraption attached to the railing where he stood.

There was a blob of silver–gray on the deck about four feet behind him and to the right — just out of range of the drips.

He welcomed us on board with embarrassed courtesy.

"Mr. Cobb; Miss Tarren. Is it time for our appointment already?" He raised his wrist, and saw he'd caught one Oyster already — a very expensive Rolex.

"Past it, Granddad, actually," Lew said.

"I'm so sorry. I see so few people these days, I lose track of the time."

I looked him over. My previous meeting with the guy had taken place about the time his grandson was born, but he didn't look any different. The hair was still polished silver, and seemed to stay in place by magic. The face was tan and smooth, and the lines in it, though perhaps deeper, only added character. The wardrobe was different, of course, but he still hung those clothes like a Man of Distinction in those old liquor ads.

The only difference was his hands. That day at the Four Seasons, I had been aware of a callous–free handshake and perfect nails. Now they were the hands of a diamond miner rather than a diamond merchant. Marinated in river water and rubbed against oyster shells for ten years or so, they were rough and broken–nailed.

He held up an oyster in one hand and a metal tool in the other. "I apologize for not shaking hands." He showed even white teeth in a grin, then bowed to Mona.

"Do you mind if I go on with this? I can explain it if you like."

"I already told them, Granddad."

Rushton looked affectionately at his grandson. "Did you laugh?"

"Not this time, Granddad," Lew said.

"I'm surprised," the old man said. "A lot of people have tried to culture pearls in this country. Nobody's succeeded, and maybe I won't either. But it passes the time."

He put the metal device near the rim of the oyster and squeezed the handle. Slowly the shell opened. "Had it made to my own specifications," he announced. "One thing I couldn't learn how to do was to open the shell without killing the animal." He took a look inside, gently pushed the shell closed, then pitched it back into the water. "No luck," he said. "I'll keep trying, though. It's my patriotic duty."

I would have bet good money Mona had her tape recorder going now, too.

"How's that, Mr. Rushton?" she asked.

"I spent forty years in the diamond business. That means I spent years dealing with a South African–Dutch monopoly. There's nothing you can do about that. The diamonds are in the ground where God happened to put them.

"But there are oysters that can thrive in all sorts of environments. The best ones to eat live in cold, salt water. Some of the best cultured pearls come from oysters that grow in warmish fresh water, like we have right here. The Japanese — and other Asians — have been at this for hundreds of years, and if you think they're zealous about protecting their car industry, you don't know the half of it. So I've got a lot of catching up to do. Besides, as I said, it passes the time, keeps me out of my wife's way, gives me some exercise, and still leaves me plenty of time for reading."

He lifted up the oyster rake, and dumped the as–yet unchecked oysters back in the river.

The cat went nuts. It sprang to its feet and ran to the rails, making loud angry meows. It looked at Rushton and gave him more of the same. Very indignant, Phluphy was, silver–gray fur bristling for emphasis.

I didn't know if I was glad or sorry I hadn't brought Spot along on this trip. Spot would have given the cat an excuse to bristle. He doesn't like cats.

I don't mind them myself, though I prefer dogs. The important thing to remember about a cat is that this is an animal that will eat four hundred dollars' worth of caviar, if you let it, then knock over your garbage can to get at a pork chop bone. Cats are interested in themselves, period. I respect that, and cats seem to respect me for knowing that about them, and we get along fine.

What I have troubles with are cat lovers, the kind of people who think cats sit on their laps to give them affection rather than to suck up some body heat. The kind who say things like "little oozy poozy," as they rub their face against the cat's fur.

Actually I can't stand people who treat dogs that way either. I was thankful that Rushton didn't go so far as to say "little oozy poozy," but he got pretty bad. He scooped the Persian up and held it to his cheek, and said, "What's the matter, Pluphkin? Something scary in the water?"

The cat showed impressive fangs as it meowed in his face.

"Okay, kitty, we'll get you right home. I have to talk to these nice people, anyway."

Phluphy didn't want to know. He meowed louder.

"Lew, take us home, won't you? I'll see to Phluphy."

He tucked the cat under his arm like a football, and he subsided long enough to use his rough little tongue to lick the oyster juice off his master's (a term you have to use loosely with cats) hands.

During the quiet interval, he asked me what I heard from old Whitten College. I told him not much lately.

He'd mentioned a murder that had taken place last time I was there. I told him I remembered it, too. He said he heard on the news that I had solved it, and I said that was sort of true, and that was all we had time for before the cat started a ruckus again.

The oyster boat pulled up to the dock. Lew jumped out and tied us up, then offered a hand to Mona, who took it and gave him a charming smile. I didn't blame her for smiling. We'd already been here longer without being thrown out than I'd thought we might be.

The old man, still carrying the unhappy and very noisy cat under his arm, hopped ashore. "Lew will show you to my sitting room," he said. "I have to get some dinner for Phluphy."

I looked at the building. The place still looked like Tara. "Does your grandfather have any help on the place?"

"Only the Jacksons live in — she's the housekeeper and cook, he's the butler and chauffeur, sort of. This is their day off. Heavy cleaning, stuff like that, comes in by the day. Why?"

"Just seems like an awfully big place for a millionaire to clean himself."

"Don't worry about that," Lew grinned.

I mentioned that the caterwauling had died down.

Lew nodded. "Phluphy always gets like that when he expects to be fed. Shall we go in?"

Inside we had to wait for a while. Mona amused herself by lining up camera angles.

"Of course, we'll have to get the cat. Everybody loves cats. And that chandelier. And we'll have the kid for pathos — lost his father as a result of the tragedy. This is going to be great." She swung around, making a frame in front of her with her thumbs and forefingers like an old-time director. "We'll start the piece with Rushton walking through that archway —"

At that moment, Earl Rushton walked through the archway in question. He looked as if he had let the network wardrobe department dress him for Mona's benefit — blazer, spotted shirt, white slacks. He even wore an ascot. The personification of the typical viewer's idea of what a rich person wears around the house.

He had a little dish with him, with something in it that clattered, like jordan almonds.

He asked us to sit down, placed the dish on the coffee table. It didn't contain jordan almonds. Instead it contained some lumpy gray–brown things that shone dully in the sunlight.

"I thought you might be interested in these," he said. "Some of the pearls I've gotten from the river." He smiled and shrugged. "As you can see, we still have a long way to go."

"That is a sort of ... unusual color," Mona said.

"The color's not important. We can adjust that with the food we put in, and the chemical mix of the water. It's that shape that's the problem. Unfortunately, the oysters don't care. We put an irritant inside, and they cover it with something smooth — nacre, we call it — and as soon as they're comfortable, they stop. There'd be no pearls at all if oysters could just spit."

We laughed politely.

"My wife'll be joining us in a minute, if you don't mind. She's getting us some tea."

Son of a gun, I thought, he really did feed the cat himself. Of course, why you'd indulge a creature who got so nuts during a boat ride that you had to head back to shore was beyond me, but what the hell.

Soon, Mrs. Rushton joined us, carrying tea things. She also belonged to the formal–around–the–house set. She was wearing a dress of perfect Barbara Billingsley–as–June Cleaver design, complete with pearl necklace. Not lumpy brown ones, either. She was a tall woman, and robust, with a handsome face. If nature hadn't blessed her with two perfect gray streaks in her dark chestnut hair, some friend had blessed her with the name of a genius hairdresser. I could see Mona nodding slightly, lining up camera angles for Sheila Rushton, too.

I was hoping for a chance to remind her we hadn't even broached the subject of the show yet, but it wasn't really necessary. Things went swimmingly. Rushton and I talked for a few seconds about dear old Whitten, then Mona launched her spiel about how *Justice Quest* had helped catch dozens of criminals, but that the worst crime of recent decades still unpunished was the holocaust at Earl Rushton Ltd. She could make no promises, but there was a *chance* the network could help, and wouldn't he please let us try?

And incidentally hype our ratings and save our jobs, I refrained from adding.

Rushton frowned, bit his lip, and at last said. "Why not? Of course. When do you want to do it?"

Mona's control was good. Her eyes widened with surprise and delight only for a few seconds before New York Career Girl was back in control. Without missing a beat she said, "At your earliest convenience," she said. "I could have a crew out here tomorrow, if you like."

Rushton's grin was tinged with sadness. "I think that's just a *little* too early, Ms. Tarren. How about — oh — one week from today?" He spoke to his wife. "Is that okay with you, dear?" he asked. "Is the whole idea okay with you?"

"I think it's marvelous," Sheila Rushton said. She turned to us. "It eats at you, you know, to have something like this happen. It's been worse for poor Earl than for me."

"What do you mean?" Mona asked, all concern and soft sympathy. She was already in film–interview mode.

It was Rushton who answered her question. "The idea that I was spared, Ms. Tarren. That's what eats at me. The diamonds were insured, and even if they hadn't been, I could have stood the loss and still lived quite comfortably.

"But the human life! Over two dozen human lives, all my employees, longtime customers and friends —"

"Your son's fiancée," I said.

Rushton nodded, seemingly as sad about her as he was all the others. I could see it. Time and death have a way of glossing over people's bad points.

"All of them," he said. "And the killer had every right to expect I would die, as well. He put the canister of gas right where it would be sucked into the air conditioning and spread through the whole establishment."

"But the cat saved your life," Mona said.

Rushton smiled in spite of himself. "That's right. Of course, at the time, I thought I was saving his. There was an outside door from my office to a courtyard between our building and one on Sixth Avenue. On nice days I used to open it from time to time. Air conditioning can get so stale — I like to leaven it with fresh air."

It took a strong effort to keep me from loosening my tie. There was no air conditioning on in here, either. Rushton was easy to please, I thought, if he considered the air of either midtown Manhattan or that of an island in the middle of a swampy river "fresh."

"Anyway, I opened the door, and Phluphy — he was just a kitten then — jumped out. I'd never been responsible for a pet before, and I had that exaggerated fear of all new pet owners. I was so afraid he'd be crushed by a car or attacked by a dog — and then my grandson would never forgive me. So I chased him outside. The cat kept me hopping around that courtyard and back alleys — in a full business suit — for over half an hour.

"Of course, just minutes after I'd left, the gas bomb went off." Rushton swallowed. "The office door had locked automatically behind me when I left, and the door was impregnable. When I finally caught the cat, I had to find my way through an alley to a side street, then walk around the block to Fifth Avenue to get back in to the building.

"That's when I ran into the police and fire department. The thief or thieves had already been in the store, of course. They put on gas masks just before their timer let out the gas, then helped themselves to the jewels. No one ever saw them. The police and emergency vehicles were there simply because a passerby had been sickened by a slight whiff of gas coming from under the front door and had told a traffic cop."

He shook his head. "And that was that. The thieves have been very clever. No identifiable stones have turned up on the world market, no unusual number dumped on the market at one time. I still have connections in the diamond world, and I check with them from time to time. Whoever did this must be living frugally, selling the goods one or two at a time."

"That could be the strangest thing of all." I hadn't meant to say it, it just popped out. Now that I had, manners compelled me to explain myself.

"It just seems a little odd that someone would commit a mass murder like that just to live frugally."

Rushton took a deep breath of unfresh river air and said, "Cobb, we've both come a long way from Whitten, but I'm older and I've seen a lot, and I tell you there is no fathoming what goes on inside the human mind."

He rubbed one eye. "Besides, what seems frugal to me might be extravagant to someone else, no?" He slapped his knees with his hands. "By God, I think this is going to do me good. I've hidden these feelings for so long, get them out in the open and maybe we can deal with them once and for all. Care to stay for dinner?"

"It's very kind of you," Mona said, "but I'd really like to start back right away and begin getting things ready for filming the interviews. In fact, if you'll let me use your phone, I'll call New York and tell them the project is a go."

Sheila Rushton stood up. "I'd better help you in the early stages, my dear. We're quite primitive here. If you want to make a credit-card call from the house, you have to go through the local operator."

Rushton and I made small talk until they came back. It reminded me of that lunch at the Four Seasons. Everything superficial and friendly on the surface, but the man was looking at me in a way that said he was searching for something in me. All he would have found at that point was a vague sense of unease. Something I'd heard or seen this afternoon wasn't hanging together with the rest, and it bothered me.

Soon Mona was back, and we took our leave. Lew reappeared to ferry us back to the rented car.

"I take it he agreed," Lew said.

It wasn't a hard guess. Mona's smile glowed visibly in the twilight.

"I'm surprised," Lew went on. "He never even talks about it."

"Said he wants to get his feelings out in the open," I told him.

Lew was deadpan. "Feelings? Granddad? Seems weird, but maybe that's it. Anyway, I'll have to lay down the law on this case to the guys back at school — no Baffle on this one. On this one it would be nice to get some real results."

All the way back to the motel, Mona didn't once ask me what state we were in. What she mostly said was, "Isn't this *terrific*?"

What I mostly said was, "Uh–huh."

"God, I wish we'd had a film crew with us today. I hope he's that good next week when the film is rolling."

"You never asked him about his son's suicide."

"I don't want him to use it all up! I want that reaction fresh. I also didn't ask him about the possibility of an inside job."

"I thought the whole staff was killed."

"Two people had the day off, one was out sick. The sick one was in the hospital, one of the guys with the day off had an alibi — he went to the track with friends, but the other one got some heavy questioning by the cops before they decided he just didn't fit it. If we use him, we'll probably change his name."

"Not to tell you your job or anything, but check into the proverbial disgruntled ex–employees, while you're at it."

"We will," she assured me. "The cops did at the time, but we'll dig deeper."

We got back to the motel, which was pretty elaborate for where it was, with a separate garage for vehicles and all, plus a restaurant where the food was actually edible.

Mona celebrated with a couple of Gibsons before dinner, and talked about how great it would be, how this was going to turn the show around.

I said I hoped she was right and ate my pork chop.

It was still early when we were done. Mona said she wanted to get some work done, and that was fine with me. I went back to my room, turned the air conditioner on full (by me, no air warmer than sixty degrees can possibly be fresh), jumped into the shower, got out and dried off, watched some college hoops on ESPN, and went to bed. Driving always makes me tired, and we had a long haul to the airport tomorrow.

About midnight, there was a knock on the door.

"Go away," I said cordially, but the knocking went on. I got out of bed, put on a robe, staggered to the door, and opened it to the extent the chain bolt allowed.

Nobody there, but the knocking sound continued. Curious. Then I heard Mona's voice say, "Matt, it's me. Open up, I need you."

I had not exactly expected this would happen, but I flattered myself enough to include it in the possibilities that Mona, with the drinks in her, might to decide to declare a little cozy celebration involving the two of us.

She was a very attractive woman, and in earlier days, I would have jumped at the chance and whatever else there was to be jumped at. Now, however, I was officially Going Steady with a young woman who happened to be the network's largest single stockholder. Roxanne was the best thing that had ever happened to me, and I wasn't about to mess that up. The idea was to get it across to Mona without winding up with her hating my guts.

I unbolted the connecting door and opened it a little, about to explain the good news that there were still faithful men in the world, and that I was one of them, when my eyes focused enough to see that she already had company.

A big, sandy-haired guy with a mustache, a butch cut (I could smell the wax), and an incipient beer belly was in the room with her. His right hand was behind his back, under the flap of his seersucker jacket, undoubtedly ready to unholster a gun. His left hand held a black leather case with a silver star pinned to it.

"You Cobb?" he asked.

"Sure am," I said. "What's up?"

"I'm Investigator Paul Albrick. Sheriff's department. I'd like you and Ms. Tarren here to get dressed and come along with me, if you would."

"Are we under arrest?"

"No, nothing like that. I know you Easterners hear 'southern' and 'sheriff' and start thinking about fire hoses and back rooms and lynching parties. But there ain't nothing like that going on. My daddy's the sheriff, and this parish wins awards, he runs things so clean. Look, if you want a lawyer, you can have one; even though y'all aren't suspected of anything, okay?"

He was as earnest as a kid talking to the father of his first date. I tried not to let it fool me. We weren't suspected of anything, but Albrick had done a fine, professional job of approaching us, all the same.

"Nah," I said. "We can save that for later, if necessary. Okay with you, Mona?"

"Sure," she said, though I sincerely think it was a simple desire to stay on the good side of the cops that kept her from screaming for a lawyer.

It was curiosity that was driving me. "Before we go anywhere, though, we do want to know what this is all about."

"Some trouble at Rushton's Island," Albrick said. "Somebody rowed or poled out there, socked the grandson, and stole the cat."

"Oh, no," Mona said.

"How's the kid?" I asked.

"Doc's with him. No telling, right now. Anyway, we're doing all the routine, question everybody who's been there, you know, and the sheriff sent me to fetch you. I'll be waiting outside till you get dressed."

I decided that if I was crossing the damned river again tonight, I wasn't going to climb back into a suit to do it. I put on a pair of jeans and a pullover shirt, and suggested Mona go casual, too. Only trouble was, I'd already left my Nikes in the rental car. I asked Albrick if we could stop by the garage and pick them up. He said sure.

Mona had a dress on ("I didn't *bring* any casual clothes"), but she did have on a pair of canvas espadrilles, which was a lot more practical in a boat than high heels. Albrick walked us to the garage so I could get my sneakers. I walked up the ramp toward the rental car, and saw that there was something wrong. I called for Albrick as I ran up to the car. I stopped about ten feet away from the nose of the thing and looked.

Liquid, black–looking in the fluorescent light, had trickled down in snaky tendrils from the windshield. Written on the hood in big ragged letters was the word DON'T. Clinging to the windshield itself like an obscene parody of those suction–cup Garfield toys was the grey Persian, Phluphy. His head had been smashed, and he'd been cut open down the belly. One yellow eye leered at us.

I heard somebody gulp. Might have been me. I turned away. "Well," I said. "That solves half the mystery."

Albrick didn't laugh, but he didn't smack me in the mouth either, so I figured I came out ahead. Driving down the highway, after the investigator had arranged to have the kitty corpse guarded and to get the lab boys out there, Albrick had a remark of his own.

"It looks," he said, "like someone don't want y'all doing this TV show, don't it?"

Mona came back at him with a very commendable load of the First Amendment, the Communications Act of 1934, and the Accepted Canons of Journalistic Responsibility, but that wasn't the point.

We got the point later, right after we were taken to the island in a sheriff's launch.

Mrs. Rushton met us as soon as we walked in the door. "Thank God you're here!" she said. "Use the phone in the hall. Call New York right away. Call off the filming!"

Mona's media persona finally got the better of her diplomacy. She looked at Mrs. Rushton and said, "Are you insane?"

It made sense from Mona's point of view — the network arrives — more violence — great television — ratings! TV people sometimes forget that real people have feelings. TV people tend to forget that reality exists.

Of course, a response like that was a good bet to *drive* someone like Mrs. Rushton insane, and I was wondering what to do about it when Earl Rushton came down the main stairs and saved the day.

"Lew's conscious, dear. He's asking for you." His wife dropped everything and ran upstairs.

"How is he?" I asked.

"Thank God, the doctor said he's going to be all right. It wasn't so much that he was hit so hard, it was that he hit a rock when he fell." Rushton shuddered in visible relief.

When he stopped, he said, "But Ms. Tarren, while my wife is perhaps a bit hysterical, she's absolutely right. Helping you with that TV show now would be out of the question. I won't take a chance with my grandson's life." He shuddered again.

"Maybe we'd better sit down," I said.

"Please do. I'm going back upstairs to Lew."

"Can we talk just a minute? I can appreciate your concern, but *we* were the ones who were warned."

"I take it as a warning to all of us. It was my grandson who was attacked. Our cat who was butchered. Poor Phluphy. He never hurt anyone."

"How did you know about that?"

"The sheriff told us. His son radioed it in."

"That's right, he did."

Rushton left us and went upstairs. He was soon replaced by the sheriff in uniform, a carbon copy of his son except that he had some gray under the butch wax and more beer under the belt. He led us, politely but thoroughly, through our day, asked if we had witnesses for what happened after we got back to the motel. I told him sure, the waitresses at the restaurant would remember us having been seen at dinner too late to have made another round trip to the island and done the mischief that was supposed to have been done.

The sheriff nodded. "As a matter of fact, she does. Lab boys say there's no cat hairs in your car, neither. So I suppose y'all are off the hook."

Then he took off his hat, said "May I?" and wedged himself a seat on the sofa between Mona and me.

"Look, Cobb," he said. "I been on the phone to New York about you. Why don't you just sit here and think awhile while I do my job, and we'll see if you come up with anything."

"That's not the way it works," I began.

"Look," he said, rising. "The only lever I got on you is that the police launch ain't leaving the island again till I'm ready to go myself, and that ain't for hours yet. I know this ain't no big murder case like on your show, ma'am — watch it every chance I get, by the way — but Rushton pays about half the taxes in this parish, and I'd appreciate any help I could get. Just think it over, all right?"

"Sure," I said.

"Good," the sheriff beamed. "Deputy Packson is at the door if you need something."

"Also to keep us from making a break for it, right?"

The sheriff chuckled and walked off. I sat down to think.

"Tell you what I think," Mona said. "I think I should have listened to my mother and become a secretary."

"Baloney," I said. "When this is over you'll realize you loved it. Nobody goes into this business without a huge ego and a love of adventure, no matter how sick."

"Not even you?"

"Especially not me. You think it's not a kick to have a lawman in a place you never heard of ask you for help?"

"All you have to do now is deliver."

"Right. So let me think."

I thought. I thought about the cat. Why smear the cat on our windshield? I mean, I have no love for cat killers, but we really didn't give a damn about the creature, except for Mona's probable delight if it turned out to be telegenic. But there was some thing off, something wrong about the cat that bothered me all day. Something that had happened on the oyster boat ...

Sure. And then the rest of it started to fall into place. Everything. All the way back to New York.

"Cobb," Mona said. "Are you alive?"

"Huh? Yeah."

"It's been hours, you know, nearly sun–up."

"Complicated thing."

"You spent all this time thinking about the cat?"

"About the cat, and an insect."

"Insect."

"The wicked flea."

"What the hell are you talking about?"

"Sorry, it's a joke. Bible quote — 'The wicked flee where no man pursueth.' That's what happened tonight. That's why the cat was killed."

"You've got something?"

"I've got a headache. I've also got a bunch of ideas so crazy they almost have to be true."

"Almost?"

"One of them, at least, can be checked. Deputy Packson! I need to talk to the sheriff."

I talked to the sheriff for a long time. For a while I thought he was going to give me a medal. For a while I thought he was going to throw me in jail. Finally he said, "I can't go into court with a bunch of noise like that. I can't even mention it to Rushton."

"I can."

Sheriff Albrick was silent for a long time. Finally, he said, "Yeah. You do that, Cobb. I don't want no comebacks on this."

"Unless I'm right."

"Right. Then I adopt you as my second son. But you mess this up, you are an orphan, you got me?"

"Yeah. Well, before I go off to find out if I can call you Daddy, let me run down what's supposed to have happened here on the island tonight. The help had the night off, and weren't around. Mrs. Rushton took a sleeping pill and went to sleep early, about nine o'clock. Lew went for a nighttime cruise on the river about the same time. When he landed, somebody jumped him, hit him, left him there."

"I told you all this."

"Just making sure. About an hour later, Rushton hasn't seen the cat or his grandson for a while, so he calls out the back door. He gets no answer, gets nervous, starts looking around. He finds Lew, who mumbles something about hearing the cat snarling before he passes out again. He runs to the house, calls you and the doctor, and here we are."

"Here we are."

"Okay, hold on tight."

* * *

I caught Rushton in his study upstairs. He was sitting in a reclining chair, looking at a gem catalog.

"Never really gave it up, did you?"

He looked up at me. "What? Oh, this? Just keeping up. Same with the pearl business, just keeping up."

"How's Lew?"

"He's going to be fine, according to the doctor. We'll just keep him in bed for a few days."

"That's got to be a relief."

"You can't imagine."

"Bet I can," I said. "Mr. Rushton, what would say if I told you I snitched one of the pearls you showed us this afternoon?"

"You didn't." He said. I was silent and he went on. "And even if you did, what difference does it make. They're worthless, anyway."

"You mean if I asked for one now, you'd give it to me?"

"No. Not now. I find your manner offensive. What's gotten into you, Cobb?"

"Something I saw the cat do."

That hit home. Rushton blanched, but said nothing.

"I didn't think about it at the time, you know. It bothered me, but not enough to keep me working at it. It was just that it struck me odd that the cat would act all betrayed, would start demanding a meal in the middle of the river. Cats get used to routine, don't they? That cat was accustomed to being fed when you dredged up a bunch of oysters. You never gave a damn about the oysters. The metal gadget was shiny and brand new, but there was a well–used knife right near you. You usually cut the oyster open, right? Then took out the pearl and fed the oyster to the cat. You didn't do that this afternoon, because you didn't want us looking at the pearls. You didn't even want us looking inside the oysters, did you? Because the seeds, the centers the pearls are built on, weren't covered yet."

He eyed me steadily. "I have no idea what you're talking about."

"You knew I didn't snitch a worthless pearl because you counted them. Why keep track of the number of worthless pearls? And why do you keep worthless pearls in a wall safe?"

"I still have no idea what you're talking about."

"No? Well, try this one for size. The sheriff is going to get a warrant for your pearls, and he's going to X-ray them. And he's going to get an expert to tell him what the shadow pattern of the seed is."

"I see."

"Yeah. Me too."

"How do you know?"

"The cat on the windshield. A warning, sure, but why that? Slashed tires would have been just as effective, and a whole lot less messy. An excuse to call off Mona's film crew? All you had to do was to change your mind. But then I latched on to the one thing I wasn't supposed to notice — that warning also served to *eliminate the cat.*

"See, old fellow alumnus, I think you know more about me than you let on; you could certainly find out. You saw me wondering about the cat, you worried that I might put something together. Or if I didn't, somebody else would. So the cat had to go. But you decided to make use of him. You've gotten more use out of that cat than most people do, I'll give you that.

"But you didn't mean to hit your grandson so hard. Probably you were just going to stun him, then tie him up. You knew your wife would be out of it with the sleeping pill she took. You got the cat, killed it — where? Now that the lab boys know to look, they'll find traces of blood in a tub drain, or on some isolated part of the island. When Lew hit his head on the rock in falling, you could have called off the plan, hidden the cat, and called off the most horrible part of your plan, but you go through with your plans no matter how horrible they are, don't you?"

"You're telling it," he said. His voice was very quiet.

"You drove off to the motel — Lew had told you what our car looked like, no doubt — left your grisly message, and zoomed back here, 'found' your grandson, and spread the alarm. You made up that

Killed in Midstream

bit about Lew telling you he'd heard the cat snarling, knowing he'd be excused for nor remembering saying it or hearing it.

"Good superficial effects, Mr. Rushton, but they don't stand up. You called my attention to the goddamn cat, and that's when I got it."

"Got what?"

"Well, everything I've told you so far, for starters."

"Well, even if you were telling the truth, what could you get me on, cruelty to animals? My grandson would never press charges."

"You forgot about the pearls, Mr. Rushton. Those X-rays are going to show diamonds in the middle of those worthless pearls. The diamonds supposedly stolen from your establishment ten years ago. You're going down for insurance fraud, at least, even if nobody can prove murder. But more than that, you're going to lose your wife, and your grandson. I'll tell Lew. This is no game of Baffle.

"He'll understand. Of course, we wouldn't really even have to wait for the warrant. Brilliant idea, hiding precious gems inside worthless ones. All we need to do is dissolve one of the pearls in vinegar or wine — *oof!*"

Without giving a hint, Rushton shot out both fists, caught me below the ribcage and knocked me over. Instead of trying to get past me, he ran for the bathroom at the end of the study. The door slammed, and I heard a bolt slide home.

I tried the door. It was no ordinary bathroom door. Rushton had been ready for this, maybe for years.

"Get away!" he said.

"Where are you going from here, Rushton?"

I heard phones ringing in the house. A few seconds after they stopped, Deputy Packson appeared with a slightly bewildered expression on his face.

"Mr. Rushton's on the phone, sir. He wants to talk to you, but only on one of the downstairs extensions."

"Okay, he's locked in there. Watch the door. But from a distance. He's tricky."

I went downstairs and took the hall phone, the one Mona had called New York from. I could see Sheriff Albrick backing out of the kitchen with that extension's receiver in his hand. "Yes, Mr. Rushton, he's on the line now. Here he is, go ahead, Cobb."

Albrick was giving me dirty looks, which I ignored.

"Go ahead," I said.

"I got you that scholarship," Rushton said. "That diploma got you your job. I sowed the seeds of my own destruction."

"I was the smallest part of that. You did it all yourself."

"I suppose so. It doesn't matter."

"Why don't you come on out of the john and talk about it?"

"Let's just talk on the telephone for a few minutes."

"Why did you do it? Business was good. You could have just retired. Why did you kill twenty–seven people, your employees and customers?"

"To protect my son. I had to kill that worthless bitch he was planning to marry. She would have destroyed him. Made him a weak fool. I couldn't let that happen. I thought if I just arranged something horrible enough, she'd be lost in the shuffle."

I looked down the hall. Albrick looked like he was having trouble standing up. I felt a little woozy myself.

Rushton was still talking. "... too late, of course. She'd already made a weak fool out of him. He killed himself over her, can you imagine that? My son killing himself over a tramp. If he was that far gone he's better off dead."

"You killed twenty–seven people to break up your son's engagement?"

"Cobb, I'd kill a million people to protect what's mine."

I was speechless. Rushton laughed into the silence. "I told you, Cobb, you can never know what's in another person's mind. Now listen. The combination on the wall safe is 22–35–51–33–19. In about twenty minutes, have the sheriff tell one of his men to put a few bullets through the window here, then wait another half hour before anybody tries to go in."

I heard a hissing noise. "Bye bye, Cobb. Tell Lew I did it for him ..."

There was a thump and a sharp click as both Rushton and the receiver hit the floor.

"Simple," I told Mona on the plane back to New York. "He deliberately cultivated the cat to have an excuse to be out of the building when the gas went off. He'd already stolen the diamonds a few at a time. Didn't even steal them — they were his. Sneaked them out of the store. Then he called the fiancée, told her he wanted to talk to her, maybe he could come to accept her yet, and so forth. Then he beat it out the back with the cat, but not before he was sure his target was on the premises."

"He — he was *evil*, Matt. Pure evil."

"Ought to make for a great show."

"Jesus, how crass can you get?"

I just smiled.

"How did Lew take it?"

"How do you think? Pretty damn bad, but better, I think, than Albrick took to the notion that he was the custodian of thirty-five or so million dollars in diamonds until the insurance company gets there."

"Did you tell Lew what his grandfather said?"

"That he did it all for him? I did not."

"Why not?"

"How'd you like to think twenty-seven innocent people, one guilty bastard, and one cat were slaughtered because somebody loved you?"

"I see what you mean." She chewed her lip for a few moments. "Matt?"

"Yeah?"

"I think we'll leave it out of the show, too."

"Okay by me," I said, and settled back in the seat to try to go to sleep.

Killed in Good Company

My eyes burned from something worse than tear gas. I squinted as tightly as I could, but I had to keep my eyes open a crack, to follow the yellow cone the flashlight made in the smoky interior of the cabin. To try to find Doug Empsey and drag him the hell out of there, even though I could tell from what was happening to me, it was surely too late.

Outside, I could hear Ethel Eden's hoarse voice telling me to hurry. It was nice to have encouragement, but it was superfluous. If I didn't find Empsey *that second* I'd have to — but there he was. He was between the small frame bed and the rough wall of the cabin, on the floor. There was a window there — maybe he'd been trying with his crippled hands to get it open. To get some air.

Air. That was the idea. I'd been holding my breath as much as possible behind a wet, thick scarf that I'd wrapped across my face, but I'd risked a few inhalations, every one of which had been a mistake. I burned inside now, and I had to get out.

There was no time to be gentle, now. I dropped the flashlight, put one knee on the rumpled cot, braced myself with one gloved hand, and with the other, I grabbed him by the collar of his T-shirt and pulled.

I cursed as the fabric started to tear, but the rip hit a seam and stopped, and Doug Empsey came flying over the cot like a marlin being hauled into a boat.

I didn't stop to admire him. Instead, I got to my feet and started dragging him. My eyes felt like chunks of meat grilled on a skewer by now, and I couldn't see much, but I could make out the rectangle of light that was the open doorway. I made for it.

Empsey had seemed to weigh practically nothing when I pulled him over the bed, but he got heavier with every step as my air and energy gave out.

Finally, with a scream, I got him out the door and dragged him about seven feet away from the cabin. I took a bleary-eyed look at him for a second, but I couldn't make out any features, just a mass of red, blistered flesh. He might still be alive, but I couldn't do anything more for him. I staggered on a few more steps, then collapsed on the cool grass, still crisp with the early autumn morning frost. Each breath was a new river of fire, and my eyes were melting and dribbling out of my head.

From behind me, I heard small footsteps and a slamming door. Ethel had shut whatever was in the cabin back inside. I wanted to applaud her, but I couldn't think of anything but the pain.

"Don't rub your eyes!" she commanded, and my hands stopped halfway there.

"I hear sirens," she said. "Help is coming."

"Uh-awww, uh-auggh," I said. That was supposed to be "What about Doug?"

Either she understood me, or she filled me in figuring I'd want to know, which seems more likely. "Doug's dead," she said. "It's ... horrible."

It flashed through my mind that this woman had covered countless wars, famines, and disasters around the world over the last thirty years, a period in history particularly rich in them. If *she* thought something was horrible, it probably was.

I wanted to ask her how I looked, but it was too much trouble. I passed out before she could have answered me, anyway.

I t was the sort of letter it would take a whole new mind-set to respond to. I wasn't especially interested in resetting my mind, but that's why God gives us girlfriends.

"You've got to do this," Roxanne said. She pulled her knees up under one of the extra-large T-shirts she liked to sleep in. It was Saturday morning, and we were at my borrowed apartment on Central Park West. The mail had arrived. There was nothing worth noting except a cream–color envelope with GO Productions and a Manhattan address printed in the corner. It was addressed to "Mr. Matthew Cobb" which usually meant junk mail. Anybody who knows me at all usually skips the "mister" and keeps it to "Matt."

Still, since it purported to be from a production company, I figured I might as well have a look. It presented a little mystery.

It's not unusual for a TV executive to get mail from production companies, and I do work for the network as Vice President in Charge of Special Projects. And it's not unusual for people to get the wrong idea about just what Special Projects is, since the name was deliberately chosen to be obscure. What we do is try to keep the network's nose — or as much of it as the public and regulators can see — well wiped. We do everything too nasty for Public Relations, and too sensitive for Security.

It *is* unusual, however, for this sort of mail to reach me at home, since I am the beneficiary of what seems to have turned out to be the longest and most luxurious sublet in the history of New York City. The original deal was that I would watch the apartment on Central Park West for Rick and Jane Sloan, college friends of mine who would rather live in a tent studying endo–cannibals in the Mato Grosso than have barbecued chicken brought to their door by the local deli, mere fools they.

In any case, I watch the apartment and their dog. Spot is an attack–trained Samoyed with black nose, black eyes, and perpetually smiling black lips the only contrast to his cloud of pure white fur. I'd been sitting him so long, I'm sure he had completely forgotten I wasn't his master.

Anyway, we were lazing around the apartment. Spot was allowing himself to be petted alternately by Roxanne and me. And I opened the letter and read it.

"Oh, for God's sake," I said.

"What is it, Matt?" Roxanne wanted to know.

I chuckled. "Maybe I shouldn't tell you. It says here it was specifically sent to me at home so the network wouldn't have to know about it."

She brushed some black hair from her eyes and said, "I am not the network."

I forbore to point out that she was the granddaughter of the network's founder, and still the largest single stockholder.

"Come on," she insisted. "What does it say?"

"Oh, all right. It's from somebody named Gary Oshen, head of GO Productions. Dear Mr. Cobb, bla bla bla, in case you prefer not to receive this kind of communication at work, bla bla bla, this letter.

" 'I have received a grant from the Max N. Serra Foundation to produce a film I plan to call *No Secrets*. In it, I plan to gather some top investigators from all fields, and have them talk about various aspects of their craft, both in individual interviews and in a roundtable format —' "

I interrupted myself. "Why is he telling me all this?"

Rox told me to read on. I did so. " 'Such famous names as Sheriff Lamar Briggs of Georgia, private eye Doug Empsey, and Pulitzer prize–winning investigative reporter Ethel Eden have already agreed to attend. Your participation would make the film complete, assembling an official policeman, a reporter, an individual private investigator, and (yourself) an investigator whose skills are at the disposal of a large corporation. The core of the film would be a roundtable discussion,' bla, bla —"

I looked up from the page. "Is he out of his mind? I'm a TV guy. The investigations are an unfortunate by–product of the job I happen to have."

Roxanne's dark eyes were big with mock innocence. "So?" she said. "Sheriff Briggs probably thinks of himself as a speeding ticket guy who gets stuck with investigations, too."

"Come on, Rox. He fights crime for a living."

Roxanne laughed. "Matt," she said, "I love you, but you're awfully dense sometimes. What the hell do you do? The only difference is that Lamar Briggs does it for the people of his county, and you do it for my grandfather's grasping corporate octopus."

I was a little defensive. "Well, trouble turns up."

She nodded sympathetically. "Funny how that happens in a glamorous multibillion–dollar corporation in the public eye."

"Yeah." I started sticking the letter back in the envelope. "No sense rehashing those old scandals for a panting public. I'll send regrets."

Rox shook her head. "You've got to do this," she said, pulling her legs into her T-shirt.

"Why?"

"Because you want to. You know you do."

"It's embarrassing."

"Hey, this is me, Cobb, remember? Your lover? The woman who knows you better than anybody on earth? You do a good job of hiding it, but you've got an ego the size of the Empire State Building. You love the idea of being included in company like that."

"They're world famous! I'd make an ass out of myself."

"You ought to be used to that by now."

"Oh, thank you, darling."

She smiled sweetly. "It's quite all right, love. Now, you go ahead and do this. I'll never forgive you if you don't."

That wasn't the end of it, of course. We argued about it the rest of the weekend. But the outcome was never in doubt. By the end, I knew that deep down I did really want to go and confer, converse and otherwise hobnob with the Master Snoopers. Giving us an excuse to do what we really want to do anyway is another reason God gives us girlfriends. Monday morning, I told Gary Oshen I'd be glad to be there.

The get-together was set for Columbus Day weekend in Maine, at Empsey's Nest, a hunting and fishing resort run by Doug Empsey and his daughter since his retirement from the private-eye business.

I got off the plane in Orinoo alone. After nudging me into the trip, you would have thought Roxanne would have come along, but she had a big exam on Tuesday (the woman's hobby is academics—she has more degrees than a Celsius thermometer by now) and she wanted the long weekend to study.

A square, solid woman about my age dressed in plaid corduroy and L.L. Bean duck boots said, "Cobb?"

Killed in Good Company

I admitted it.

She put out her hand. "Hi. I'm Sharon Empsey. Since I was in town anyway, I thought I'd meet you and take you to the lodge."

I told her thanks, and climbed into the passenger seat of an Isuzu Trooper, the back of which was filled with groceries, it was a tight squeeze to get my little suitcase in.

"Doesn't look like you brought a gun or any tackle with you," she said.

"Nope. I had my fill of guns in the army."

"Nam?"

"Fringes. I was an MP."

"Important job," she offered. Her utterances were clipped, but her voice was lovely, low and smooth. She had dark hair drawn back in a no-nonsense ponytail, and her cool blue eyes were glued to the road.

I shrugged. "It got to be a drag," I said. "Two million Americans sent over there to fight Communists, and they send me over to fight Americans."

"So you don't shoot. Don't fish, either?"

"I'm a city boy. Never got the urge."

"We don't have a lot to offer at the lodge outside of hunting and fishing," she said. "Hope you don't get bored."

"I've brought a few books to read. And the company should be interesting. If all else fails, I can catch up on my sleep."

"You don't look that tired. As for the company being interesting, don't count on my old man. He doesn't talk much, and when he does, he's usually asking questions. Private-eye habit, I guess."

That made sense. Since I, too, was supposed to be one of the ace investigators I figured I'd uphold my image and ask a few questions myself.

"Am I the first one here?"

"Nope. Lamar Briggs got in yesterday. Gary Oshen has been around for days, making a nuisance of himself. Right now he's painting the lobby."

"Don't tell me. He has a color he thinks will look better on film."

"Yeah." Sharon Empsey smiled a little. "How'd you know that? Most people I tell about it think I put him to work."

"I work in television," I said. "He's doing the painting himself?"

"He's doing everything himself. Far as I can tell, he's a one-man show."

"I guess the Max N. Serra Foundation didn't overload him with money."

"Nah. He's not even paying for the lodge. I agreed to let him use it — figured it would be good publicity. And it will be nice to see Dad back in the public eye again. Not that you could get him to admit it."

"Your father's being difficult?"

"When is he not? But this time he's been impossible. According to him, I shouldn't have let anybody use the lodge without his permission — hell, I've been running this place single-handed since I was twenty. He never pays attention to what I do, and I've kept the place profitable every year, which is more than he ever did. Now he just stays in his cabin halfway up the mountain and comes down a couple of times a week to complain about something."

"Shame."

Sharon smiled again. "Yeah, well, I think he misses the chase. Now, with his arthritis, he can't even hunt and fish as much as he used to. Anyway, he came around. You're here, the movie is going to be made, Dad is going to participate."

Her face was suddenly serious. "Though that was a near thing, too."

"How's that?"

"When he found out Ethel Eden was going to be here."

"I thought they were great friends."

"Once they were. At one point, I thought Dad was going to marry her. Then the Skeggens case got between them."

"I remember hearing about that one, but I didn't catch up on all the details."

This time, the smile was a little twisted. "I'm sure you will before the weekend is out. Suffice to say, my dad and Ethel wound up on opposite sides. There may be some fireworks when the two of them set eyes on each other again, though I wouldn't bet what kind."

"You're eager to see it happen, though, aren't you?" I asked.

"What are you talking about?"

"You want to see them back together. That's why you let Oshen use the lodge and talked your dad into going through with it. You're playing matchmaker."

"Oh, I am, huh? In the marriage sense or in the boxing sense?"

I sized her up. I had hit a nerve, no doubt about that, but she wasn't giving anything away. "I don't know," I said at last. "Could be either. You tell me."

"I've told you too much already. It's a gift with you detective types, isn't it? People just shoot off their mouths to you. Well, forget it. If I were making matches, I'd make one for myself. As much as I love the wilderness, it's no place to meet guys. Are you taken, cutie?"

That called for a double take, and I did one. I saw she was smiling, which made me feel better.

"As a matter of fact I am," I said.

"Figures. Here's the lodge."

She checked me in, then showed me to a room that was clean, comfortable, and rustic. No phone, no TV, no radio. It was, as she said, a place for people who wanted to get away from it all. She told me there'd be a get-together in the lobby at six o'clock, and left me to my book.

I read for a while — *Justice at Nuremberg*, by Robert E. Conot. Now *there* was a criminal case. Of course there wasn't a whole lot to do in the way of investigation, since the Nazis were so proud of themselves they kept detailed notes on every depraved thing they did.

When it was time, I headed for the lobby. On the way downstairs, I tried to remind myself that these people, as much as I might admire them, as much as they had accomplished, were still just people, and I shouldn't embarrass myself or them by gushing on them. It was the sort of thing I used to have to tell myself a lot in my early days with the network, when I kept meeting the Greats of Show Biz. Since then, I've become pretty blasé about show biz. But finding killers and exposing corruption are slightly more important than pretending to be a frontier doctor, and the people I was about to meet had been doing it for years.

Actually, the first person I met was Gary Oshen. If you move in certain circles anywhere in the United States or Canada, you've met dozens of him — he was a Filmmaker. One word. Capitalized. Two m's. They run around, documenting the things in life that the networks never get around to covering, living on grants and small film festival prizes, and occasionally doing a commissioned film for a charity or government project or something. I probably sound as if I'm putting them down, but I don't mean to. Part of what's wrong with the media in this country is that too few people produce it. These men and women redress the balance a little.

Gary Oshen was a recognizable subspecies — somebody with ambitions beyond cheap documentaries. He might make it, too. He was pushy enough.

"Matt," he said. A hand stuck out from the forest of photographic gear that hung about his torso. "I'm so glad you could come. I hope you had a pleasant trip."

"Not bad at all. Nice color you picked for the lobby."

"Good, good. The airport's pretty busy for a town this size, because the University's nearby, of course. Listen, would you mind going up to the top of the stairs again and coming down? I want to get the entrance of all the participants — you know, 'Cobb takes the case!' "

I looked at him. He was smallish, with coarse black hair, wire glasses and the youthful smile of a Jewish Howdy Doody.

"I thought we were going to talk, and you were going to film what happened."

"Oh, well, you work for the network. You know we've got to open up the film a little. Let in a little air."

I decided to give him a chance. I went back up the stairs and descended again. He passed. He didn't try to ask me to do it again. Then he gave me a release to sign.

"Okay, after this, forget I'm here, okay? Just mingle. The rest of them are in there." He pointed to a room off the lobby I hadn't been to before. "Have fun!"

I heard the camera whirring behind me as I went. I was glad he was using high film. I didn't need some hot spotlights cooking my eyeballs while I was trying to be natural.

"You're wrong," I said to Oshen as I went in. "They're not all here."

"You're not supposed to talk to me now."

"Where's Empsey?"

"He'll be here. Talk to the other guests."

So I did. A tiny woman with short, soft brown hair and a tall, white-haired man were sharing a drink with Sharon Empsey, who in a long skirt and a silk blouse looked rounder and softer than she had in flannel and corduroy that afternoon.

They were talking about the weather — Oshen was going to love that for cinematic potential. I waited for a lull, then I said, "Hi."

Sharon introduced me to Ethel Eden and Lamar Briggs. Miss Eden — she'd been married a couple of times, but she'd always remained "Miss Eden." Those birdlike brown eyes of hers and that thin little beaky nose had been poked relentlessly into the business of everybody from starlets to dictators, mobsters to athletes, for the past forty years, and they always seemed to see or smell crime or scandal. In her sixties, she was still at it. The network news had recently had pictures of her scrambling across rooftops in Bosnia, following up information on a phony charity that was bilking relief-minded contributors in the States.

She was wearing her trademark jodhpurs, riding boots, and safari shirt, and she looked at me like a teacher with a promising but so far disappointing student.

"Mr. Cobb!" she said. "I've researched you. You're good. Why do you waste your talents helping *management*, for heaven's sake?"

"Management has the money," I said blandly.

"Nonsense!" she sniffed. "I've made more money than you ever will. If you must work for that network, get on the air! Expose some corruption! Make waves!"

I told her I'd keep it in mind, and turned and shook with Lamar Briggs. He was tall, much taller than my six-two, with a tall man's slouch and an air of slow competence about him. He was dressed in rumpled tweeds, and he looked a lot more like a college professor than a lawman.

"Don't you mind Ms. Eden," he said in a deep drawl. "Seein' me just brings back bad memories for her."

"How's that?"

Briggs showed me a sly grin. "Back in nineteen hundred sixty-three, she come down to my county lookin' to find out who killed this fellow from up North who was gettin' Nigras out to vote. She come lookin' because she didn't think I would be, you see. She was what you call prejudiced."

Ethel Eden took in a sharp breath. "I don't appreciate that, Lamar."

"Sorry, ma'am. Anyway, the day she breezes in, askin' me what I intend to do, I brought her in the back room and showed her I'd already done it."

"Done what?" I asked.

"Found the killer. It was a peckerwood named Sam Pettison. I guess you'd call him a white supremacist, which is kind of pathetic considerin' Sam probably wasn't superior to a single livin' thing on earth. Anyway, I caught him, we prosecuted him, the good people of the county convicted him, and he's in the penitentiary yet. I bet you never heard about this."

I admitted I hadn't.

Ethel Eden sniffed again. "I wrote about it. I wrote all about it. I told the truth."

"Yes, ma'am. I think it appeared on page forty-seven of *The New York Times*."

"A reporter has nothing to say about where her story appears," the journalist protested.

"No, ma'am," Briggs said. "But, Ethel, darlin', as I've told you before, I remain convinced she learns real fast what kind of story makes the front page and what kind doesn't."

"You're impossible," Ethel Eden said, but there was affection behind the asperity in her voice. "Almost as bad as Doug Empsey."

"Yes," Sharon Empsey said. "I wonder where Dad is?"

"I'm here, I'm here," said a hoarse voice, familiar from dozens of TV interviews. The well-known form of Doug Empsey followed. He wasn't tall, but he was impressive, even into his seventies, square and stocky and powerful-looking. There was a little softness around the middle, but he still looked tough enough. He wasn't wearing his trademark dark suit and fedora. He was wearing a blue plaid sport jacket over an open-necked sport shirt, and his unruly mop of hair had gone gray. The face was still the same, though, nose mashed slightly to the left over a good-natured crooked grin.

Then we shook hands, and I knew the difference. Sharon had mentioned her father's arthritis, but I hadn't figured it would be as bad as this. He sort of reached over my hand and pinched it with his fingertips. I didn't squeeze back — his fingers felt as fragile as a handful of breadsticks.

It was kind of sad. The fists that had laid waste to the Brooklyn mob, the hands that had held the famous .45 that ended the career of the kidnappers of three-year-old Nancy Salliman, now probably needed a tool to open a can of beer.

It didn't seem to bother him. Of course, he'd had a while to get used to it, over twenty years since he'd retired, I realized. He told me he was glad to see me, patted Briggs on the back and said, "Lamar," then put an arm around Ethel Eden's waist and gave her a large and enthusiastic kiss.

It was a bit of a shock — I mean, *I* wouldn't have dreamed of kissing her, but then again, I didn't know her when she was young and cute. Ethel Eden, it is fair to say, was not revolted. She, in fact, kissed back in a way that said she'd been down this particular road before, and hadn't minded the trip in the least.

When they broke she said, "Hello, Douglas. I see you haven't changed."

"You either, doll. I hope the kid got that on film. It'll help his movie."

That was disingenuous, since Gary Oshen had been popping in and out of everybody's line of sight, sticking a camera in our nostrils at the slightest provocation, and telling us to ignore him anytime one of us looked in his direction.

"No one," Ethel Eden intoned, "wants to see two old relics kissing."

"Except the old relics themselves," Empsey said.

Sharon looked at her watch and said dinner was ready. As she chivied us into the dining room, her father called over his shoulder to Oshen, "Don't worry, kid, we'll find something to liven up your film."

I woke up. I couldn't see. I tried to rub my eyes, but I couldn't move.

I tried to call for help, but I made no sound. There was something in my mouth, but I couldn't spit it out.

I didn't think I was dead. Dead people didn't get this mad — or this scared. I had visions of myself in total, insensate paralysis trapped inside my own head, getting crazier and crazier from isolation, with no one knowing it until I died.

I started thrashing around. I could move that much, even if my arms seemed to be tied down. I shook and twisted all I could until someone came and stuck a needle in me, and I was gone again.

I don't know how long I was out this time. I still couldn't see or move my arms. I think I began to cry, but I made no sobs.

The only sounds I heard were metallic rasps.

I could feel the panic welling up in me again, but I fought it. It hadn't done me any good the last time.

A woman's voice said, "Mr. Cobb? Mr. Cobb?"

I could turn my head a little. I turned it in the direction of the voice.

"Mr. Cobb, I'm Dr. Clara Connor, you're in the University Hospital, and I've been treating you. Nod your head if you understand."

I nodded.

"Very good. Now, I suppose you want to know what's wrong with you." She didn't wait for an answer. "You have been severely poisoned — by poison ivy, to be precise."

Poison ivy? I thought. Impossible. Of course, I'd seen some on the way up to the cabin with Ethel Eden, but I'd been careful to avoid it. In the fall, when the shiny leaves are bright red, poison ivy is even easier to avoid than it is the rest of the time. And if you're wondering how a city boy like me knows about poison ivy, I'll take you to Central Park and show you at least six lovely patches of it.

"Someone had burned a large quantity of poison ivy in the fireplace of the cabin you entered, and droplets of the irritant oil were disseminated by the smoke. You were lucky you got out of there when you did."

I'll bet I was. The doctor's words also informed me that Ethel had been right — Doug Empsey had to be dead. I thought of the blisters all over him, on his eyes and lips, and shuddered. What the hell did *I* look like?

Dr. Connor was psychic. "You have a serious skin rash on your face, head, neck, and part of your chest, a slightly lesser irritation on the palm of your left hand."

Every place she mentioned began to itch. I wished she'd shut up.

She didn't. "In addition, your eyes and throat were severely affected. Don't worry though, there should be no problem in getting completely well. Your eyes are bandaged, and your hands have been tied to the bed frame to keep you from rubbing your eyes in your sleep. There is an oxygen tube in your mouth. For the first thirty-six hours, we had an airway to your lungs, but we were able to remove that."

The *first* thirty-six hours? What the hell day was it? How long had I been here?

Either the doctor's psychic powers failed her, or she didn't want me to know. Instead she said, "You have been receiving intravenous medication — lidocaine, Demerol, and an antihistamine to fight swelling. You have responded well to the medication. Now, I'm going to run down a list of symptoms. You nod for me if any of them applies to you."

She did. The only one that made a difference was sore throat, of which I had a beaut. The doctor explained in the talking voice she used that that was the result of pouring almost pure oxygen on a throat already irritated by poison ivy. Still it was important that I get as much oxygen as possible because my throat was still swollen, and if I liked, she could increase the dose of painkiller.

I thought about it, but realized it was probably the painkiller that had made me act so crazy the first time I woke up. I was figuring out a few things in spite of the fog that surrounded me. For instance, poison ivy doesn't grow wild in fireplaces. If it had been there, somebody had put it there, and Doug Empsey had been deliberately murdered. Furthermore, the fact that I wasn't dead as well seemed to be only the rarest good luck. Therefore, I owed somebody a major stomping, and I wanted my wits about me to make sure it got delivered to the right address.

I shook my head no.

"Sure now? All right then. Now, I want to remove the bandage from your eyes."

I nodded enthusiastically. I could start to rasp in the respirator.

"All right, calm down, now. Lean back and let the nurse and me — that's it."

I heard scissor blades grate softly near my ears, then I felt gauze being unwrapped until I felt a cool breeze on the bridge of my nose and around my temples.

I still couldn't see. I tried to grab for my eyes.

"Relax, relax," the doctor said. "You still have gauze pads on your eyes. Please keep both eyes closed until I tell you to open them."

I didn't obey her, but I didn't jump the gun by enough to make her mad. At least I waited until both pads were gone.

I blinked against the light, though I didn't want to, because the light was glorious. Colors and fuzzy shapes, at first, then after a few more painful blinks, colors and sharper shapes.

Dr. Clara Connor was pleasant enough looking, in a fatigued sort of way, but in that moment she was beautiful. If I had my arms, I would have hugged her. If I'd had my voice, I would have proposed.

She saw the look on my face, and decided not to replace the bandage. "But," she warned me and the nurse, "this room must stay dim." She turned to me exclusively. "You get some more rest. We'll take out that air thing and see how your throat is this evening. The police will want to talk to you."

That was fine with me. For a New York blabber–mouth such as myself to have his mouth taped shut was sheer torture, especially when I had a murder to catch up on. The cops? Hell, I'd be happy to talk to the Nuremberg Tribunal or the Ronkonkoma, L.I., PTA as soon as I could get my pipes working again.

The nurse immediately dimmed the lights, and I could see even better. I just enjoyed looking at things for a few minutes — the competence with which the nurse adjusted the drips on my IVs, the red rubber bellows whose falling and rising matched the rasping noise of the respirator, the neat white boxing glove of gauze on my left band, the soft but strong pieces of cloth that bound my wrists. Eventually, if I knew myself, I'd come to hate it all, hate the hospital, hate myself for being sick.

Right now, though, I was just happy to be more or less alive. I put my head back on the pillow and let the respirator lull me to sleep.

There's a saying in the TV biz that controversy makes a good show. There's no doubt Gary Oshen believed it — he was practically licking his chops behind the camera when the subject of the Skeggens case came up.

It was Lamar Briggs who raised the topic, which was a surprise, considering how intimately both Doug Empsey and Ethel Eden had been involved in the thing. On further consideration, though, it occurred to me that they both might just have been avoiding it.

"... A lawman, you see," Briggs said with a sly smile, "has to go by the *rules*. He can't go *houndin'* someone to death the way you did that Skeggens boy out in Ohio."

Doug Empsey ran his tongue around his cheek, but said nothing.

It was the early seventies, the height of anti–Vietnam protesting. A high school kid named Chucky Scott blew himself to bits in the closed offices of Mycroft, Ohio, draft board, apparently attempting plant a bomb. There was suspicion that Chucky had been provided with the bomb by a friend, a college sophomore named Lester Skeggens, who was a science whiz (which Chucky definitely was not) and who had fallen in with some very radical pals on campus.

Suspicion, but no proof. The cops had had to leave it there, but Chucky's father hadn't. He'd hired Doug Empsey to find out what had happened. Empsey had proceeded to investigate. He questioned everybody. He questioned Lester Skeggens four or five times. The media picked it up, including Ethel Eden, who heretofore had been a close friend of Empsey's (a lover, if Sharon could be believed). Her position was that she had "sources" who told her that Chucky had been sacrificed by a group of right-wing plotters who wanted to discredit legitimate war protests.

Doug Empsey had had one comment for the record — "Bullshit." He'd gone on with his investigation. He questioned Skeggens one more time.

Later that night, Lester Skeggens took poison. The case sort of petered out after that. Empsey took expenses but no fee from Chucky's father. A short while after that, he retired.

"That's not fair," Ethel Eden said. "Doug might have been hopelessly wrong in that case, but he did what an investigator has to do. Gracious, if I worried about how my subject's feelings would be affected by my investigation of something, I'd still be writing up tea parties for the society page.

"Of course, my forthcoming autobiography, *What's She Doing Here?* will have what I consider to be the final word on the topic." She smiled demurely. "You'll all have to buy it to find out."

The conversation went on to other things. I noticed Doug Empsey didn't say much. He just kept looking at Ethel with an expression it was impossible to read.

Eventually we broke it up for the night. I was eager to talk with my fellow guests off the record, but by the time I found a phone, called Roxanne, and wished her good night, they'd all dispersed. Only Sharon Empsey was left in the lounge.

"Where'd everybody go?" I asked.

"Lamar Briggs claimed age and walked off to his cabin. He asked for one of the cabins, you know. Dad and Ethel went for a walk."

"Oho."

Sharon grinned at me. "Oho yourself. They haven't seen each other for a long time, and they've got making up and catching up to do. Did you see my father looking at her?"

"I did. I don't know what he was thinking, but he was thinking it hard."

"Must be wonderful to be fascinating to men," she said.

"You just have to get to a place where you can meet more men. If I'd met you a couple of years ago, who knows what might have happened?"

"Is that supposed to cheer me up?"

I smiled and shrugged and decided I might as well get to bed, too.

Dr. Connor came in next morning and took the respirator out. I had a drink of water. It was fabulous. I got to take about five natural breaths when Stephen King walked in. Well, it wasn't really Stephen King. It was investigator Harry Terzo of the state police. But he was tall, with an angular face, deepset blue eyes, black hair, and a weedy Maine–tinged voice, the mistake was natural.

"Do you know you look like —" I stopped. My voice sounded weird — weak, rough, and far away. I realized it was the first time I'd heard it in days.

"Yeah, yeah. Are you up to a few questions, Mr. Cobb?"

"Sure," I said. "I've got a million questions."

"I meant are you up to answering a few? Then maybe I can answer some for you."

"Okay. What do you want to know?"

"Just tell me what happened that night in your own words." He frowned. "What's the matter?"

I grimaced. "They must have cut my medicine down. I'm starting to itch. Especially my left hand." I looked at it, but of course all I could see was the gauze mitten. I flexed it a few times, just to bring the flesh in contact with the fabric of the bandage and get some scratch action that way. It helped a little, not much. I did much better concentrating on my story.

There must have been something in the air up there. I slept like a rock until four a.m. Then there was a knock on my door. Something in my brain always knows what time it is within ten minutes or so, but I checked my watch anyway. "Who is it?"

A woman's voice said, "Cobb, open up. It's important."

I came wider awake now. "Ethel?" I was puzzled. I hadn't been expecting a woman to come calling in the middle of the night, but if it was going to be one, I'd have expected it to be Sharon Empsey.

"Yes, it's me. Open up."

"I'm not dressed."

"I've seen a naked man before. This is important."

"Wait a second." I pulled on my pants and got the door. "Come in," I said.

Ethel Eden was fully dressed in her trademark jodhpur outfit. She'd added a leather jacket and a battered safari hat to the mix. She looked like Indiana Jones's mother.

She pointed at my pants. "That's a good start," she said. "Keep getting dressed. And do it right. We're going through the woods."

She was so sure of herself that I kept getting dressed, even though I didn't have the slightest idea what she was talking about. That much, I thought, I could fix. "Will you kindly tell me what the hell is going on?"

"I got a phone call."

"A phone call? There's a phone in your room?"

"There's a phone wherever I go. Cellular. Communications technology, young man. I thought that was your field."

"Only peripherally. What was this phone call?"

"From Doug. He's in trouble. He's hurt. Or something. He didn't say much before he stopped talking."

I sat on the bed and started pulling on my shoes. "Shouldn't you tell his daughter?"

She made a noise. "Her. She hates my guts. She'd waste too much time talking. Not that it looks as though I've done much better with you."

"Ha, ha."

"I'd get Briggs, but he's way out there in the row of cabins somewhere."

"All right," I said. I pulled on my nylon wind breaker, stuffed a pair of gloves into my pocket. Let's go."

It was a steep path up the hill to Doug Empsey's private cabin. In the false dawn, it was just possible to pick your steps. Empsey, according to his daughter, ran this path like a mountain goat — no wonder he was in such good shape. The path was crossed constantly with roots and vines, and I could hear creatures out there in the underbrush.

At one point, Ethel missed her footing, and if I hadn't spun around and grabbed the right sleeve of her jacket, we would have gone rolling backward to the bottom of the hill.

Doug Empsey's place was in a clearing on a ridge. Light leaked from around wooden shutters. There was nobody around, no screams, no outward signs of trouble.

As I got close to the door, I smelled something nasty. I backed away and pulled on my gloves. Ethel wet a scarf in a puddle, and gave it to me to put over my face.

"I'm going to have to get this door open," I said. "I'll probably have to bust it in."

"Try the knob," Ethel Eden said. "He keeps it open. With his arthritis, it's hard to work a key."

"You stand back a little," I told her. "If I run into trouble, you get more help, I don't care who hates your guts."

She patted the phone in her pocket. "I called the police before I woke you up," she told me.

"Yeah," I said. I twisted the knob, hit the door with my shoulder, and walked into the poison–ivy fumes.

"If I can add a personal comment," I told Terzo, "this is about the nastiest goddamn murder I ever heard of."

Terzo's mouth was a tight line. "You got that right. The poor bastard in there with his useless hands. All the killer had to do was climb the roof, drop a bunch of poison ivy down the chimney — no big trick to climb that roof by the way."

"I know. I saw it. Go right up the side of the chimney. A fat lady could climb it in heels."

"Right. Then slide down and hold the door closed until you were sure he was unconscious. What could he do about it with those hands?"

Terzo scratched his jaw. Then he pulled a visitor's seat close to the bed and said, "Cobb, I'm going to let you in on this. You don't actually have an alibi, but nobody would have gone in there like you did if he knew what would happen. You nearly got killed yourself."

"Tell me about it. But you never know. Remember that schmuck in Boston who killed his wife, then shot himself in the stomach."

"Not the same thing. He was aiming at his leg. Also, you don't have the ghost of a motive."

"Okay. You convinced me. You should let me in. In on what?"

"It would have been even easier. Empsey used to take painkillers at night, according to his daughter. Strong stuff. Knocked him right out, slept like a log."

"So if the killer knew, he could just waltz in with an armload of poison ivy and dump it on the fire. Even light a fire if he needed to."

"Exactly."

"Who knew?"

"Too many people. The daughter and the whole staff of the place. How many outsiders could they have told? Infinity."

"How's Sharon taking it?"

"Hard. I get the impression her whole life has been wrapped up in her old man. But she'll be okay. She's tough. I like her."

"What about the rest?"

He shrugged. "Your fellow guests? Professionals. Deadpan. Of course, they don't have motives, either. I suppose Eden could be nursing a broken heart from way back, or something, but I doubt it. And I saw the videotape. Briggs was busting Empsey's ass on the Skeggens thing, but if that was anything more than some innocent ball busting, I'd have to have it shown to me."

"What about the young producer?"

"Oshen? He's eating this up with a *spoon*. Keeps following *me* around with a goddamn camera. I'm about an inch away from punching him in the mouth. I'm almost ready to believe he did it to liven up his goddamn TV show."

I told him that was true to form both for Oshen and for a cop. "Find anything else?"

"Like what?"

"I don't know. Footprints on the roof? Threads snagged in bushes around Empsey's cabin? Anybody come down with poison ivy and can't explain it?"

"Just you, and you've got an explanation."

"Tell me about it," I said again.

"All we found was some stuff in the fireplace. Hard wood ash, from the regular fire, you know, poison-ivy ash, remains of some papers somebody burned in there, and some burned-up leather. Probably the killer's gloves."

"Smart," I said.

"Yeah. Use them to protect your hands, then burn them, so you don't get poison-ivy juice on things and give yourself away. You can't really wash that stuff off leather very well."

I closed my eyes. I couldn't believe how tired I was.

After a few seconds, Terzo said, "Well?"

I opened my eyes. They still took a few seconds to focus. Not all better yet.

"Well what?"

"You had your eyes closed. I thought you detective types did that to concentrate."

"Don't listen to Gary Oshen, all right? I closed my eyes because I was tired."

"Oh. Maybe you want to sleep."

"I suppose. It's hard to read with your hands tied up."

"Well, you've got another visitor out here. Been making a nuisance of herself for days. Threatened bodily harm to the doctor."

I could feel my irritated face stretching in a big smile. "Roxanne is here? Send her in for God's sake!"

"Sure. I was just going. You think about this, okay?"

"Yeah," I said grimly. "I'll think about it. Terzo, this joker almost killed me, too, remember?"

"I didn't think you'd need to be reminded of that. See you."

He opened the door. Roxanne almost bowled him over running into the room.

"Hi, honey," I said.

She came to the bed and stood over me. Her face got more and more frantic.

"What's the matter?" I demanded.

"Shit!" she said. "There's nowhere to kiss!"

"We'll make up for it later."

"Darn right we will. Oh, Matt, I'm so glad to hear you talk. They let me in here during the first couple of days. You were a mess."

"I don't want to hear about it," I told her. "Let me think."

"All right. You can even go to sleep if you want to. I'll just sit here and watch you." Then she reached out and gave my hand a little squeeze. My left hand.

"Ow!" I said.

Rox was apologetic, but I wasn't listening to her. I was looking at my left hand, my poison–ivy–infested left hand. And, as promised, thinking. Really thinking about how Doug Empsey died.

It took about a half hour. "Rox?" I said.

"Yes, Matt. I'm sorry about your hand."

"Don't worry about it. You solved the case."

She looked at me. "I did, huh?"

"You sure did."

"Gee, I must be brilliant."

"A genius. But I still need more help. I assume everybody is still around."

"Sure. Terzo won't let them go."

"Good. Here's what I want you to do …"

The killer came carefully into my room. "You're looking better. Sorry I haven't been by. Things have been hectic."

"That's okay," I said. "Lying here helpless is a full–time job. Nice jacket," I said. It was white canvas, still stiff.

"Yes, I decided the old image had to go."

"Right," I said, "and you can pop that one right into the washing machine, can't you, Ethel?"

"Yes, you can. Not that there are always washing machines where I travel."

"There isn't always poison ivy, either. What did you do with the leather one?"

"I got rid of it. Really, you're not making any sense."

"No? Then I'll be more specific. I've got poison–ivy rash all over my head and neck and face, and inside my throat from being exposed to the irritating oil in the smoke from Doug Empsey's fireplace. Fine. I've also got poison ivy on my left hand. Only my *left* hand. How did that happen? Not from the smoke. I put my gloves on when I went inside. I didn't get it on the path when we were headed up to the cabin. The only thing I touched on the way up was the sleeve of your jacket when you lost your balance heading up the hill. I caught your right arm with my left hand. How did I get poison ivy from your jacket? Because of the sap left on it by your carrying armloads of the stuff to put in Doug's fireplace.

"He never had a chance. When you went for your walk, did you go up to his cabin? Were you going to sleep together for old times' sake? Or did you leave and go back, after he'd taken his painkiller and you knew he'd be sound asleep? It didn't really matter, did it?"

"You're a sick man, Matt. It's the drugs they've given you. They've affected your brain."

"I don't think so. Nobody considered you for the crime; you had no motive. We'll get to that in a second. The crime itself was easy. Nobody would have an alibi; you'd have my swollen body — dead or alive — to prove you tried to help. All you had to do was to wait outside and listen. When the agony of breathing poison woke him up, as we know it did, all you had to do was hold the door closed while Doug scrabbled around with his crippled hands trying to get free. Did you enjoy it? Did you imagine the pain he was going through? I have to tell you, there's nothing quite like it."

"I find this very offensive."

"Too bad. You also made a big mistake. When, in the course of choking to death, and thrashing around trying to get out, did he have time to phone you?"

She ignored it. "You admit yourself, I have no motive."

"That's what everybody thought. But a possible motive occurred to me when I thought about what you'd said that night. About how your book was going to reveal the truth about the Skeggens case, how —"

Just then the phone rang. I chuckled and looked at my hands. "Would you mind getting that? Usually the nurse picks up and sticks it by my ear, but we don't want to be interrupted, do we? Just take a brief message, if you would."

Ethel Eden was still looking disgusted, but she'd decided the pose of humoring me was the best way to handle things, so she picked up the phone.

She listened for a second, then put the phone against the front of her shoulder. "It's someone named Roxanne. She says she and Sharon found it."

"That's great!" I said. "She probably heard that. Tell her I said not to open it."

Ethel put the phone back to her ear. "She heard that, too." She said good-bye and hung up the phone.

I was grinning. "Motive. There's your motive."

"I think you've been seeing the wrong kind of doctor."

"Well, the envelope will tell. I assume it's an envelope. Could be a box, I suppose. Duplicates of the papers Doug showed you the other night. The ones you burned with the poison ivy. What were they? Proof that Skeggens was guilty?"

Ethel was silent.

"I knew it had to be that. Doug had proof all along that Skeggens gave Chucky Scott that bomb, but he sat on it all these years. Quit the business. The poor bastard must have really loved you. Fat lot of good it did him.

"He'd taken the heat for years, let your reputation grow with your big conspiracy theory. Sacrificed his own reputation for you. But when you started touting a book that's going to 'tell the whole truth' once and for all, when he knows all you're going to do is enshrine a lie — that was too much to take.

"So he showed you the proof. Or reminded you he had it. And you killed him. In the nastiest possible way. You're really something, woman."

"He was a pig," she said. "How *dare* he cover up the truth for the sake of my reputation! I didn't need his *protection*. Said he did it because he *loved* me. He pretended to respect me and my career, but he treated me like a little mindless girl–creature. God, I wanted to kill him *then*.

"I deliberately talked about my book to get him to show me the paper — it was Skeggens's suicide note, by the way. Doug went there after Skeggens killed himself, found the body and note, and stole the note. Skeggens admitted his guilt. I wanted to lay my hands on it. Then I could destroy it, and Doug Empsey, and the hold he thought he had over me."

She sniffed and drew her head up. "I am not sorry. I would have gotten away with it, if he hadn't lied to me to the end, and said there was only one copy."

"Oh, that," I said. "No, he didn't lie. You burned the one and only copy. The call from Roxanne was a bluff. She's in the waiting room downstairs. I told her to watch you come in, wait five minutes, then call."

"Then you have no evidence. No evidence at all."

"There's my hand."

"That won't convince a jury of anything."

I gestured with my chin. "There's also this little black thing on the bed. It looks a lot like the button you use to call the nurse, but it's not. It's a miniature TV camera, the kind they put inside football players' helmets. Communications technology." I smiled. "My field. If you lift my sheet, you'll see a microphone there at the foot of the bed. And if you'll look out the window, you'll see Gary Oshen out on the fire escape, getting it all on tape. And drooling. Right, Gary?"

"Right!" The reply was a little muffled through the window, but came through clearly enough.

"You can't use this. It won't be admitted as evidence."

"Think again. We all signed blanket releases allowing Gary Oshen to videotape and air all our activities 'in the community of Orinoo, Maine.' This tape may not make it to court, but it's for damn sure making it to the network. You're through, Ethel."

"I've faced down dictators. You don't scare me."

"I don't care if I scare you. On behalf of my lungs, I just want to punish you. Which I have done."

She turned and walked out, but when she opened the door, the space was filled with Harry Terzo. Roxanne must have called him for the payoff, afraid that Ethel would slit my throat or something.

"Please come with me, Ms. Eden."

She turned and looked pure hatred at me.

"I suppose you think you've proved something."

I couldn't resist a parting shot. "Sure," I said. "I proved I can outsmart a very nasty killer ... even with both hands tied behind me."

Hero's Welcome

There would have been a hero's welcome for him in any case. A high official of the Soviet Union had stood by his side as he'd told the press how the Americans (or rather the CIA — it was important to remember that no blame be attached to the American People, only to the government that deceived and victimized them) — how the CIA had kidnapped him in Rome, and spirited him off to the United States, and held him captive and drugged and tortured him in an attempt to wrest from him secrets vital to the defense of the peace-loving government he had served so long and faithfully.

That was the story he had told; that was the story the high official of the Motherland had endorsed. Therefore, it was pravda. Truth. Now that he was home, he would hear or read nothing to the contrary. He would leave that to the West, where the habit of fruitless public speculation over the failings and weaker of those in power was as ingrained and ultimately debilitating as the drug abuse they allowed to flourish in their cities.

Of course, if the speculation had been true, if he had simply been a defector who had become homesick, the story would still have been told, and the hero's welcome would still have taken place. And he would have been sent on a lecture tour, speaking to the masses about the decadence, the corruption, the moral bankruptcy of the West. He would be One Who Knew, and his words would be endorsed at the highest level — more Truth. It was good for the masses to hear Truth of that kind — it was something for them to ponder as they waited in line to buy shoes, or to use the toilet when the people in the next flat were taking a little too long.

And when the freshness had worn off the story, and the speeches were no longer worth the time of the KGB men who would travel with them, and write the speeches, and make sure he delivered them properly, he would disappear, perhaps without a ripple, perhaps with a small announcement to the effect that he had become "exhausted from his labors on behalf of the State," and that he had "decided to retire from public life." And he would, in that case, remember the (unearned) hero's welcome on his return until his dying breath.

But he had no fear of that. The medal they gave him, the speeches they had made in praise of him, had all been earned. He had not, perhaps, been kidnapped, or tortured, but he knew himself to be a hero all the same.

Tirov came to the airport to meet him. Not in public, of course. Tirov was one of the new Chairman's new breed, lean and quick instead of massive and strong. A ferret more than a bear. He did not care for public ceremony, and in truth, he would have looked out of place at one. But when the photographers had gotten their pictures of smiles and embraces and kisses on both cheeks, two men who were not smiling whisked the hero off to a waiting limousine. Tirov was inside. "Welcome home, Comrade."

Vitaly Sergeyevich began to tell Tirov how honored he felt (it was the wise thing to say), but Tirov cut him off. "No, the honor is mine. You, after all, are the hero."

"It was your plan, Comrade Tirov."

Tirov shrugged and smiled with affected modesty. "Well, if you insist ..." Both men laughed, then fell silent. Vitaly Sergeyevich looked at Russia through the window. He would never leave again — the Truth demanded that he stay safe behind the borders of the Motherland, where the ogres of the CIA couldn't find him. He didn't mind, at least not very much, though he would miss the foreign assignments that had always made him appreciate his homeland all the better.

He heard Tirov sigh. "Yes, Comrade Tirov?"

"I was thinking of your triumph."

"Your triumph. Ours, if you insist."

"I do insist. Do you know that they argued against my assigning this mission to you? Not because you weren't trusted, but because you are too high up to risk, should the Americans really take it into their heads to drug or torture you."

"There was no need for them to do that. I sacrificed the expendable agents; the Americans were happy for as long as we needed them to be happy."

"Do you know what finally convinced them? Your uncanny resemblance to the Pole. I am sure, in fact, that many of those who ignore the news reports have some vague idea that Walesa has flown smiling to the Soviet Union." Tirov showed him the modest smile again. "And even if I'm wrong about that, the operation has still been a success, has it not?"

"A great success."

"And then the cowboy actor meets the Chairman knowing that you have made fools of his intelligence agents."

"That we have made fools of them," Vitaly Sergeyevich amended. "Yes, great fools."

"Yes," Tirov echoed. "One might almost say their foolishness approaches the incredible."

"I have often thought so," the hero said.

"I meant it literally," Tirov said. He was no longer smiling.

"Comrade?"

"Incredible. Incapable of belief. How many pages was the plan of your escape? Twenty? Thirty? Yet you just walk out of a restaurant and stroll to the Embassy."

"The Americans can't believe anyone would want to leave them. It is a blind spot with them. I was fortunate."

"Ah, but they were fortunate, too. How strange they did not avail themselves of their good fortune."

"What do you mean, Comrade?"

"The woman in Canada who killed herself."

"But she has nothing to do with me."

"Of course she didn't. But there were already rumors of your affair — yes, yes, I know to give you a motive to 'defect,' and this suicide was custom-made for them. They could have announced this was the woman; they could have made you out to be a heartless scoundrel who broke a woman's heart and drove her to her death. They could have snatched the propaganda victory away from us."

"But the Americans don't think that way —"

"Comrade Yurchenko, I have not your experience with the Americans, but I can only make sense of this on the assumption that they do not think at all. They have done nothing to mitigate the propaganda disaster they have suffered. They could have said they knew you were a fraud, and let you escape to see whom you would contact. They did not. They could have said you asked to go home, and they let you go as a gesture of good will in anticipation of the summit, and that we turned it into a piece of cheap propaganda. They did not."

Tirov scratched his nose. "How stupid are the Americans, Comrade? Are they so stupid they cannot think of two courses of action I come up with off the top of my head? Or a dozen more I could conceive in a half hour? Or are they shrewd? Perhaps they are standing this humiliation, doing nothing about it, looking like fools in the eyes of the world, because they want to."

Vitaly Sergeyevich said nothing. He had been a spy long enough to know when that was appropriate. Tirov went on. "It gives one to wonder, doesn't it? Why they might do that. Have you any ideas?"

Now he had to talk. "Interrogation methods," he said. His voice sounded dry.

"That is a possibility that has occurred to me. We sent you to America, in part, to learn how they debrief defectors these days. Perhaps they saw through your charade, used false ones, and now want nothing to impede your report.

"Or perhaps they used real ones, and are keeping silent — making it seem as if they don't care about their humiliation — in order to ... to discredit me. With you." Tirov laughed. "As if they could, Comrade! As if they could! Why, you might as well think they are keeping still because they have turned you, that you are now a double agent, and they want no flaws of your triumph, to keep you from getting your hands on fresh secrets to pass to them! That would be foolish, wouldn't it?"

Hero's Welcome

"Madness, Comrade," Vitaly Sergeyevich said. He had never been more sincere in his life. Hero in headquarters

The car was pulling up at KGB headquarters. The hero would be staying there for a few days. That was to have been expected no matter what the Truth was.

"Ah, well," Tirov said. "It is an amusing game, trying to read the minds of the Americans. We must have another go at it on your return."

"My return, Comrade?"

Tirov snapped his fingers. "Now I am the foolish one." He reached into his case and drew out a thick sheaf of papers. "I forgot to tell you. I have taken the opportunity of arranging a series of lectures for you to deliver throughout the nation."

"Lectures," the hero said. His voice was dead in his ears.

"Yes. Don't worry about a thing. They've all been written for you, and you will have ... ah ... assistants. They will get you safely from city to city, even as far as the podium itself. You don't mind, do you?"

"No," Vitaly Sergeyevich said. "No. Of course I don't mind."

Tirov smiled at him one last time. "I'm so pleased. It does the masses good to hear the Truth from someone like you. From a hero. Welcome home, Vitaly Sergeyevich."

Sabotage

M*other Gaia,* he wrote, *the being that is the Living Earth Herself, is the most beautiful of the Universe's Wonders.*

The computer screen reflected his frown. He rubbed his lip for a moment, then moved the cursor to change "Universe's Wonders" to "Wonders of the Universe." What the hell. It was trite, but it flowed better.

But She is not perfect, he went on, *for She harbors within Herself a virus, a poison, a parasite that, left unchecked, will destroy Her and all Her Beauty. That parasite is the evil and arrogant creature called Man.*

He smiled at that. He always referred to the human race as "Man" when he was talking about what a bunch of scumbags they were. It subliminally let the feminists off the hook; he got a lot of support from feminists.

Man, the destroyer of Mother Gaia's other helpless children. Man, burner of forests, polluter of waters, befouler of air. If any species deserved extinction it is this insane ape. Unfortunately, there is as yet no way to be rid of pestiferous Man without doing irreparable harm to Mother Gaia Herself.

Therefore, Man, like the idiot–genius he is, must be kept in check. He and the plague he pleases to call "progress" must be slowed down and scaled back, he must be forced, if necessary, to take his proper, humble place at Mother Gaia's generous banquet until that happy (if unlikely) day when ungrateful Man repents and learns to properly love his Mother.

Allen Prince read over the last few words again. He was pleased. He hit the save button, then ordered the computer to tell the laser printer to make a hard copy to be faxed to the magazine that had commissioned the article. If the idiots' modem had been compatible with his, they could have had the thing already.

Prince went to the thermostat and lowered the temperature. He liked the place extra cool when he came out of the shower. Prince exulted in the shower, letting the clean, perfectly heated mountain water wash the work and fatigue off him. Carefully, he shampooed his graying hair and beard. He would have liked to shave the thing off — it did get to be a nuisance — but he didn't dare. A "clean–cut" look, as his father, the bookkeeper, would have called it, would have clashed with his image, and his image was all the leverage he had.

Prince smiled. Right, he thought, like all the leverage J.P. Morgan had had was a billion dollars. There were levers and levers.

He stepped out of the shower and dried himself off. He put on a set of sweats and a pair of wooden shoes, and headed for the secret kitchen. The shoes made muffled clops on the thickly carpeted floor.

He really liked wooden shoes. When he'd first started wearing them, they had been a gimmick, a way to get a message in the press to the animal rights folks that he was One Of Them, No Foolin'. He had suspected, and rightly so, that there was a lot of zeal among the animal rights movement that could be useful to him.

The fringe benefit was the wooden shoes. Amazingly, they weren't uncomfortable at all, and you could slip in and out of them with no fuss. They also added about an inch and a half to his height without exposing him to the stigma of wearing lifts. And they gave him a trademark the press could always talk about, like Ralph Nader's rumpled suits.

Prince opened the stainless–steel, restaurant–style refrigerator, and took out a can of Diet Coke. He'd just popped the tab and taken the first pull at the soda when, surprise of surprises, there was a knock at the door.

Prince smiled ruefully, took another swig of soda, and stuck the can back in the fridge. He slid the door to the secret kitchen shut, and locked it. Then he went to answer the door.

It didn't happen often, but every once in a while some intrepid soul ignored the KEEP OUT signs (and the bears and the mountain lions) and made his way up the twisting dirt road to Allen Prince's retreat, on the bare top of a wooded plateau. Usually, though, Prince heard them coming — it took a powerful four-wheel-drive vehicle like the one in the garage to make it up that hill. Whatever their virtues, such vehicles weren't known for quiet motors.

Of course, his visitor (or visitors) might have driven up while he was in the shower, but he'd been out for a while now. Had they been there, gawking at the house, since before he'd gotten out of the shower? All the better. The awestruck ones were the easiest to deal with. He'd bring them in, give them a gentle lecture about the no-trespassing signs being there to protect the habitat, not humble Allen Prince, pour them a cup of herb tea (sun brewed), then see them on their way full of the warm fuzzies for Allen Prince and all his works in defense of the planet. It was a pain in the ass, but once or twice a year, he could stand it for the sake of the good PR.

Prince went to open the door. The closed-circuit monitor assured him that it wasn't a lawyer, or somebody else in a suit, come to make trouble for him. Allen Prince *sent* suing lawyers; he did not receive them.

However, it wasn't one of the awestruck gapers, either. This one had the look of a mountain man; at least the weekend variety thereof. His hair was shaggy and covered his ears; his beard grew down to where his neck joined his torso. His eyes were set and determined. Though his mouth was invisible behind the beard, the eyes would have gone with a grim line of lip and a set jaw.

Prince had this kind of visitor, too, though more rarely. This was the kind who came and wanted him to stop the city folks from pulling all the trout out of Peapack River. Prince gave them the tea, told him he'd look into it, and sent them on their way. There wasn't enough ink in fighting recreational fisherman to make it worth Prince's while. He'd get around to them, but way later.

Prince swung the door open, thereby learning that the mountain man's plaid flannel shirt was red, his corduroy pants were green, his backpack was blue, his hair and eyes dark brown.

"Hello," the mountain man said. The voice was calm and cultured. It didn't go with the look, and it certainly didn't go with the expression Prince had seen on the TV monitor. "My name is Peter

Knox. Of course, I recognize you from TV. I've come a long way to talk to you. May I come in?"

"I didn't hear you drive up," Prince said. He craned his neck into the warm mountain air. "Where's your car?"

The mountain man smiled and showed a mouthful of even white teeth. Something else that didn't fit the image. "I came on foot. I knew you didn't like cars on the freeway; I figured you wouldn't allow them on your mountain."

"Ordinarily, I don't," Prince said, joining quite involuntarily in the smile. "But I don't want my visitors to get heart attacks, either."

"Let them," Knox said. "What's a couple fewer pollution spewing Man–creatures, right?"

"Ahh, right. Right. The mountain is posted against trespassing, you know. For the sake of the environment, you realize."

"Oh, naturally. It's just that what I wanted to tell you is so important, I took the liberty. I came up the south face of the mountain."

"Through the array?"

"Yeah. Very impressive."

"Very dangerous," Prince told him. "You could have been fried."

"The mirrors were too bright to look at," Knox conceded. "Like looking at the sun."

"At the peak, they reflect a beam of almost six hundred degrees."

Prince's retreat was once a millionaire's home. Prince had caused his foundation to buy it in order to conduct an experiment: Was it possible to run a home on solar power alone? To find out, Prince had had engineers come in and put in the array. This was a group of focused mirrors on motorized mounts. The motors would keep them focused in synchronization with the sun, reflecting concentrated beams of sunlight to an egg–shaped water tower at the top of a long shaft. The heat from the mirrors boiled the water and sent it down the shaft under pressure where it spun a turbine and generated electricity — plenty of electricity, it turned out, to run Prince's computer, his air conditioner, anything he wanted, including the mirror–motors themselves.

So the experiment was a success — you *could* maintain a twentieth-century lifestyle on solar power — if you had twenty acres of land to put up an array to power one house, and about two million in capital to get the thing built. No, Prince sometimes told his followers not quite sadly (*they* weren't sad about it, after all), the only way out was to march backward, to give up electricity and live as our ancestors did, in harmony with nature. He was always applauded warmly for this.

He continued to use the retreat, he told them, because, alas, the monster of progress has to be fought with the weapons of progress — computers and mass media. At least he wasn't ripping off the planet to do it, he told them to more cheers.

Except in the winter, when he had to fire up the gas generator to keep things going after a few short, overcast days. He didn't tell people about that.

"May I come in?" Knox said again.

Prince looked down on his visitor's feet. "I don't allow leather in my house," he said. "Or meat. It's a symbolic gesture, but one that is very important to me. If you'll take off your boots, I'll go and get you some wooden shoes."

"Oh," Knox said. "I have my own." He slid the blue nylon backpack to the ground and opened it.

Allen Prince couldn't tell *what* all was in there — papers, books, something that looked like a large tool kit, the usual socks and underwear — and at last, one large wooden shoe.

"Damn," Knox said. "I must have lost the other one."

"Never mind," Prince said. "I'm touched that you made the effort. I'll get you a pair. About an eleven for you? I keep them in all sizes."

"Eleven is perfect," Knox said. "I'll take off my boots out here, like you said."

Knox was wiggling stockinged toes when Prince came back. He slid into the wooden shoes and joined his host in clomping across the lush rug to the vast living room. Prince settled down on his favorite armchair; his guest perched on the edge of the sofa. They chatted politely about weather until the herb tea was done. Prince waited until his visitor took a sip, then said, "Now, Mr. Knox, how can I help you?"

The mountain man reached into his pocket. For one horrible instant, Prince thought he was going after the makings of a hand-rolled cigarette or something equally dangerous to the rug. When he saw the small white rectangle of a business card come out instead, he was relieved, but no less puzzled.

"Actually," the man said as he handed over the card, "it's *Doctor* Knox. I'm a psychiatrist."

And not just a psychiatrist, Prince saw, but one with a fancy Park Avenue address.

"You have me at a loss, Doctor," Prince said. "I'm sane. I don't mean to sound immodest, but I believe my work makes me one of the sanest men on earth."

"I suppose you're right," Dr. Knox said. A strange smile played on his lips. "I would say so. Of course, 'sanity' is a legal term regarding degree of responsibility for one's own actions. It has no medical or moral significance whatsoever."

Knox waved the thought away with the back of his hand. He no longer looked like a mountain man. He looked like a professor who'd been roughing it for a while. For a purpose.

"It's not important. We'll talk about that later, if at all. Right now, I want to consult you about a patient of mine."

"Ah," said Prince. "I see."

"Do you?"

"Oh, yes. This has happened one or two times before. You have a patient who is in severe anxiety over the state of the world; is thrown into panic at the thought of nuclear powers and global warming, and acid rain. You want me to tell you how to reassure this person, keep your patient from being paralyzed with fear."

Prince leaned back and took a deep breath. He was enjoying this. "I'm afraid I can't do it."

"You can't?"

"I won't. Anxiety and panic are the *proper* responses in the face of the world situation. Those of us who can calmly go about their business — even a business such as mine, fighting the criminal society that causes the problems — are the ones who are insane. Sorry, let me say *unhealthy*."

"You are aware, aren't you," Knox said, "that even factoring in Chernobyl, nuclear power is the cleanest, safest, and most efficient source of power in the history of man kind? That there is no scientific evidence of any global warming whatever? That a five-year study failed to find a single — even *one* — organism that was harmed by so-called acid rain?"

"I have heard lies," Prince said with dignity.

"Well," Knox said wryly. "Somebody's lying."

Allen Prince was accustomed to being spoken to with more respect, especially here. He was about to put Knox in his place, but the psychiatrist didn't give him a chance. He grinned and waved this matter away, too.

"But that's not important, either," Knox said. "That's not the kind of patient I have in mind."

"Then why *are* you here?" Prince could feel his impatience rising. It was something he'd discovered in the early days of building his movement — it wasn't worth the effort to be polite to the opposition. Treat them with contempt, and you reinforce the beliefs of your own followers. An open mind on your part simply raises the danger that the minds of those you've already convinced might open as well. It was a tactic well learned by the associate professor he'd once been, and one that had proven invaluable ever since.

"I'm a busy man, and you are trespassing. Perhaps you should go now. I can't help you with your patient."

"How do you know? You don't even know who it is yet."

"What difference does it make?"

"It's Dwight Noring," Knox said.

Prince was silent for a few moments. He stared hard at Knox. The psychiatrist had no trouble meeting the stare.

"Dwight Noring," Prince said quietly, "is dead."

"So many people are," Knox said. "Including Dwight. But a person's death doesn't end his significance, does it?"

"Depends on the person. Poor Dwight had unlimited potential, but he was ... misguided. I don't know if it's sad or fortunate he died before he accomplished anything."

Dr. Knox rubbed his nose. "Oh," he said. "Well, *Dwight* thought he'd accomplished something. He thought he'd accomplished something so big he couldn't figure out how to live with it."

Peter Knox remembered sitting at his desk before his first appointment with Dwight Noring. As he read the file, he kept thinking that the boy was too good to be true. First of all, he was a genius, the child of parents who themselves had been gifted children. They had taken care to try to keep their son's childhood as normal as possible, while not neglecting the appetite of a giant intellect.

Dwight spoke six human languages, and all computer languages. He had built (with a little soldering help from his father) his first computer at the age of six, and programmed it himself from scratch.

("I made a lot of mistakes doing that," he was to tell Knox. "I learned a lot before I got it running right.")

He played piano, guitar, and trumpet. He composed music, and wrote science fiction stories. In Knox's admittedly inexpert opinion, the music was excellent; the stories suffered because the science they hinged on was insufficiently simplified for the lay reader (like Peter Knox, for instance) to understand.

Dwight played soccer (All-State prep) and basketball ("I wasn't really tall enough, but I was a good passer.")

Dwight was the shining light of the gifted students program at a local university. Or rather, he had been.

Because two years ago, he had dropped out of the program; had dropped out of his whole life. He now spent virtually all his time in his room, watching old movies on his VCR. He wasn't angry, or violent, or defiant. He just brooded.

Attached to the file was a note from Allen Prince, Ph.D., professor at the University, and director of the Gifted Students Program. Knox had heard of him — he was getting a lot of ink lately because of some militant environmental stands he had recently taken.

The note said that Dwight had showed no signs of "burnout" prior to his dropping out of the program, that he had been eager and energetic right until the end of the previous January. Dr. Prince went on to say that in his experience the most brilliant young people *did* have periods in which they let their talents lie fallow. Under no circumstances, in his opinion, should Dwight be "pushed," or made to feel as if he were letting anyone down.

Dwight's parents were inclined to agree, having had their share of being pushed during their own gifted childhoods. So for a little over two years, they let their son be, and did nothing.

Until the morning their son, now sixteen, took a razor and cut his wrists.

He had been discovered in time and rushed to the hospital. The M.D. in charge of the case, as well as the psychiatric resident, recommended Dwight be sent to Knox, who'd treated gifted children successfully in the past. Everything Knox had heard or read said that this was a kid worth helping.

Then Dwight Noring came into the office. His wrists were still bandaged. Other than that, he looked like a healthy, handsome kid of medium height. The first thing he said when he sat down was, "You can't help me."

Knox got a look at the boy's eyes. They were old and sad and beaten.

It was in his tone of voice, too. Nothing belligerent, or even challenging. Just hopelessly matter of fact. "You can't help me. I wish somebody could."

"That's a good start," Knox said. "I spend about seventy-five percent of my time trying to get patients to admit there's something wrong to need help about."

"I don't *need* help," Dwight insisted. "Anyway, the term is meaningless, with all due respect."

"I don't understand."

" 'Help' for me doesn't exist. Can't. It would involve time travel. Violation of free will and causality. All sorts of impossibilities. How can you 'need' something that has never been and never will be?"

"Good point," Knox said. "A bit of a sophistry, perhaps, but nicely done."

"I thought you guys were never supposed to argue with your patients," Dwight said.

"Is that what I'm doing?"

"An accusation of sophistry implies disagreement. And disparagement. Is that wise? I mean, they made me come here because I tried to kill myself. You shouldn't call me a sophist and break down my self-esteem any more than it is."

"A couple of things. You may not believe this, but you do want to be helped."

Dwight clenched his jaw. "Don't pretend to read my mind, Doctor, okay?"

"I'm not reading your mind. All I have to do is read your record. I'm supposed to believe somebody with a brain like yours doesn't know or can't find out fifteen quicker and less painful ways to commit suicide than by cutting his wrists? Or, if he were determined to cut his wrists, he'd know not to cut them across?

"I know you know how to research. You've read some psychiatry texts in preparation for coming here — that much is obvious. You could have checked up on anatomy just as easily. Believe me, Dwight, if you'd really wanted to die, you would be dead."

The boy stared at him.

"To answer your other question," Knox said, "now that you've read the books, and know what I'm *supposed* to be doing, you'll have nice walls built up to keep me out. I'll have to improvise. What do you want to argue about?"

Dwight gave him a crooked smile. "That was good," he said. "It might even turn out to be interesting. You come on more like a cop than a doctor."

"Is that appropriate?"

"How do I know what's appropriate?"

"I mean, is it appropriate to what's troubling you? You might as well have a neon sign over your head flashing GUILT. Did you do something bad? Something criminal."

Dwight laughed, but there was no mirth to it. "Something bad. Oh, God, yes. I can't think of anything worse than what I did. Criminal? Well, no policeman would arrest me. Wouldn't believe me if I confessed. Even if he did, a court wouldn't try me and a jury wouldn't convict me."

"But who needs them, right?"

Dwight looked unblinking into Knox's eyes. "Right. I know I'm guilty. That's enough."

"What did you do? Care to tell me?"

"Sure?"

"Are you serious? Yes, I'm damned sure, Doctor."

"Why don't you want to tell me?"

"I can't even stand to think about it, for God's sake!"

"You're thinking about it now, aren't you?"

Again, the crooked smile. "Uh uh. You're not going to get me that way. Drop it, Doc. If we do these sessions for fifty years, I won't tell you. Just drop it."

"All right, let's change the subject. Why did you cut your wrists."

Dwight shook his head. "Well, gee, Doc, when I walked in here, I thought I knew the answer to that one. Now I'm all confused. According to you, it was a cry for help. Which doesn't exist and will never come."

"No," Knox said. "I mean, why did you cut your *wrists*, as opposed to say, your throat? Or, going with the cry–for–help theory, take a not–quite–fatal overdose of some chemical you cooked up in the lab?"

There was silence for a few long seconds, then Dwight said, "I'm having a strange experience, Doc. I think I may have run into someone too smart for me."

"I thank you for the compliment, but let's cut the bullshit, shall we? Will you answer my question?"

"I can't."

"Can't or won't?"

"All right, I won't. Let's just say it seemed 'appropriate.' "

"Appropriate?" Knox asked.

Dwight Noring wasn't listening. He was looking at his hands as if they were some sort of slimy creatures he'd found under a rock. Tears came to his eyes, and he muttered something.

Knox let it go on for a full minute, then gently said, "What are you saying?"

No luck. Dwight snapped out of it. "What? Oh, nothing. Nothing."

"Something about the future, right?"

"Forget it," Dwight said.

"You wanted me to know, or you wouldn't have mumbled it in front of me."

Dwight got to his feet. Seeing the near–tears look on the boy's face, Knox realized that no one was a genius when it came to dealing with his own emotions.

"I told you I won't talk about it!"

"Okay, okay. Don't talk about it. Think about it."

"All I do is think about it!"

"All you do is think about the guilt and fear it causes you — whatever 'it' is. I want you to think about the thing or event itself. I want you to realize that you are breaking your back, staggering around under the weight of it. I also want you to remember that your parents are paying me a whole lot of money, maybe more than they can afford, so I can help you shoulder this and get on with your life."

"Get on with my life. Somehow it doesn't sound very attractive, Doctor."

"Just promise me you'll see me one more time before you do anything drastic, okay? Just show up next week. Call me if things get particularly tough."

Dwight said he would, and kept his word. He showed up the next week, and for many weeks after that.

Many in Knox's profession measured progress in terms of getting the patient to tell you things he's hidden from himself. In the case of Dwight Noring, that didn't really apply. He wasn't hiding all that much from himself. He was so immersed in self–loathing, he was hiding everything from the rest of the world.

There were moments when he'd let something slip. Once Knox had asked, "What do you want to *do*? 'Genius' is not something you can put on your income tax return."

"I used to want to be an astronaut," he said. "How's that for a laugh, now? They don't recruit nut cases who've tried to kill themselves, do they?" Dwight laughed bitterly. When Knox suggested he might still do something for the space program, Dwight became hysterical. He laughed until he sobbed; sobbed until he had to stumble to the bathroom to throw up. He came out wiping his chin. He wore a sick grin on his face. "I touch the future, huh, Doc?"

Every few weeks, Knox came back to the central question. He asked it in many different ways; he hid it in a maze of other questions, or disguised it as case histories or parables.

But the heart of the question was always the same: "What in the name of God do you think you did?"

A couple of times, Knox even got answers. Once, Dwight exploded, "You want to know what I did? I did my *homework*. I was a good little boy, and I did my fucking *homework!*" Another time, much more calmly, with a sort of laughter of despair, he said, "I saved the Earth, Doc. I made it possible to save Our One Earth." Generally, after such an outburst, the rest of the session would be spent in silence.

And on it went. Knox grew to like Dwight (an indulgence not really good for a psychiatrist's own mental health), but he never came close to really helping him. He used to like to tell himself he was functioning as a safety valve for the boy's emotions, which if he just kept Dwight hanging in there long enough, his own brainpower would pull him through.

He was wrong. At the end of the next January, the twenty-eighth, to be precise, a year to the day after he'd slashed his wrists, Dwight Noring, now seventeen, succeeded in killing himself.

Prince's face was bland. "So how can I possibly help you, Doctor? It seems your failure is complete."

Knox nodded. "As far as Dwight's concerned. But there's always the future, isn't there?"

Prince smiled. "My entire life is dedicated to ensuring that there is one."

Knox returned the smile. "I disagree. Your entire life is dedicated to marching humanity triumphantly back to the past, where every day was a backbreaking struggle to get enough to eat; where woman's life was in peril with every pregnancy; where filth and terror were the only release from the mind–destroying boredom of unending physical labor."

"A lot of people call those the good old days."

"Some," Knox agreed. "Even some people who lived that kind of life. Understandable. The human mind has an almost miraculous capacity for blotting out past, pain. There'd be no second children, otherwise. And there's no denying the present has its problems."

"Hmph. Kind of you to admit it. But what about the young? Almost all of my followers are young people."

"That's easy. I was the same way in the seventies. I did my sit–ins and my shouting. Vietnam was the 'cause' then. It was all a young jerk could desire — the opportunity to feel really virtuous without doing anything to earn it except make trouble for people who are really dealing with the problems of the day. You declare the moral equivalent of war, Mr. Prince, then demand that the human race do the moral equivalent of surrender. You offer these kids a chance at feeling warm and toasty about themselves as they're driving some poor schmuck out of business because he can't afford to spend a quarter of his time filling out EPA forms. You take legitimate concerns about progress and the environment, blow them completely out of proportion, and sell doomsday to a bunch of people who won't check facts or think for themselves."

"Are you done?" Prince asked.

"Except to tell you that you make me sick, yes."

"Fine. You came here to tell me I make you sick. You've told me. Will you go now?"

"Not yet. I'm just done with my *tirade*. It felt good, by the way. I want to tell you that I know why Dwight killed himself."

"How? Did it come to you in a dream?"

"It came to me in Dwight's will."

"He left a will?"

"Well, not a legal one. Holograph wills aren't legal in New York, but Dwight had left a note saying he wanted me to have something."

"What was it?"

"I'm not sure. The note called it the 'red metal toolkit on my desk.'"

"You saw the note?"

"Yes. Dwight's parents called the police then me. My apartment was just in the next block. I got there first. I saw the note. I saw the toolkit. I saw the body."

"He shot himself, didn't he? Must have been a terrible mess."

"That was the interesting thing. No mess at all. There was a small black hole about the size of a pencil point in the middle of his forehead. If he shot himself, he didn't use a bullet."

Knox started rummaging in his backpack.

"Be careful, Doctor," Prince said.

Knox looked up to see himself looking into the barrel of a .38 caliber revolver.

He grinned. " 'Appropriate technology,' right, Prince?"

"I don't know what you've got in the bag. I'm being prudent."

"I'm not armed. Or bugged, either, if you're interested." He kept talking as he looked. "Neither Dwight's parents nor I touched anything, you know. When the cops came, they took a look at the note, then they looked inside the box. They closed it up, sent us all to another room, and called the bomb squad. And that was the last I heard of the box I was supposed to get. Ah, here it is."

Knox pulled a red metal toolkit from the knapsack. "Look familiar?" he asked.

"Never seen it before in my life," Prince said.

"Not this one, of course. Yours might have been a different color. Or maybe it was a lunch box. Something you could carry unobtrusively."

"If you never heard of the box, where did that come from?" Prince asked.

"Glad you're still paying attention. That was the last I heard ... until about six months ago. It showed up in the mail, with a photocopy of the note. The return address was the Department of Defense, Arlington, Virginia."

Prince's eyes opened wide. "They wouldn't!"

"Wouldn't what?"

"Wouldn't just send you … in the mail …" His voice petered out. He seemed to forget he had the gun. He drew back in his chair, as if to get away from the toolbox.

"I don't see why not," Knox said. He flipped open the lid. "It's empty, see? An ordinary tool box, just a couple of extra holes drilled in it. Like wire–size holes."

Knox scratched his nose. "Of course, I knew the New York Police hadn't called the bomb squad over an empty box. I got curious about the contents, and I started calling and writing the Pentagon. I got a royal runaround — bureaucracy — but eventually, I would up talking to a lawyer attached to the research department. That's when I learned three things — the phrase "classified information" is no joke; holograph wills are not valid in the state of New York, and even if they were, all I'd been left was the box, which I now had, and not the contents; and three (unofficially), that somebody working for the Pentagon had so much respect for the late Dwight Noring that he directed the kid's last request to be honored to the extent possible, and that's why they sent me the box in the first place.

"Then they told me to shut up and not to bother them anymore."

Allen Prince was back to his old self now that the box had proved to be empty. "I admire the sentiment."

Knox grinned at him. "So? You've heard enough? Maybe I should go now?" He bent over and began to remove the wooden shoes.

"Stay, stay," Prince said. "There's a certain pulpish ingenuity to your hallucination. I'd like to see how it turned out."

Knox sat up and grinned. "I knew you would. Anyway, I didn't bother the Pentagon anymore, but I was plenty bothered myself. I started doing what I should have done after my first session with Dwight."

"Go ahead, I know you're going to tell me."

"I listened to the boy. I started acting like a cop instead of a shrink." Knox sighed. "Unethical. We're not supposed to pry into anything but the patient; we're not even supposed to try real hard to ascertain whether what he tells us is fantasy or reality, on the theory that the emotions are the same. Sometimes theory should take a hike.

"So I decided to treat every hint Dwight had given me as gospel. Of course I had help in reaching that conclusion. I don't expect the Pentagon's research department spends a couple of years examining a fantasy it found in a toolkit. Or bends procedure to honor the fantasist's last wish, do you?"

"I wouldn't presume to guess what goes on in someone's mind. That's your profession, Doctor, not mine."

Knox looked at him. "Don't sell yourself short, Mr. Prince. You're a master at guessing what's in other people's minds. That's how you manipulate them so well."

Knox shrugged and went on. "I'll give you this. From what I could tell, you were an excellent teacher for these kids. I tracked down a few of your former students. I especially liked your practice of having each kid at the beginning of the term pick something they felt would be impossible for them to accomplish, then assigning them to accomplish it as well as they could by Christmas break. That's exactly the kind of challenge a gifted student needs."

"I've always thought so."

"You don't have any of your former geniuses working for your organization, though, do you?"

"As a matter of fact, no. What of it?"

"Just interesting. Are smarter people somehow more selfish about the resources of Mother Gaia, do you think, or are they just better at sifting facts from propaganda? Where was I? Oh, yes, the assignments. For Janey Chang, it was to write a cantata in the manner of Bach. She's first cello with the Phoenix Symphony these days, you know. For Arnie Barheim, it was a novel. He has his own PR firm, now. Works for Mammoth Oil."

"Pity."

"They were good friends of Dwight's before he dropped out. They seem to recall that Dwight's impossible project was to build a laser small enough and powerful enough for a soldier to use in combat. They finished their assignments, but they didn't know if Dwight ever managed to complete his. But we do, don't we? I know because Dwight told me he did his homework; you know because he handed it in to him."

Knox leaned back with his hands behind his head. "What did you do, tell him it was dangerous and should be kept a secret? Until what? I can't see your turning it over to the Pentagon — not with your track record. On the other hand, you couldn't flunk Dwight, either. He'd make a stink, and *build* another one for the Pentagon. So that was one annoyance you were facing."

"Have you found more? In the course of your imagining, I mean?"

"I certainly have. I've found out where you were at the end of January the year Mark dropped out of school."

Allen Prince was a True Believer in those days. The evening before the launch, he sat on the patio swatting bugs and sweating in the Florida sun while he wondered what he was going to do with young Mr. Dwight Noring. There was no denying the boy's brainpower. Dwight was undoubtedly the most brilliant student who'd ever passed through the program. But that mind had been saddled with the most disgustingly bourgeois values and attitudes. One of the reasons Prince had taken this job was to try to stem the flow of the greatest minds to the profit beast that was oppressing the masses and eating up the planet's resources.

Young Mr. Noring treated everything wrong with the world as an opportunity for someone to be great. Pollution? Cars that run on hydrogen gas, and make fresh water as exhaust. Overpopulation? Not a problem for thousands of years, yet all long–term famines in this century deliberately caused by totalitarian governments, here are the figures to prove it. He always had the figures to prove it, and Prince just wasn't mathematically sophisticated enough to find the mistakes that must be there. It was a constant irritation.

Then there was the class trip. The university budgeted a certain amount of money to take the participants in the gifted–students program away somewhere between terms. Students usually voted, but the vote was almost always a rubber-stamp approval of Prince's recommendation. This year he had arranged for the students to spend a month at the Dawn of Man Commune in Idaho, where the participants lived life at a technology level of the late Stone Age. It was a magnificent way to gain an appreciation of nature.

Dwight Noring would have none of it. He led a revolt, and insisted that the class have a chance to vote to go to Florida to watch the launch of the space shuttle Challenger.

This was to be the one with that woman on board, the civilian. The schoolteacher. The one who said her job let her "touch the future." Allen Prince hoped she had more effect on her students than he had on these ungrateful snots. They backed Dwight enthusiastically.

Prince hated the space program. Usually, he echoed the standard line, and decried the waste of sending all the money into space to take pretty pictures and to bring back a few rocks when there were people starving on earth.

When he'd tried that on the class, Dwight had raised his hand and said, "Excuse me, Mr. Prince, but nobody ever sent a penny into space. The money remained on earth, creating jobs and stimulating the economy. Furthermore, the space program has more than paid for itself with the development of minicircuits, plastics, new medical technologies ..."

And on and on. As usual, Dwight had the figures to prove it.

None of that mattered of course, because of the *real* reason he hated the space program. In fact, all these so-called miracles were themselves the reason. Allen Prince hated the space program because it allowed the bourgeois to delude themselves into believing there was *hope*. People who were convinced there was a Universe to explore and conquer and be learned from were unable to focus on the severity of the problems here on Earth. They kept pushing for *progress*, when it was progress that was killing the helpless snail darters and the owls; they wanted more technology instead of less. They wanted to continue to make their parasitical lives *easier* and longer, instead of harder and shorter, as an all-wise Nature intended.

The space program was the symbol of all this insane looking forward, and Allen Prince hated it. And here was Dwight Noring, ready to devote his amazing brain to that nonsense.

And now what had the boy done? He had delivered to him, all smiles, a powerful laser with a nearly invisible beam. The whole thing fit in a tool box. He had had Dwight show him how it worked the weekend before they left. Prince had watched in horrified fascination as Dwight burned his initials a half-inch deep in a boulder two miles away. The letters were two inches high; the lines that made them up about a quarter-inch thick. If this could be done to a rock at half a mile, what could it do to a human body at close range? What was Allen going to do with the thing? Dwight wouldn't let him suppress it, and he couldn't reveal it. He hadn't even dared leave it back in New York. He'd thrown it in the suitcase and brought it along.

Allen Prince thought. He had a few drinks, then thought some more. An idea came to him, and made him laugh. He had another drink and laughed some more.

What the hell, he'd do it. Pitting one of his problems against the other wouldn't destroy them both completely, but it would pass the time and make Prince feel a little better.

He drove his rented car a few miles to a nearly deserted beach that had a clear view of the launch pad. He grabbed the toolkit from the beach beside him, placed it on the roof of the car, aimed it as well as you can aim a toolbox, and pushed the button on top. A thin line of light was visible for about a pencil's length in front of the opening in the front of the toolbox as the beam hit some dust. That was all. Prince gave it about five seconds.

Combined with the drinks in him, it felt good. "Take that," he said, then, laughing, got back in the car and drove back to the hotel.

The next morning, he had a better vantage point. He and his group watched from a NASA-approved viewing site as the challenger took off. Prince was disappointed as it cleared the launch pad. He'd been hoping his little prank last night would have screwed something up enough so that the launch would have to be delayed past the time they'd budgeted to stay in Florida. Serve young Mr. Dwight Noring right.

Then the ship blew up. Six astronauts and a civilian plunged to their deaths; a whole nation went into shock.

Including Allen Prince, though his reason was slightly different. It didn't last very long, either. Before he'd even gotten his stunned little geniuses back to the motel, Prince had realized that this incident was his step up to the big time in media awareness. The loudest and most extreme voices would make it into print and on the air. He made sure his was among them. He started with a statement accusing NASA of murder, and went on from there. That gave him the notoriety he needed to build a local organization into the vast movement it was today.

There were two flies in the ointment. One was his guilt over seven human lives. He soothed himself with the knowledge that what they were doing was harmful, a crime against the Nature of Things, and that they had served the world much better in death than they would have in life. Besides, when the official investigation blamed O–ring malfunction for the disaster, he was off the hook.

The other was Dwight Noring. He wanted his laser back. And he wanted a grade.

"You can't have it," he said. "I destroyed it. I smashed it and threw it in the ocean."

"You can't do that! It's my work, and the material wasn't cheap, either! I'll build another one! My father will go to the chancellor about this."

Prince grabbed the boy by the shirt. "Listen, you little bastard, you say one word about this, and I'll testify to the authorities you were down there in Florida with your little laser weapon. They'll love that."

The kid turned white. He went limp in Prince's hands. His face wore a look of horror. "You," he said. "You had it. You —"

"No, Dwight. *You*. *You're* the genius. *You* built it. Everyone will know *I* couldn't have. And you're a frustrated spaceboy, aren't you? Everybody knows that. They'll remember that John Lennon was shot by somebody who called himself his 'Number One Fan.' So you just keep your mouth shut and your parents happy, and have a nice life."

It was a risk, but it worked. Prince left the university to run his movement full-time, and Dwight dropped out, accompanied by a concerned note from his former teacher, suggesting oh-so-subtly that Dwight had burnt out on his own brainpower.

Aside from the news of Dwight's suicide, which reached the busy Allen Prince months after the fact, he hadn't heard another word about it.

Until today.

"Do you know where the word 'sabotage' comes from?" Peter Knox asked.

"Huh? Oh, from French, I think."

Knox chuckled. "So it was unintentional. 'Sabotage' comes from French, all right. At the beginning of the Industrial Revolution, when weaving machines were first brought to France, the weavers stormed the factories, destroying the machines by throwing their *sabots* into them. Do you know what a *sabot* is?"

"I studied German."

"A *sabot* is a wooden shoe."

Prince started to laugh. "Does it really? Oh, marvelous! I wish someone had told me sooner."

"I accuse you of sabotage, Mr. Prince. I accuse you of damaging the space shuttle *Challenger*. I accuse you of sabotaging the promising young life of Dwight Noring. Even more, I accuse you of trying to destroy the human race's entire reason for living."

"Damn! I must be a terrible person. What is this reason?"

"To learn. To grow. To build. To face problems as they come up, and *defeat* them, damn you, not run away like a puppy who's been slapped on the nose. But you're just like the original saboteurs. You might delay progress, but you'll never stop it."

Prince rubbed his chin. "No, it usually takes a war to do that."

"War's a lot less likely than it used to be."

Prince was silent for a few minutes, thinking. "I'm going to tell you a few things that may surprise you, Dr. Knox."

"Like you're not going to kill me?"

"This gun is for defense only. I have better methods of attack. Take off all your clothes, please." He smiled at the look on Knox's face. "You see, I *did* surprise you. Relax. I just want to make sure you're not concealing any recording or transmitting device. I know you said you weren't, but you might be lying now, mightn't you?"

Knox complied. As he stood there naked, Prince walked behind him and tugged at Knox's hair and beard. "Can't be too careful, you know."

"I just grew them in order to look like somebody you might let in up here."

"Well, it worked. Sit down, Doctor." Prince went through the clothes Knox had taken off, then threw them back. "Get dressed now. Your knapsack stays here when you go. Oh, and I'll take your watch, as well."

Knox took a look at the dial before handing it over. "I ought to be going soon," he said.

"This won't take long. I'm going to confess. You see, I did fire the laser at the rocket." He went on to tell the whole story. "Of course, when they found out about the defect in the O–ring," he concluded, "I slept better. No one will ever know whether it was my tipsy escapade that did the damage or the O–ring as all the experts said."

Knox snorted. "Dwight didn't have any doubts. And it would have been better for you if they'd *never* found any defect in the O–rings."

"Why do you say that?"

"Because they would never have launched another human into space before they found the cause of the disaster. And how would they have found a little pinhole, especially after it had been the focus of an explosion? You would have destroyed manned space flight permanently. As it is, you may have saved future disasters by inadvertently bringing the O–ring problem to light."

"I'd never thought of it that way. I don't suppose that earns me any credit with you."

"None."

"Good. I don't want any mixed feelings here. You may be wondering why I told you all this."

"It's crossed my mind."

"It's because I hate you, Mr. Knox. I hate you most of all because on your last point, I have come to know you are right. The human race *is* a pack of greedy gluttons who won't rest content until they exterminate everything on the planet, and then themselves with their *progress*.

"So be it. Let them have their suicide party. But I have arranged things so that it's being held in *my hall*. Any of your precious so-called progress will have to pass through *me*. I'll collect what I can from the spoiling bastards, and I'll drive out of business those I can. I'll drive them to suicide, if I can manage it. You call me a saboteur. I want to tell you it is my intention to be the greatest saboteur in the history of economics — before the end comes."

"And you want me to know that."

"I want just one of you smug, destructive bastards to know that. And you're the perfect one, Dr. Knox, because no one will be able to prove we ever met. You have no evidence of *anything*. And if you take this to the media, who do you think the media will believe?"

"You can be fought, you know. You can be fought the same way you fight."

"Go ahead, Doctor Knox. Try to speed your inevitable victory. Fight. I'm not going anywhere, except back to my writing."

"I'm counting on that," Knox said.

Peter Knox finished lacing up his boots, then walked away from the house, moving quickly but not running. He went back the way he came, through the solar array. All the mirrors had moved with the sun, in order to keep their burning rays trained on the water tower.

All but one. This one hadn't moved since Knox had walked by here before. It was still angled for the morning sun, and it shot its afternoon beam in the direction Knox had calculated during the days he'd spent on Prince's mountain, scouting and figuring. He could see the brightness now, slashing across the house, leaving a trail of fire, sealing off the study wing. Knox could see Prince now, banging against the windows of his study. Within a minute, the beam hit the window itself. It wasn't quite a laser, just five or six hundred degrees of concentrated heat. Knox thought he could hear a scream.

A puff of smoke obscured the window. When it cleared, Prince was gone. Knox shuddered. It was, he had to remind himself, probably an easier death than that suffered by the Challenger crew.

This would be, he reflected, a perfect opportunity to make a fuss, call a press conference, denounce solar energy as dangerous, and call for its banishment. He could see the NO SOLAR buttons, and the picketers.

But he wouldn't do it. Someday, someone, maybe someone like Dwight Noring, would figure out how to use solar power economically. *That* would be progress. *That* would be how humanity is supposed to work.

In the meantime Knox bent, and with an effort, pulled loose the object with which he'd jammed the movement of the mirror.

It was a wooden shoe.

A Friend of Mine

One

Every day they were locked into the room below the ice. They sat in their swivel chairs and looked at the screens. The men had been psychologically matched for compatibility; the chairs were ergonomically designed for comfort, the screens a soothing orange-on-gray to ease eyestrain. The people who'd designed this system didn't want something as avoidable as human discomfort to lead to any ill-considered actions.

There was no way to engineer out the boredom.

"Don't you ever wish somebody would launch a goddamn missile once?" Corporal Mike Alvarez asked.

Sergeant Hank Peeters scratched his nose. "Who?" he asked. "Us? That's up to the boys in the mountain in Colorado. All we do is watch the screens."

"You got that right. All we do is watch the screens. No, I didn't mean us, I meant them. It would make it seem worthwhile sitting around here, at least."

"What do you mean, 'them'? There is no 'them' any more. The Cold War is over, and our side won. We're sort of like a leftover."

"A frozen leftover," Alvarez said. "Doesn't it ever bother you that we spend our whole lives on, in, and around *ice*?"

"The compound is warm enough."

"I'm not talking about the compound, man, I'm talking about the fact that we're sitting on a glacier a quarter of a mile above the nearest earth. It's like floating in space."

"Depends on how you look at it," Peeters told him. "Ice is a mineral, you know. And ground is made up of minerals, right?"

"You like it up here, don't you?"

Peeters was silent for a few moments. "Yeah. Yeah, I do."

"I heard you signed up for another hitch up here."

"It's not allowed. They're afraid we'll go stir crazy."

"Hah! But you tried it, didn't you? You went to the old man and asked to stay, didn't you?"

"What if I did?"

"Don't you miss civilization? Goddamn, man, the *Greenlanders* don't even come around here."

"There's a tribe not too far away."

"I'm not talking about a tribe, I'm talking about *you*."

"No, then. If you absolutely have to know. I don't miss civilization. Civilization has become a big ugly mess of crime and dirty politics and people whining about how hurt and victimized they are, and how society ought to be restructured to help *them*. There's not a kind of person out there who's not doing that."

"Except your kind, right?"

"I don't know. I don't even know if I have a kind. But I suspect that if I go back there, I'll be pissing and moaning just like the rest of them. And there's nothing worse than being the kind of person who makes you sick."

Alvarez looked at him for a few seconds, then said, "I was just kidding, you know."

"What about?"

"When I suggested I wished somebody would actually fire a missile. I didn't mean it."

"I know you didn't."

"I just wanted to make sure. Because, my friend, you are getting strange enough to do it yourself."

Peeters smiled. "Never happen," he said. "I just said I was sick of it. Didn't say I wanted to destroy it."

"Maybe so. But I think our hitch up here has lasted long enough. Maybe if you re–up they'll put you on some desert island someplace. Then you can be lonely *and* warm."

When the shift was over, Peeters had attended to his paperwork, then checked out a halftrack for a little drive to clear his head. That wasn't strictly according to regulations, but the CO understood the grind here, and he knew that a little open space — even a little frozen-solid open space on top of a glacier — can be better than fifty bottles of tranquilizers.

It certainly was for Peeters. As usual, he invited Alvarez along, and some of the other guys, but, also as usual, they were busy playing ping-pong or watching videos, or, in Alvarez's case, looking at the sunny scenes on the postcards his mother sent him from Miami.

Peeters was just as glad. There was something he had to do, and he couldn't share it with anybody, yet.

It was May, so daylight wasn't a problem. He gassed up the crawler and warmed up the engine until the heater would almost melt lead. He grabbed a couple of extra twenty-liter jerry cans, just in case, checked the compass on the dash, and headed off. North. There was something he had to check on. Something he had seen the last time he was out this way.

He'd been about fifteen klicks north of the base when the blizzard came up. In Greenland, a blizzard isn't something the weather boys can warn you about. Peeters had learned, to his surprise, that it is possible for blizzard conditions to prevail without a snowstorm being in progress. A blizzard, it turns out, requires only low temperatures, strong winds, and snow, but the snow doesn't have to be falling from the sky at the time. God was frugal here in the Arctic Circle. He could make the same snow do for any number of blizzards.

Anyway, the wind had kicked up, and Peeters' soothing vista of bright blue sky and weird, wind-sculptured ice was gone in seconds, replaced by a nightmare of white streaks as the snow rose and blotted out the weak sunlight.

Peeters shrugged. He reached for his clipboard (when you go anywhere in that country, you make sure you keep track of how you got there, because there's no highway back), and was just about to turn the crawler around, when something thumped heavily against the glass cab of the arctic vehicle. Then another thump came, then another. Somebody was throwing rocks at him.

A freak shift in the wind gave him an instant of visibility, and he saw ten or twelve figures in anoraks running across the snow at him.

It was Eskimos, for God's sake. Attacking him now with gloved fists and clubs, yelling at him. Angry. Hostile.

Peeters had tried to pull away, but he was afraid to gun it, for fear of running over one of them or something worse.

The glass was case hardened and thick, and the locks were good (these things were designed to be polar bear–proof), but Peeters was getting nervous anyway. Every so often, a club would rattle the glass. The angry faces outside showed no sign of letting him go.

And there was something else. This was not just a hunting party. There were women and children, along with men climbing the crawler, trying to get inside.

Then a sound came. Peeters told himself it was the wind. He'd been telling himself ever since it was the wind, howling through some whistle it had carved for itself in snow and ice. There were arctic wolves, and Peeters supposed they howled, but no wolf had ever howled this loud or this low.

Whatever it was, the Eskimos heard it, too, and turned as one to face it. Then, as quickly as they'd attacked, they climbed down off the crawler and disappeared into the wind.

Peeters looked over his shoulder all the way back to camp.

He duly reported the incident. The CO scratched his crew cut and said, "Well, Sergeant, I'm damned if I know what to make out of it. The Eskimos aren't hostile."

"Yes, sir."

"Far from it. They're the friendliest people on Earth. The non–fraternization rules are to protect them from us, not us from them. Hell, the first white men who came up this way kept getting the use of the Eskimo wives. It's like a custom. At least it was."

"Yes, sir."

Though the interview wasn't over, Peeters already knew two things. He wasn't in trouble, and this report wasn't going to go any further than this office. He was pleased at the first, not so happy with the second. What had happened out there had been weird. An anthropologist or somebody else who knew about these things should check this out.

Peeters said as much.

"Sergeant," the CO said, "I know you've got the best interests of the service at heart. But keep in mind the song and dance that we have to go through with the Danes and now the U.N. to keep this place open, won't you? That we're not having an adverse effect on the 'indigenous peoples'? That we're not screwing up the ecology?"

"Yes, sir."

"Those are good rules, Peeters. I believe in them. Though how the hell anyone could screw up this godforsaken ecology is beyond me.

"In any case, some pencil pusher who goes home to a wife every night might take a report of what happened to you out there today and twist it so that you've done some irreparable damage to their noble primitive psyches or some such crap, and then we'll all be in the soup. You'll get a black mark in your record, and I'll have to put an end to crawler excursions, morale will drop, men will become lackadaisical at their tasks. Some nut in Moscow will get nostalgic for Communism. He'll fire off a missile. We'll miss it. Washington will be destroyed. One thing will lead to another, and all the missiles will be fired. The human race will be destroyed, maybe all life on Earth."

"Yes, sir."

The CO looked at him.

"Peeters," he said.

"Yes, sir?"

"Have you been listening to a goddamn thing I've said?"

"Yes, sir. The human race will be destroyed, sir."

"I was kidding, Sergeant, okay? You were supposed to laugh."

"Sorry, sir."

"I was trying to lighten things up a little around here. Don't go back to the men saying the old man thinks the human race is about to be destroyed, will you do me that favor? Because I don't really think that."

"Certainly, sir. I didn't really think you did."

"Sergeant Peeters, you're a good man, and your record speaks for itself, but you've got to loosen up a little. If we can't laugh in a posting like this, we go nuts."

"Yes, sir."

"What happened today was probably some sort of welcoming ritual or something, or initiation, you know? I'll pass along your report if you want me to, but I think the best thing is just to let it drop. All right?"

"I won't push it through channels, sir."

"Excellent, Peeters, excellent. Now go to the rec room and watch a dirty movie or something."

"Yes, sir."

Peeters went to the rec room, but he didn't watch a dirty movie. Instead, he sat down at a computer terminal — not to play Tetris, but to plug into one of the truly amazing array of data bases this little machine at this isolated outpost could reach.

He started simply; he dialed up an encyclopedia program and looked up ESKIMO. That gave him a cross reference: see INUIT AND RELATED PEOPLES.

Peeters cussed himself. He should have known that much. He read the article, but it didn't tell him much he didn't know. A lot about hunting for seals and whales and the like, some stuff about ice fishing. A lot about Alaska and Canada, just a passing reference to the peoples of Greenland and Russia.

But at the end, there was a bibliography. He followed that up, then chased down *their* bibliographies. It took him every free moment for several days, but finally, he found a reference to a paper entitled "Description of Some Aspects of Unexplained Religion–Caused Behaviors Among Inuit and Related Peoples," by D.K. Olsen. He tried its data base call up number, and from the bowels of some computer somewhere, the information scrolled up on the screen.

In Danish.

The CO would have approved. Peeters sat there and laughed for about twenty minutes. Well, he thought, it was a good try. He scrolled through it anyway, hoping that somehow combining his native English, his grandparents' Dutch, and the German he'd learned in college, he could make something of it, but no dice.

Well, it had been a good try.

Wait a minute, he told himself. There was a note at the end that seemed to say the article was also available in German, English, Russian, and Japanese.

He tried for the English version, but it wasn't there. Okay, he thought, last chance, and punched the numbers that would bring him the German version. Even if he could read Russian or Japanese, he doubted this terminal could show the characters on the screen.

And then, *ach du lieber*, there it was.

Peeters rubbed his eyes — he was going to go blind, peering at a CRT for hours at a time like this — then plunged in. It was tough slogging. His German was rusty, and each sentence he decoded had to be decoded again from academic jargon. That part was harder than reading the German.

Peeters didn't want to have to do this again, so he took notes.

Beginning in the 1930s, when polar exploration settled down to becoming less of a race to some arbitrary geographical spot and more like science, there had been reports of rare but real anomalies in the behavior of various tribes of what were for many years called Eskimos, but more recently have come to be known by their preferred name of Inuit peoples.

Since the Inuit represent a number of more or less discrete populations, numerous variations in language and culture were to be expected, but *in general*, their religious beliefs tended to be a form of animism, ascribing spiritual traits to the wind, the snow, and the various animals they deal with in their lives, as well as a belief in the survival of the soul after death.

Except.

Except some tribes admitted to having known a personified god "long ago." He was a giant called Veektuk, and he rescued abandoned hunters from ice floes. He provided meat when hunting was bad. He loved children. And he disappeared after the white man came.

The amazing thing about Veektuk is that those rare tribes who knew him weren't imprecise about *when* they knew him. It was frequently pinpointed as during the lifetime of a member of the tribe, more often as during the lifetime of a parent or a grandparent. There was a mosaic of Veektuk reports totaling a hundred fifty years or so, from the 1840s to within a few decades of the date of the report.

The other remarkable thing was that the tribes who knew Veektuk were scattered haphazardly around the pole. This wasn't a story that diffused in the normal manner of folklore. It was a story that arose again and again, at widely scattered locations throughout the Arctic.

And that was about it. This was one of those academic papers that was basically a call for help. Before Peeters let the thing go, he checked the date of the report. Nineteen seventy–nine. He wondered what, if anything, had happened in Veektuk scholarship in the ensuing fourteen years. If anything.

He knew that if he played his cards right, though, he'd be able to add to it. Not that he cared.

What he cared about confirming was his sight and his sanity. He hadn't told the CO his whole story, and a good thing, too, considering the reception he'd gotten. He hadn't told about what he'd seen through a split–second break in the blizzard when the people had been storming the crawler, a glimpse too quick to leave much more than an impression. The possibly imaginary sight of an impossibly huge man, howling in the snow.

As the crawler chugged along, Peeters made a fetish of watching the compass, of matching exactly the route he had taken the last time. He wished he had more to concentrate on, because the rest of his brain was racing madly.

What if he ran into the Inuit again? What if it got back to the CO? Hell, his hitch here would be done even sooner than it was doomed to be.

But how could he *not* go? He had a chance to track down a god, a small "g" god, to be sure, but how many people even achieved that? And a benevolent one, besides. Peeters didn't even want to think of the need he had discovered in himself to find somewhere, anywhere, a benevolent god.

A Friend of Mine

Gracious. Going out to call on a god. I should have worn dress blues.

And, of course, as a contrapuntal bass line to the whole composition was the stubborn and undeniable knowledge that he was a fool. That he was chasing a lie, or an optical illusion around which some tiny minority of the tiny slice of mankind known as the Inuit had created a myth. If he found so much as a crude ice sculpture in the form of a man, he'd be lucky. As it was, he probably wouldn't find —

He found dogs.

Four of them, staked down by leather leads and bone rings into the ice, at almost the exact point he'd come to before.

He'd nearly run them over as he approached, in fact, because they were sleeping, buried in snow to keep warm. Their keen sense had warned them of the approaching crawler, and they'd sprung to their feet, barking and snarling at him.

Peeters knew enough about the people who lived here to know that they killed only what they hunted. But life was cruel, and polar economy was harsh. A dog too old to pull a sled was staked out like this and left to starve.

One dog at a time.

This was different. These dogs weren't old or sick. They were young animals, prime specimens, strong and square and active even now.

Peeters needed air, even in this frigid weather. He pulled the snorkel of his parka tight around his face, and opened the door of the crawler. Before he climbed out, he clipped a rope to his belt, in case a sudden blizzard sprang up on him again. He jumped down from the tread, and his boots crunched snow.

Peeters had loved his stay in the Arctic. His days spent staring at a radar screen served to remind him of the absurdity of so-called civilization and why he hated it. The rest of it was order and simplicity.

Until now. This made no sense at all. What was this supposed to be, a sacrifice?

But that was nonsense. Those same harsh economies that dictated the death of an aged dog precluded the needless death of four superior dogs like this. The people here just couldn't afford it.

Peeters stood there, feeling useless. The thought of the waste of the dogs' lives oppressed him, but there was nothing he could do. The animals were bred for strength, not for gentleness. If he approached, they would certainly tear him to pieces. If he somehow did manage to set them free, they'd still starve. Or they'd run into a bear and go down fighting. A better fate, but still not an enviable one.

Air Force issue cold-weather gear was good — Peeters didn't feel cold, just numb with helplessness and bewilderment.

He forced himself to think. What did he have?

Well, he had a gun in the crawler. He could shoot the dogs. That way, at least, they wouldn't suffer. But the dogs would be just as dead.

Then he thought of what else he had in the crawler. He had emergency rations — MREs, the great-grandchild of the K-ration. According to the Pentagon, MRE stood for Meal Ready to Eat, but in the service it was widely understood to mean Meals Rejected by Ethiopians. They were horrible, but they might seem pretty good to a starving husky. Even with a hefty dose of morphine from the emergency medical kit in each one.

Sure. He could dope the dogs, tie their legs and muzzles in case the dose wore off en route, throw them in the crawler, and hightail it back to base. He'd catch hell for it, but it would be worth it.

Of course, it also meant giving up the Great Veektuk Hunt, but that had been foolish on the face of it. Besides, if he got through the hiding that awaited him from the CO, there was always next time.

It would be nice to dope the dogs, if only to shut them up. Their howling and yapping had attained amazing volume. He turned back to the crawler.

That's when he saw the bear.

It wasn't the biggest polar bear in the world — it was about as high as the bottom of Peeters' rib cage at the shoulder — but it would do. And it meant business, eyeing Peeters and the dogs alternately, getting ready to start that almost comical shamble that turned into a lightning fast, deadly lunge at the end.

Peeters started telling himself exactly how big a fool he was, but he realized there was no profit in it and made himself stop.

He wasn't getting back to the crawler — his path would brush the bear's nose. The thing to do was to back around the dogs, get the dogs between the bear and him. So much for saving the dogs, you hypocrite. He excused himself partially by telling himself that if the dogs tied up the bear, he'd be able to beat it to the crawler in time to get the rifle and save all of them.

He kept telling himself that until he slipped.

Men were not designed for walking backward on ice. Peeters slipped and went down. He heard a kind of slapping noise — no more — as the bear ran for him. He smelled hot breath and felt pain, across his chest, across his face.

Then the howling came, the noise he'd heard before. What came next was like a magic trick. His vision had been filled with the open jaws of the bear, approaching his head. Then they vanished, leaving him with a vision of a clear blue sky. Snarlings and gruntings filled his ears, with the dogs yapping background vocals.

Painfully, Peeters twisted his body to see what was going on. What he saw was a nightmare vision — a fur–clad giant wrestling with the bear, holding it to him with one arm, pushing back on its head with the other.

Peeters heard the crack, then the bear flopped forward like a rug.

Peeters flopped himself, back to the snow. He had no strength. This, a part of his brain knew, was a fantasy concocted in his last split seconds to keep the horror of his death from himself.

It was quiet now. He was going. The last thing he saw was the scarred gray face leaning over him.

Two

"**D**on't try to move," a voice said. It wasn't hoarse so much as stiff, as if from lack of use.

Peeters sank back down. He didn't especially want to. His head felt heavy, his whole body tired, as if he'd been drugged. Or dreaming.

That's it. Definitely dreaming. The warmth I feel is the freezing–to–death feeling. The whiteness above my eyes means I don't have enough blood left in my eye–lids to make things look red in the sunlight. He resented it that his last dream should be of a strangely accented voice telling him not to try to move, but at least he wasn't in any pain.

Then he did move. And the pain was staggering.

"I warned you," the voice said. It wasn't quite "I vond you" but it was close. "If you must move something, move your left arm. That has not been injured."

Peeters had heard something like this voice before. Sure. It was like a slowed down version of Arnold Schwarzenegger, with echo effects. Whoever this was had an Austrian accent.

"Sprechen zie Deutsch?" Peeters asked.

"Ja, gut," the voice said. "Whichever you prefer. You have been crying out mostly in English; I assumed that was your language."

"It was," Peeters said, then he heard himself, and said, "Am I dead?"

There was a strange noise, something between a bark and a wheeze. It went on for a long time, and Peeters had trouble recognizing it as laughter. "Do you ask me that? Do you think I am God, then? It would take one wiser than I to stake out the line between life and death. What is your name?"

Peeters told him. "How about you."

Shadows on the sky told Peeters he'd been mistaken. His eyes had been open all the time. He was in an ice cave, or an igloo — an igloo, more likely because smoke from the fire whose reflection he could now also see dancing on the ceiling didn't fill the place — lying on a bed of soft furs. His boots were off. He tried to turn his head to look for them, but the pain was too much.

"I warned you," the voice said again. "Just your left arm for now."

Peeters listened this time. He raised his left arm, which didn't hurt, except for the fact that it weighed a ton. He brought it to his face, and found, to his surprise, that he had a good start on a beard, some two weeks' worth.

"I've got to get back to base."

"You are too ill to go anywhere. Besides, I must talk to you. I must decide."

"Decide what?"

"What I am to do with you."

Peeters was suddenly cold. "What you're going to do with me?"

"That is what I said."

"If you wanted me dead, you could have left me with the bear."

"I know. I should have. Compassion, of necessity, is alien to me. I have left others to die as you were going to die."

"For now, at least, I'm glad you changed your mind."

"Do you know why?"

"I don't know anything."

"I watched you, you and your ... engine. I watched for a long time. You had come too close to me before — that was you, was it not, some weeks ago?"

"I suppose."

"And now curiosity was driving you back. I could have killed you, but it would do no good. I would have to leave here, cross the pole yet again. I have done it too many times. I am weary of it."

"But you saved me, anyway." Peeters tried to sit up in his excitement. Pain forced him back down. "Ow. You saved me. From a polar bear. No weapons."

"I have a large knife. Do not concern yourself with that."

"I'd like to know how you did it."

"I am very strong, and I have had much practice."

The way he said it dissuaded Peeters from pressing the point. "Okay," he said, "*why* did you save me?"

"I do not know. I think it might be because you were taking a large risk to give the dogs their chance. In reality, the people of this place staked them out there as a gift for me — I need good dogs — but you had no way of knowing that. I could see you suffering over their plight, ready to take a risk for them, when you owed them nothing.

"It has not been my experience before now that a European would have such a gesture in him."

"I'm an American."

"I know of your wars, but you remain Englishmen."

Peeters decided these things didn't make sense because he was too weak.

"And so I decided," the voice said, "to give you the chance you were giving to the dogs. I brought you here and kept you warm, and bound your wounds as well as I could — I sewed you up with seal gut and a fish bone."

"Listen, you've got to get me back to my people," Peeters said. "I thank you for what you've done, but I need antibiotics quickly."

"What do you need?"

"My wounds are going to fill with pus; I'm going to develop a high fever and die."

"No. I know of these things. The People got the proper medicine from the missionaries. You have no fever now, do you?"

Peeters felt his forehead. "No," he said. "I don't think I do."

"And, of course, I boiled my instruments. My teacher was ahead of his time in that regard."

Peeters decided to stop trying to make sense of it.

"Are you Veektuk?"

Again, the laughing noise. "That is what the People make of my name. If you must call me anything, call me Victor."

"Victor."

"After my father. Victor Frankenstein."

Victor Frankenstein, Peeters thought, and he found it all very encouraging. Obviously, he was not in some igloo on top of Greenland's ice mass; he was in some military hospital somewhere, probably back in the States. There were probably pretty nurses running in and out, giving him the shots of morphine or demerol or whatever that were giving him such interesting dreams. The bear'd fucked him up, no doubt about that, but they'd found him and plunked him back to the States, and now he could lie on his butt and dream and accumulate his pay until he was in shape to spend it.

Of course, there was another possibility. What if he was lying in that hospital bed and the pretty nurses were running in feeding nutrients to him through tube in his nose because he was in a permanent coma. What if he was going to spend the next thirty to forty years inside his own head? My God, the *first* thing he dreamed up was Frankenstein's monster. Where did he go from there?

"I wish I knew," he said aloud.

"Wish you knew what?" his host responded.

"Never mind. How did you get to be a god?" He *was* a god, right? Sure. Veektuk. That was from before the bear, wasn't it? Unless he was imagining the whole thing.

He made himself stop. He was, as far as he could tell, physically paralyzed, at least temporarily. Too many doubts would freeze his brain, and then he would be as good as dead. Just stay calm and take things at face value.

"A god?"

"Sure. You've become obscure folklore. You turn up in stories all around the Pole, rescuing Inuit, bringing them food in hard times."

"I do what a decent man would do for his neighbor. It costs me nothing. It gains me fine furs and good dogs that they leave for me in gratitude. Fair trade, Englishman. Isn't that your creed?"

"You're kind of out of touch, if you don't mind my saying so. How long have you been doing this?"

"What is the year?"

Peeters told him.

"Then I have made my home in the Arctic — it is hard to keep track of time here, since I do not age — for something over one hundred eighty years."

"Of course," Peeters said. "The book came out in 1818."

"I am glad I rescued you. You represent a problem to *think* about. I have solved all the problems of mere survival long since."

Peeters laughed. "You think *you've* got a problem to think about."

"Yes. For one thing, why are you so unafraid? You can see, can't you?" The great, gray, scarred face loomed over Peeters.

"I can see."

"And yet you do not draw away. Am I not ugly to you? Once, all fled from me for my ugliness."

"My mother used to say, 'Beauty is as beauty does,' and you saved my life. Besides, I —" Peeters was going to go on to say that he probably didn't look so hot himself, after being mauled by a bear, but a strange noise cut him off. The creature was sobbing.

It went on for a long time. Finally, the Austrian–flavored tones returned. "I am sorry. I have always believed that to be true. I — I once needed very badly for it to be true. But the world showed it to be a lie. Perhaps men have learned since I walked among them."

Peeters thought it over. "A little, maybe. Some people have learned to be ashamed to hate for no reason. Little enough. Too damned little."

"That is another puzzling thing. You accept all I say. Are you humoring me?"

"No. Myself, a little, maybe."

"I think I must tell you my story, so that you can understand."

"I think I know your story," Peeters said, and he went on to tell the story as best as he recalled it from his teenaged reading of the book.

"How could you know this?"

"The book I mentioned. *Frankenstein, or: The Modern Prometheus*. Mary Wollstonecraft Godwin Shelley, 1818."

"Godwin! Of course! The anarchist. My father knew and corresponded with him! News of Frankenstein's death on the whaling ship undoubtedly reached that family."

Peeters could see the creature's shadow shuffling uneasily. "It is well known, this book?" he asked almost sheepishly.

"It's a classic."

"Then people will understand."

"No. I'm sorry, they won't. They see you as a soul–less, murdering monster. Most have never read the book, just corruptions by popular storytellers. They miss the point."

"I should not have killed the child, Frankenstein's brother. I have been tormented for years that I killed the child. But I was *myself* a child, and I was banished and denied. It is not right to reject those for whom you are responsible. They call me the monster? Well, perhaps they are right. And since it seems I do not age, I may not die; thus I may never know if I have a soul. If I do, it undoubtedly is corrupted by hate, for to this day I hate Victor Frankenstein for what he did to me."

The creature's voice got very soft. "But I also know this. My hatred is no deeper than the love I could have given him. He could have taught me, ugly as I am, to be a man. Instead, he drove me to be a monster."

"That's the way I always read the story," Peeters said.

"Here, drink this. You must sleep some more now."

Peeters drank and slept. There were no dreams.

Days passed. Peeters grew stronger. He could sit up, now, if he supported himself with his good arm.

He was also coming to grips with the idea that this dope dream of his (if that's what it really was) had a quality of consistency no other dream he'd ever heard of possessed. There was just the igloo and the fire and creature. And the talk. Hours and hours, about everything imaginable. Peeters' host had a hunger for knowledge, especially about science and technology. He had a low enough opinion of mankind that no history of war or brutality surprised him.

"Tell me more about the flying machines," the creature would say, "I have seen them." What impressed him most about men going to the moon was the idea of carrying air to breathe in bottles.

The time came when Peeters could sit up and feed himself. That day, there was little talking. Victor — Peeters had come to think of him as Victor — sat brooding, staring at Peeters sometimes, flexing his great, strong hands.

"Tell me," he said at one point. "With all the wonders men have achieved, are there — have there been — others like me?"

"No. I think people are afraid."

"Afraid of making monsters?"

"Perhaps. But also afraid of not being able to help treating them the way your father treated you."

"You are honest, Peeters. Perhaps too honest."

"You owe it to your friends to be honest with them."

That brought a few hours of silence. Then Victor said, "You call me your friend, Peeters. Don't you know I have been sitting here trying to decide whether to kill you?"

"See? You're honest with me, too."

"There have been more of the flying machines. Many more. The kind you told me are called helicopters. They are looking for you."

"My body, you mean. They must figure I died weeks ago."

"If they keep looking, they will find us."

"If they find my body, they'll stop looking. Is that the way you're thinking?"

"Why are you not *afraid?*"

"I don't know. I don't want to die, but from your point of view, I wouldn't blame you if you did kill me." Peeters didn't tell him that a part of his own mind was still convinced he was already dead.

Victor said, "Look at me."

Peeters struggled to a sitting position and looked Victor in the eye. The eyes were the only part of him that looked alive.

"I have considered," Victor said, "bringing you to them."

"You have?"

"Yes."

"Don't do it."

"You want me not to? It would save your life."

"They'll catch you and cage you and cut you up to see what makes you work."

"Is that so bad? You say I am already famous, or a version of me is. Perhaps I could write my own book. And tell the truth."

"Victor. It would be awful. Don't do it. They won't fear you now, but they won't respect you either. Here, you're nearly a god. If you came back to civilization, you'd just be another guest on the *Oprah Winfrey Show*."

"The what?"

"Never mind. I'd rather have you strangle me and get it over with than submit you to that." Peeters bit his lip. "God, I don't want to go back there myself. That's why I volunteered for Arctic duty in the first place. I don't fit into the world I was born into any better than you fit into yours."

"You must go back."

"I what?"

"You must go back. Your world is your responsibility, just as I was the responsibility of my father. If it is monstrous, it is because you — and all the other men and women — have driven it into being monstrous. Am I not the living evidence of the sin of turning one's back on one's responsibilities? You must go back. You will go back and fight for a better world. If you and enough others do that, I shall not mind captivity or curiosity or whatever awaits me so much. Perhaps, some day, I won't need to be a monster or a god. I will be a man, which is all I ever wanted."

"Victor, don't do it."

"I have decided. After you have slept, I will bring you south, to your people."

Peeters had had no choice but to drink, but he fought off the sleepiness. He had to stay awake, had to think of something to do. Victor slept, he knew that. He was sleeping now, in fact.

But what difference did that make? He couldn't overpower him, couldn't restrain him, even if Peeters were in the best condition of his life.

Whatever he did would have to be simple and stealthy.

He had an idea that made him smile. It was simple, and he could manage it easily.

He crawled over to where Victor lay and made his preparations. Then he slipped into furs, some of his and some of Victor's giant-sized ones. He pushed open the snow block that plugged the entrance and stepped outside. The cold, fresh wind was intoxicating after God knew how long breathing seal-oil fumes.

The dogs that had frightened him so weeks ago were now well trained and docile. They dug out from under the snow and took their place in harness in a matter of seconds.

Peeters found the whip, cracked it, and they were off, in the direction Peeters best judged to be south. He heard a bellow from the igloo.

Over his shoulder he could see Victor trying to chase him, but stumbling and falling. No shoelaces in the People's-style boots Victor wore, perhaps, but it was still possible to tie someone's ankles together with a leather thong. It took only a second for Victor to break the leather. He scrambled to his feet and yelled, "Come back, you fool. Don't die for me!"

"Good-bye, my friend," Peeters yelled back. "And thanks."

Peeters had no stamina. He was exhausted in minutes, and close to death in an hour. He had fallen off the sled and was lying in the snow when, miraculously, they found him. Alvarez was part of the search party.

"Hank!" he said, "Hank, you sonofabitch, you're alive! Where have you been? Where'd you get them clothes? Who sewed you up? You're a mess, man, but you're alive! We'll get you fixed up, don't worry about that."

Even as Peeters muttered thanks, he felt a twinge of fear. This was the first time of thousands those questions would be asked. What could he say? What could he do to let his friend keep the role he had heroically created for himself on the fringes of the humanity that had scorned him?

Then it came to him. It would mean time and treatment in a mental hospital, but he could take a year or so of that — long enough for Veektuk to work his way around the pole to another place.

It was an answer that would stand up under any test — lie detector, truth, drugs, whatever.

"I've been with Victor," he whispered. "Victor saved me."

"Who's Victor?" Alvarez demanded.

Peeters put a childish smile on his face and said, "Victor is a friend of mine." Then he began to chant. "Victor is a friend of mine, he resembles Frankenstein ..."

The Adventure of the Cripple Parade
(ascribed to Mickey Spillane)

I

Watson was a bloody mess.

It was so bad, that when I entered the surgery, where three of his brother medical men were working feverishly over his body, trying to staunch blood and rearrange bones, that I instinctively doffed my deerstalker, as though in the presence of death.

Angrily, I pushed the thought away, and turned to my brother, Mycroft.

"I found your note," I said. It had been in the rooms I had once shared with Watson at 221B Baker Street. I'd come back from a three-day chase of bank-note forgers, to find big brother's small but very neat handwriting pinned to the wall in front of my favorite armchair with the knife I usually use to secure my current correspondence to the chimneypiece.

Looking at poor Watson now, I could think of better uses for a knife.

"I knew you would," he said. He hardly moved his mouth enough to make his chins wobble. When we were children, Mycroft who was seven years my senior, had been left the task of raising me almost single-handedly. It was one of those situations the parents are too busy, and the governess just can't match her charges in the intellect department.

Mycroft had taught me the Code of the English Gentleman, and the first item of that code was "Never show your feelings." It was a hard lesson, but I learned it well. It served me in good stead in my chosen career as a consulting detective. I'm sure it served my brother equally well, in his career of arranging difficult situations for the Crown.

Of course, at this stage of the game, there's no way to know. We're grown up now. We don't talk about our emotions, at least not with each other.

This code came with its price. You learned how to hide your emotions, but not to stop having them. They came to me, just as they came to anybody, but they got bottled up like steam in an engine, and up and up, until the valve seems like it's about to pop, but you lean on it a little harder, and it never quite does.

Tonight, I was leaning on the valve with all my strength, but I could feel the bubbling inside.

"What happened?" I demanded.

Mycroft made a sour face. He might have been leaning on his emotional valve, too, but heavy as he was, he had a lot more to lean with.

"We're not sure," Mycroft said. "Of course, the superficial deductions are obvious. He was attacked from the front, then mercilessly beaten with an unidentified instrument."

"From the angle of the wounds, wielded by a right–handed man." My monograph on *Contusions and Lacerations Caused by Severe Beatings With Non–Edged Implements* was fresh in my mind as I elbowed my way past a doctor who was walking away from the table, took my glass from my pocket, and had a good look.

"Certain similarities to a cricket bat's marks, but whatever did this is harder and more flexible than ashwood. Either that, or the person who swung it must be a giant."

"Then there would be fewer blows along the legs and more on the upper body."

"Correct," I said. "And Watson would be dead."

I stepped aside for the doctor, who was returning with a bottle of laudanum. That was a good sign. You don't fetch painkiller for a corpse.

I asked the doctor with the bottle what Watson's chances were.

"I just can't say," he said. "The beating he took was ferocious; most people I've seen this bad were already dead. But your friend

Watson has the heart of a whole pride of lions, and a solid constitution. He may be all right. He may be in a coma from which he never awakens. He's in God's hands, now. He has had one stroke of luck already, though — they dropped him just two doors down from our surgery, just outside the Diogenes Club."

"The Diogenes Club," I echoed. I shot Mycroft a look; he returned one that said he'd explain all in good time. *He* was a member of the Diogenes Club.

Suddenly, the man on the table groaned.

"Watson," I said.

Watson's voice was a breathless thing, each sound forced into the world past pain. "Holmes," he said. "Is that you, Holmes?"

I took his hand. He smiled a little. "Trying a little detective work on my own … crippled … shouldn't have tried to do so much … wanted to impress you … crippled, all crippled, all the same place … I have to tell you … clubbed, clubbed. Doomed …"

Like a game bulldog in the pit, Watson strove to get up and give it another try, but the doctor was shaking his head so hard, almost made his eyeballs rattle.

I held Watson by the shoulders and eased him back to the table.

"Quiet, old friend," I told him. "And don't you worry about a thing. You're bashed up, but you're not crippled."

"No, no … not me … all, all crippled … must find out …"

"You're going to be fine, Watson, I know it. You need some rest. And while you're resting, let me tell you what's going to happen. I'm going to find out who did this to you, and I promise you they will pay, through the law or otherwise."

I thought I felt him squeeze my hand. "Sorry, Holmes … made such a mess …"

"Stop talking rubbish," I said. "Listen, not only will I bring in whoever did this to you, I'll also write it up for your files, so you won't miss a thing."

He squeezed my hand once more. Then the laudanum took hold, and he sighed and sank back into a heavy slumber.

II

The only place in the Diogenes Club in which talking is allowed is the Strangers' Room. Mycroft had signaled the porter to have our brandies and sodas brought there. I poured some amber liquid for myself, wielded the gasogene, then took a healthy swallow. It traced a warm line from my mouth to my stomach, but did nothing to thaw the cold hard thing in the pit of it.

"Has Mrs. Watson been notified? She's visiting relatives in the country. Cumberland, as I recall."

"Yes, Watson's locum told me. Everything is in hand, as far as that goes."

"Tell me the rest of it."

"I suppose in one way, it's all my fault. There's a flap on in the Ministry of Defence; stolen plans for troop movements and some technical innovations — I don't need to be any more specific than that. The plans have been recovered, and the foreign spy who bought them is under lock and key. But we have not been able to lay our hands on the thief. He collected forty thousand pounds, and must surely plan to smuggle it and himself out of the country."

"Has the foreign spy named him?"

"He says he's only seen the man in disguise."

"What sort of disguise?"

"The man the foreign agent met with was always disguised as a heavily bandaged cripple."

"Watson was raving about cripples. Mycroft, you had better not be trying to tell me that since I wasn't around, you sent Watson out to catch this spy."

"Sherlock, I am insulted. My admiration for Watson as your friend, as a physician, as a man of action, even as the recorder of sensational tales of your adventures, is unbounded. Only a dunce would send him alone on a confidential mission of this kind."

"Well, you're not a dunce."

"Thank you," he said. He surreptitiously slipped one hand inside his waistcoat as if he wanted to scratch his huge belly. He came out

The Adventure of the Cripple Parade 143

holding a piece of paper in his hand. He didn't mention it, so I didn't either.

"All I said in this matter was that I rather badly wanted your assistance in a matter of smuggling, and if he should hear from you, I asked him to tell you to call on me at any hour of the day or night."

"How did Watson take this?"

My brother pursed his lips. "He was much as usual, eager at the prospect of another of your adventures together, however vague that prospect might have been. But there was something more, a musing quality. At one point he said, 'Smuggling? I hadn't thought of that, but it might be an explanation.'"

"That's just like him," I said. "Watson is always looking for a mystery or a menace, even where they don't exist."

"They existed here," Mycroft said.

"Do you think Watson stumbled on your Ministry Problem on his own?"

"I believe I do, Sherlock. It's a remarkable coincidence but the coincidence of two possible smuggling plots involving bandaged cripples is even worse."

"It seems to me that a bandage would make a fine place to hide diamonds or gold coins, or any other portable form of wealth. All right, it's a lucky day for you."

"Why do you say that?"

"Because I'm working on the theory that your government secrets and what happened to Watson are connected. If they weren't, I'd be after Watson's attackers, and I wouldn't give you the time of day."

"I try always to know the time of day. Besides —"

"Besides you haven't shown me that piece of paper you took from your waistcoat."

Mycroft treated me to one of his rare smiles. "This will establish a connection to your satisfaction, I think."

I took the paper and read it. "MYCROFT HOLMES — TELL YOUR BROTHER TO STOP MEDDLING, OR THE NEXT BODY WILL BE HIS."

I held the paper up to the light. "There's most of a watermark here. I'll have to consult my files."

"In due time."

I leaned even harder on the steam valve. "Watson is lying unconscious. He may never wake up. The time, Brother Dear, is long past due. I need to examine this watermark, and I need to have all the details of what was stolen, for whom, and why."

"Would you mind getting the details first? The sub-Minister is waiting in his office for us."

III

"Aluminium, Mr. Holmes. Or as the Americans persist in mis-calling it, aluminum. Are you familiar with the subject?"

"I've studied chemistry, and I read the *Times*," I told him. It was from reading the *Times* that I knew about the sub-Minister, himself. He was touted for Great Things in the future, maybe even a stint in Number Ten. I knew about his trademark white side-whiskers, but then, everybody did. Sir Carl Berin-Grotin was one of the rising stars of the Empire.

But rising star or no rising star, if he couldn't shed any light on what had happened to Watson, I had no time for him.

To speed things up, I told him what I knew about aluminium.

"It's a chemical element, a silver-white metal. It's strong, light, elastic, malleable, ductile and a superb conductor of electricity. It's also one of the most expensive substances on earth. The Americans acquired a large portion of all the refined aluminium in the world to top off their Washington Monument. Tripled the cost of the structure, I believe."

"It might well have done," the sub-Minister conceded. "But here at the ministry, we are not concerned with the cost of the metal. Or rather we are, but only insofar as we can attempt to drive down that cost."

He pointed a finger at me, a rude habit, especially when a finger is as ugly as his were. They were thick and almost globular at the tips, and the nails didn't grow out straight, but curled tightly over those rounded fingertips like the claw of an animal.

"You see, Mr. Holmes," he went on, "aluminium is not so precious because it is scarce — indeed, a ministry chemist tells me it is one of the most abundant elements in the crust of this planet. The problem is, it is bound so tightly to bauxite, its ore, that it takes temperatures virtually impossible to sustain by conventional methods to melt it free."

"I take it that what has been stolen is an unconventional method. The troop movement information was a smoke screen."

"Yes. When this sort of crisis is on, rumors inevitably start. Not everyone can appreciate the value of an electrically powered furnace to refine aluminium on a scale hitherto impossible. Let them rest content with troop movements. It sounds more … dangerous somehow."

"Fine," I said. "Plans for an electrically powered furnace to refine aluminium were stolen. Mycroft says they were recovered. Obviously the plans are simple enough for a man to carry in his head."

"A man with a trained memory," Sir Carl said. "Or time to study. We can't be sure our quarry didn't have a chance to copy the plans. More than one country would be interested in this. Cheap aluminium would make possible gigantic Dreadnoughts. Body armour for soldiers. Airships. Heavens, one could even hammer it out flat into sheets and preserve food in it."

"Besides Watson's … misfortune, how do you know our man is still in the country?"

Sir Carl scratched with his odd claw–nails at the trademark side–whiskers. That told me something about the man right there. He was willing to put up with an uncomfortable growth, just for show. "We have sources, Mr. Holmes. There would be elation in certain foreign circles it would be impossible to hide. Our man is still in England. The question is, can you apprehend him before he leaves the country?"

My face was hard, like a mask of stone. "Count on it," I said. "The only place he goes from England is Hell."

IV

She was a brunette, tall and cool, and her smile was a challenge that was almost an insult. Watson thinks I'm immune to women, and I don't correct him because there's no advantage to it. But Lizabeth Parkins had the stuff to overcome anybody's immunity, and she dressed to show it, the thick wool hugging every curve, the smoothly turned ankles shamelessly exposed.

"It's unusual to find a woman in a shipping line's office," I said.

"I'm an unusual woman," she told me. "What brings you here, Mr. Holmes?"

What brought me there was the watermark on the paper and Watson's day book, but she didn't need to know that. Watson's book showed me he had several cases that brought him down to the docks in recent weeks, and there was enough left of the mark on the paper to let me know it was the stationery of the Trans–Global Line, one of the biggest of the new shippers.

"Routine investigation," I lied. "What ships do you have in London right now?"

She licked her red lips. Suddenly, it got hot in the room, and there was a buzzing sound in my ears.

"Why do you want to know, Mr. Holmes?" She was still wearing that cool smile, but there was a thin sheen of sweat on her forehead.

"Come on, Miss Parkins, I could find out in a second from the shipping desk at any newspaper. I'm in a hurry."

"Oh, well, if you're in a hurry. We have only one at the moment, the *Peruslavia*, leaving tomorrow for Hamburg. It is not too late to consign a shipment. You can see it if you like. Pier Sixty–one."

I thanked her and went to leave.

"Do come again, Mr. Holmes. When you have more time."

I found a convenient corner out of sight, and watched the *Peruslavia*'s gangplank. The first bandaged cripple went up after I'd been there about twenty minutes, then at fifty–minute intervals for the next three hours. It was the kind of thing you wouldn't notice ordinarily, but it would stick in your mind if it happened more than once. I'd checked out Watson's patient, and from his window the gangplank was clearly visible. Three visits here, Watson must have seen five so-called cripples go on to the ship.

A nice racket. You give them a crutch, and a bandage load of something expensive, send them up the gangplank, unwrap them, and send them down as ordinary seamen.

I timed myself on the next one and planted myself at the bottom of the gangplank.

"Here," I said. "Let me help you up."

He recognized me, and he ran. He wasn't just fast for a cripple, he was *fast*. Through the back alleys of the docklands, in and out of doorways. I might never have caught him if he'd had sense enough to throw the crutch away. He obviously didn't need it, but he held on. It slowed him down, made his passage through doorways harder. Finally, I had him cornered at the end of a blind alley. Like a rat, he turned to fight.

He held the crutch like a weapon. That would have been fine with me, if I'd had a stick, too, but I didn't. I let him take one wild swing, ducked it, and delivered a terrible right cross to his face. I felt bones in his nose go to gravel, and redness squirted in all directions.

When he was down and out, I took a look at him. A typical thug, not somebody I recognized. Then I unwrapped the bandages on his arms and legs and head. There were no injuries underneath them, but I'd been expecting that.

There was nothing valuable in them, either.

Not so much as a miserable farthing. A beautiful logical construction came crashing down. They weren't smuggling things in those bandages, so what was the parade of cripples all about? I had to get on that ship.

There was enough privacy in the alley to do what I had to do. I got rid of my cap and Inverness cape and jacket and tie, and proceeded to wind the bandages around myself. I wiped some grime from the sooty walls and smeared it on my hands and face. Then I picked up the crutch and headed for the ship. The hardest part of the whole thing was using the crutch. It was too short, and didn't seem to weigh as much as it should.

I remembered to limp, and to do it consistently. It was probably just some mistake that had caught Watson's attention in the first place. He may not be much of a detective, but he's a perceptive and dedicated doctor. And the best friend a man ever had.

Anger started bubbling up in me once more, but it was vital to keep under control. Even more vital, because suddenly, I had it. The reason for the bandages, the heat and the humming, everything.

I could have gone to Mycroft; I could have gone to Lestrade at the Yard. But this was personal, and I wanted to do it all by myself. I kept limping, but I changed direction back to the office of Trans-Global lines. I limped through the door into the empty office. The place was still stiflingly hot. Lizabeth Parkins was buttoning the top buttons of her dress as she came to the office.

A look of anger contorted the beautiful face. "What are you doing back here in that — Fred! Nigel!"

Two more cripples came out of the back room. One of them had a shotgun, but it was pointed at the floor. I didn't give him time to regret his mistake. I pulled the revolver from my pocket, and fired. He went to the floor. His friend didn't know whether to attack me with his crutch or grab for the shotgun. I had the pistol against his eyeball in a split second, and suddenly the decision didn't matter so much anymore.

I took the crutches, both as light as mine. I herded everyone into the back room. In there was the crucible, filled with a glowing yellow–white liquid, like a piece of the sun.

"I see," I said. "You weren't just going to sell the secret, you planned to present a working model. How did you plan to get that on board?"

"We were going to call it machine parts. Even if customs opened the box, that's what it would look like." Her face was amazing in that unearthly glow. "What happens now, Mr. Holmes?" she asked coyly.

"It's over," I said.

"It doesn't have to be. *Someone* is going to get rich with this technology? Why shouldn't it be us?"

"Who besides you and me?"

"Just you and me. We could share the money, and … and much, much more."

Treachery can wear the mask of beauty, and her mask was exquisite. Somebody with less experience might even have believed her. I didn't come close. The buzzing I'd heard before was the electrical generator, making the heat. The pile of metal on the floor was aluminium.

"Don't insult our intelligences, Miss Parkins. You didn't set this up all by yourself. The electricity, the furnace, the mold, the snap–together pieces of wood veneer. This took organization. This had to be planned even before the secrets were stolen. It was brilliant. You weren't smuggling anything in the bandages. The bandages were just a blind. *You were smuggling crutches*. Aluminium crutches, each worth five hundred to a thousand pounds, covered in a thin layer of wood, and brought on board the ship. Watson stumbled onto the secret, and a few of your cripples beat him with the metal. The wood covering kept us from recognizing the marks. You'll pay for that, my dear. You'll get old and ugly spending years picking jute in prison."

There was something wrong. She wasn't scared enough. She had the smug confidence of a punter who knows the game is rigged.

Now, I knew it, too, and that was all I needed. "Thank you," I told her. "Now I know who —"

Just then, the door burst open, and a figure with a gun started spraying bullets around. I ducked for my life, even as I saw Nigel (or Fred) go down. Parkins made a big mistake. She ran for the doorway, yelling, "Darling."

Darling shot her, then disappeared from the doorway. She spun away and fell back against the crucible.

Her scream was more than the scream of a woman's throat. It was as though it was being torn from her soul. She was in flames as she fell, rolling and still screaming. I ran to her and beat out the flames, but it was too late.

"You're done for," I told her. I mentioned a name.

Her voice was a croak, it came from somewhere in the middle of a charred and blistered mess, but it was still a human voice. "I … loved … him," she said.

"Obviously, he didn't reciprocate," I said, but I don't think she lived long enough to hear it. I left. I had a report to give.

V

A commissionaire was waiting for me outside the Ministry, and pressed a note into my hand, I tipped him, but I didn't bother to look at it.

Mycroft met me outside the sub–Minister's office. "Well?" he said.

"You'll hear it," I told him, and went inside without knocking.

The sub–Minister was scratching at his side–whiskers when I walked in.

"Ah, Mr. Holmes, results so soon?"

"Many of them, sub–Minister. And here's another one." I walked up to him, grabbed him by his trademark facial hair, and pulled with all my might.

He screamed, but not as loudly as he would have if I were pulling roots from skin, instead of false hair from spirit gum.

"I knew it," I said. "The way you kept scratching. A man who has had whiskers for years gets used to them. But they weren't your whiskers anymore. You shaved them off so you could do your dirty business around the docks without being recognized, gluing them back on when you came here."

There was hate on the reddened face, the hate of an evil man who could betray his country and take pleasure out of watching his men pound a good man like Watson into jelly.

Mycroft, as usual, was right there with me. "Sir Carl had the easiest access to stealing the plans."

"Of course he had. You were there when Watson was beaten near to death, weren't you, Sir Carl?"

"You petty fools, what do you think you can do to me?"

My face wanted to smile, but I kept it grim. "Answer my question. You must have watched. At least, Watson must have seen you, because he told me something about you, something I didn't recognize at the time. I'll make you an offer, sub–Minister. You answer my question, and I'll answer yours."

The Adventure of the Cripple Parade 151

He drummed his strange fingers on the tabletop. "Very well. Yes, I was there. Your friend begged us to stop."

I went icy inside. "So will you."

"Are you going to answer my question?"

"A true Englishman keeps his word," I said. "Here's what's going to happen to you. The Prime Minister will be told. The Queen will be told. Your immediate superior will be told. That's all. The Crown would just as soon avoid scandal, wouldn't they, Mycroft?"

"Naturally, but we just can't let a murderer —"

"He'll be punished," I said. "He'll come to the office every day. He'll have no appointments. He'll make no decisions, or speeches. He'll be a shell, a nothing."

"And all the while, he'll be waiting."

I snaked out a hand, grabbed his drumming fingers, and squeezed. "Have your fingers always been like this, Sir Carl?" I asked, shoving the blunt, nail-covered tips in his face. "Never mind, I see from the portrait of you on the wall that they haven't been."

I threw his hand down on the desk. "Watson said to me, 'Clubbed. Clubbed. Doomed.' I assumed he was talking about himself, but he's too good a doctor not to have assessed his own condition properly. He was talking about you."

I grabbed the hand again. "These are called *clubbed fingers*, and they are an outward sign of a deadly heart disease. Watson called my attention to a paper on the subject in the *Lancet*."

And finally, the valve popped, and all my hatred of the traitor poured out in face and voice. "And so, every day, you'll leave the gilded prison that is your home, and come to the gilded prison that is your office, and one day, a year from now, perhaps six months, maybe less, Providence will swing its hammer, once, twice, crushing your black heart, making you cry for mercy, and you'll die, clawing at the carpet and whimpering."

He was whimpering now. I turned in disgust and left him to Mycroft.

Outside the door, I remembered the note the commissionaire had given me. I fished it out of my pocket and read it.

It was from the doctor. Watson was conscious. He was going to be all right.

I ran to the street to hail a cab.

The Adventure of the Christmas Tree

Over the years of my association with Mr. Sherlock Holmes, he strove constantly to present himself as the perfect reasoner, divorced from all human failings and concerns. And it is true that his perception and deductive abilities were unparalleled in at least the recorded history of our race; it is also true that Holmes was not devoid of those becoming and manly sentiments which distinguish the true English gentleman.

In perusing my notes, I see that I have already recorded a number of cases that illustrate my point, among them "The Adventure of the Yellow Face" and "The Adventure of Charles Augustus Milverton." There are others, recorded and unrecorded, that point in the same direction. Holmes scoffs, but I believe his ability to feel, albeit tightly controlled, enhances his genius as an investigator.

We were in our rooms at 221B Baker Street on the third day of winter of 1889, I reading the *Lancet*, and Holmes standing in the bow window scratching out tunes on the violin as he looked out at London. The weather had obliged the calendar by delivering at the advent of winter the first important snowstorm of the year.

The downy whiteness had muffled the usual bustle of the metropolis. I found it quite soothing, and it augured for a peaceful Christmas to come.

"I believe we are to have a visitor, Watson," Holmes said. "Two of them, to be precise."

"A case, Holmes?" I inquired.

I looked up to see him smile. "Bill collectors do not travel in the company of young ladies, and the charitably minded, collecting for a worthy cause, would stop at other doors than ours. I think we might safely say that these are potential clients come to see us."

I put away the *Lancet* and tidied up the area in which I had been reading. Soon Mrs. Hudson knocked to tell us that the visitors were Joseph Camber, and his daughter, Nancy.

Camber was nervous and embarrassed. He kept his hat, an old-fashioned high beaver, in his hands as he sat, and constantly turned it by the brim. He wasn't a tall man, but he was a muscular one, particularly in the arms and shoulders. His hair was brown, shot with gray. He was dressed for church, or for business, but he seemed uncomfortable in city clothes, as evidenced by the times he ran a finger around the inside of his collar.

The daughter was much more self-possessed. She was also brown haired, and she had a softer version of her father's strong features, rendering her handsome, rather than pretty. Still, she had an air of health and confidence about her that was most fetching.

"Good afternoon," said my friend. "I am Sherlock Holmes, and this is my colleague, Dr. Watson. Pray, how may we help you?"

Camber looked at his hat. "I feel a ruddy fool," said he. His accents marked him as a Highland Scot.

His daughter had the same soft burr. She laid a hand on Camber's arm and said, "Now, Father, we've come here. The decision has been taken."

"Ach. I know, but it *sounds* so daft."

"Perhaps I can help you get started," offered Sherlock Holmes. "You are the forester on the estate of the duke of Balleshire in Scotland. You are left handed, and a widower, and you have come to consult me on a matter which will leave your mind no peace until you have got to the bottom of it."

The eyes of our younger visitor went wide with surprise; the elder visitor began to sputter. The only intelligible sounds he uttered were, "But how …?"

Holmes gave the merest suggestion of a bow. "A trifling matter, really. The callosities on your hands are those of the man who wields the saw and the ax. Since your left hand is more heavily callused on the webbing of the thumb, that is the hand in which you hold the saw. As for being a widower, an outdoorsman will frequently seek the support of a woman in dealing with problems with which he is not familiar. Since your daughter is here with you instead of a wife, I assume that the lady in question is not available. Her having passed from the world was simply the most likely explanation. Am I perchance in error?"

"No, my Aggie's been gone these seven years. By gaw, I would have liked to have her advice now. She was never o'er thrifty with the givin' of it when she was alive, ye ken."

"Father!"

Holmes's amusement could be seen only in his eyes. "I'm sorry, Mr. Camber," said he, "but you shall have to make do with only my advice."

"How did you know about the duke?" the daughter demanded. "And about how this has been preying on his mind?"

"Your father is wearing a stickpin in his cravat bearing the duke's crest. Unless His Grace has developed a hitherto secret passion for woodsmanship, I knew your father must be in the duke's employ, and that the pin is some sort of gift."

Camber nodded proudly. "Aye, man and boy forty years in the service of the duke and the old duke before him. The pin was given me from His Grace's own two hands Christmas last." His face turned grim. "Christmas in Scotland ye ken, is not the spectacle of it the Sassenachs make. We're more apt to save our celebrations for Hogmanay, when a man can see in the new year and get behind a wee nip or two. But His Grace's mother was from across the border, and he likes to keep the holiday in the ways she preferred. As a good servant, I've always done my best to help him, but this year it's landed me up to my ruddy ears in a mystery. And as you say, it preys on my mind till I'm sleepless over it."

Holmes's nostrils had flared at the sound of the word *mystery*. The ineffable scent of that particular phenomenon was the breath of life to him.

"Indeed," said he, "I deduced as much when a member of such a canny race as the Scots would travel to London to consult me in the matter. I adjust my fees according to my interest in a case, Mr. Camber, but I do charge them."

Camber closed his eyes as though enduring great pain. "Ah know it," he said with a sigh. "But I have no choice. The regular police, both in Scotland and here, laughed in my face. By gaw, we'll see who's laughing at the end."

"Now, please, tell me the details of your mystery. I know from the *Times* that the duke is keeping Christmas this year at his house in London. Does it have to do with him?"

Camber turned to his daughter. "You tell it, Nancy."

"Very well, father." She turned to us. "Yes, Mr. Holmes. We believe it does have to do with the duke. You see, His Grace spends alternate Christmases in London, and when in London, he follows the practice so many have adopted in emulation of the late Prince Consort. He erects in the hall of the building a Christmas tree. He supervises the hanging of the decorations and presents, and lights the candles himself."

"Yes. An invitation to the destruction of the house by fire, but I suppose it has its charm. How do you know of this?"

"I have the honor of being the personal maid to Lady Caroline, His Grace's eldest daughter."

"I see. Pray go on."

"In those years when His Grace celebrates in London, it is his pleasure to cause a tree from his own estate to be shipped up to town for decoration. A week or so before Christmas, my father selects the most robust and symmetrically formed tree of the proper size from among the large stand of Scotch pines on the grounds of the estate. He then makes preparations for the preservation of the tree in transit — something I do not understand, I'm afraid."

The outdoorsman shook his head in a gesture of dismissal. "Earth and ice in alternating layers, with burlap between and canvas outside. It's really elementary."

I cleared my throat. "The workings of the expert mind," said I, "while perhaps seeming elementary to the experts themselves, do not always appear so to those who lack that expertise."

I had been wanting to say that for years.

The Adventure of the Christmas Tree

"Thank you, Doctor," said Nancy Camber, "that expresses a thought I've never been able to articulate. In any event, my father made the usual trip out to the woods, marked the tree for cutting, then went to the railway station to make arrangements for a crate to ship the tree in."

"Upright and braced," said Joseph Camber decisively. "So that the branches might not be marred."

"But the next day, when he went with the horse and sledge to cut it and bring it away —"

"It wasn't *there!*" interjected Camber. "The ruddy thing was *gone*. I mean, I've heard of poachin', but I've never heard of anyone daft enough to poach a *tree*."

"Is there any reason someone might want to do that, in any case?"

Camber shook his head. "I've been bruisin' my brain on just that question, Mr. Holmes. Pine is no good for firewood; too much resin, gums up the flue. Ye can make decent, rough-hewn furniture from it, but not from a tree small enough to keep in a house."

"You say you marked the tree. In what manner did you do this?"

"I just put a wee nick in the bark at eye level. It's easy to spot if you know what to look for, but it doesn't mar its decorative properties, ye ken."

"What did you do when you discovered the tree missing?"

"Well, I'll tell you, Mr. Holmes, I spent quite a while goin' back and forth between scratchin' my head and cursin'. When I left off doin' that, I did the only thing I could do. I found the next-best tree, and cut that and sent it to be shipped."

Holmes rubbed his chin. "Hmmm," said he. "Mr. Camber, your case presents certain elements of interest, and I think —"

"Oh!" said Nancy Camber. "Please, Mr. Holmes, forgive me for interrupting you, but we haven't got to the mysterious part yet."

"Oh," said Holmes in his turn. He began to fill his pipe. "I shall smoke if you've no objection. Pray continue."

"You see, sir, I prevailed upon my father to travel to London to keep Christmas with me. He is great friends with MacBurney, the duke's valet, and His Grace is rather fond of Father himself, so there was no problem about Father's staying with MacBurney in his room, and sharing our servants' Christmas fare."

"Then I took a notion," Camber said. "For years, I'd been cutting the trees, but I'd never seen one in place. I reckoned this'd be my one chance to do it, so Nancy and MacBurney ganged up on the butler, a Sassenach named Havering, and he let me into the hall where the tree was."

"The hall is closed off before Christmas Eve," Nancy explained. "And no fire is lit there until then, to aid in keeping the tree fresh. Father went in and —"

"It was the *missing tree*! The very one that had been stolen in Scotland!"

"How can you be sure of that, Mr. Camber?" I inquired. "Your mark might have been copied after all."

"Dr. Watson," said he. "A medical man?"

I nodded assent.

"Do you deliver bairns, then?"

"Frequently," said I.

"Do you ever deliver more than one bairn in a day?"

"Of course."

"And if, at the end of that day, someone showed you one of the bairns, could you tell which one it was?"

"Of course."

"Well, Dr. Watson, trees are my bairns. I plant 'em when that's needed, and cut them down when that's needed. I watch 'em and take care of 'em, and spend my life around 'em. I made a study of that tree before I picked it. I'll take my oath that that is the same tree."

Holmes drew deeply of the aromatic shag in his pipe. "We'll take that established, then, Mr. Camber. Do you have any idea of what happened to the tree you cut and shipped?"

"Not a glimmer."

"Miss Camber?"

She looked surprised. "I? No, I have no idea at all. I am simply worried that someone is playing some sort of nasty joke on my father, seeking to spoil the fine relationship he and His Grace's family have always enjoyed."

Camber thumbed the top of his beaver hat. "Ah think this is summat much worse than a joke. It's mighty *expensive* for a joke, even for people of quality. *Ah* think it's some kind of evil plot, aimed at His Grace. He's quite an important figger in diplomatic circles, ye ken."

"Yes," Holmes said dryly. "I was aware of that." Holmes jumped to his feet. "Yes!" cried he. "The outré nature of this puzzle is quite refreshing. I shall investigate, Mr. Camber, and report to you at the earliest opportunity. You both remain at the duke's residence in Ounslow Square? Good."

"Well, now, Mr. Holmes," said Camber. "I don't — that is, I'm not a wealthy man."

"Don't worry about a thing, Mr. Camber. I shall leave you enough for bread and a ticket back to Scotland. On your way now. Charmed to have met you, Miss Camber."

When they were gone, Holmes threw himself into his seat and said, "For the first time, this looks as if it might be a tolerable holiday after all. What do you make of them, Watson?"

"Oh," said I. "They seem quite devoted to each other, and they are obviously sincere."

"Yes, Watson. You may trust me to notice the obvious for myself. What do you think of their story?"

"I hardly know what to think. At first blush, such machinations with an emblem of the festive season seem sinister, but has the final result been? The tree Camber wished to be in the duke's house is now in the duke's house, and an inferior tree is missing."

"Forget the inferior tree," said Holmes. "The inferior tree is now a pile of ashes, or flotsam in the Thames. What we must concentrate our attention on is how the original tree reached its destination on its own, like some vegetable version of a homing pigeon. And why."

"How are we to do that?" I inquired.

"Facts are the bricks from which deductions are built, Watson. Come, we go to seek facts."

We sought them in the Diogenes Club, that remarkable collection of unsociable men, who go there to read or eat or drink or relax in a comfortable chair, but who never, on pain of expulsion, allow one word of conversation to be passed one to the other.

Talking is allowed only in the Strangers' Room, and it was there we spoke to Holmes's elder brother, Mycroft. The corpulent elder brother was what he sometimes liked to describe as a "facilitator" for the British government. He had no title, nor even (so far as I knew) an office, but he seemed to know everything about any current crisis.

Mr. Sherlock Holmes informed his brother about Joseph Camber's mysterious story.

"Suggestive," said Mycroft Holmes.

"I found it so," averred his brother. "It is common knowledge that the duke moves, as my client says, in the 'highest diplomatic circles.' Is he engaged in anything of importance at the moment?"

"He is involved in something of the first importance. He is engaging in unofficial, preliminary talks concerning South West African mineral concessions with the Germans. The German government has brought Herr Stefan Geitzling over from Africa to begin the talks."

Mycroft Holmes pressed the tips of his fingers together and pursed his lips. "I need not tell you gentlemen that since the uniting of the German States under the kaiser, relations with that country have been strained, and the strain is felt most strongly in our respective empires. The problem under discussion may be a relatively trivial one, but if such trivialities cannot be worked out amicably, they will fester over time and, one day within our life times, burst out into a horrible war."

I privately wondered what this had to do with Christmas trees, but I held my peace.

Holmes said, "I intend to call on His Grace this afternoon. I shall not, of course, allude openly to what you have told me, but I will keep it in mind. I answer for the discretion of Dr. Watson."

A rare smile disturbed the folds of Mycroft Holmes's face. "My dear Sherlock, I am quite prepared to answer for the doctor's discretion myself. Do, please, communicate with me again if you learn anything the government should know."

Holmes indicated he would, and we bade Mycroft farewell.

"Now, to Ounslow Square, I imagine," said I.

Holmes was already hailing a cab. We clopped along through the whitened streets. The weather seemed to have accelerated the rate at which the usual glumness and irritation of city life are replaced by goodwill as Christmas approaches. In this case, the cabbie seemed to be smiling even before he received his tip.

According to Holmes's wish, we alighted in the business area of South Kensington before proceeding to the square. Much to my surprise, he bade me wait on the sidewalk whilst he went into an ironmonger's shop, emerging a few moments later with a parcel wrapped in brown paper.

A butler at the duke's residence informed us that His Grace was in a meeting at the moment. Holmes asked that his card be brought in to him at the next opportunity and asked if we might wait in the meanwhile.

The butler reluctantly assented.

In the event, we did not have to wait long. The butler returned, and asked us to accompany him to a room on the first floor. When we arrived, we saw it was fitted up as a conference room, with a large table in the middle of it. The table was littered with maps and charts and documents, some in English, some in German. Having no wish to surprise my country's secret affairs, I looked no further than that.

The butler began to announce us, but he had barely gotten our names from his mouth before a round, squat little man with an imperial beard and a monocle came forward and pumped my companion's hand vigorously.

"Mr. Sherlock Holmes, what an honor it is to meet you. Even in the Godforsaken desert, we have of your adventures read, as recorded by the so-good Dr. Watson."

He let go of Holmes's hand to pump mine for a while. "When we send for brandy and soda, and the so-good Perkins bring in to us the card of yours, I am beside myself with joy. I am neglecting my task, which is talking with my new good friend, His Grace, but I claim a guest's indulgence and say meet you I must do. And here you are."

"Here I am, indeed." Holmes turned to the duke, whose youthful face under a crop of snow white hair showed a not–quite suppressed smile of amusement. "Your Grace, I do not mean to interrupt your work, but I wish to have a few words with you, on something of importance. A matter has come to my attention which concerns you."

"It's quite all right, Mr. Holmes. I believe Herr Geitzling" — here the round man bowed, still beaming — "and Herr Untermeyer, his aide" — and now a handsome, blue–eyed young man with dark curly hair bowed — "were beginning to feel almost as stale as I do myself. That was why I rang for refreshment. May I be excused to talk to Mr. Holmes, Herr Geitzling?"

"You may on one condition be excused, Your Grace."

"Even now, *mein Herr*, you remain a tough negotiator. What is your condition?"

"That after your talk, Mr. Holmes and Dr. Watson to this room return and the brandy and soda share with us. Furthermore, we shall talk not about our business while they are here, but about their adventures."

The duke made a conciliatory shrug. "You must appreciate, Herr Geitzling, that Mr. Holmes is a busy man —"

"But not so busy that we cannot spare some time for such a distinguished visitor to our shores, Your Grace. We will be delighted to join you."

We repaired downstairs to the duke's study, a fine, masculine room of leather and books.

He told us to be seated, and took a chair behind a large square desk. "So, Mr. Holmes, what is the matter that needs my attention?"

"I believe your life may be in danger, Your Grace."

His Grace seemed as shocked as I was.

"I beg your pardon, Mr. Holmes. My life? In danger? From whom?"

"How important is the matter which you are discussing with Herr Geitzling?"

"Moderately important. I cannot go into details."

"That will not be necessary, for the present. Would events be dire if these talks were to fail?"

"Concealing nothing from you, Mr. Holmes, I don't think so. Expensive, yes. Inconvenient, certainly. But dire? No. Nothing irrevocable here."

Then His Grace smiled slyly. "If the failure of these talks — which, by the way, I do not anticipate, they are going quite well, thank you — if the theoretical failure of these talks was to have a dire effect on anyone, it is likely to be Stefan Geitzling. His wife is a distant relative of the kaiser's. It is undoubtedly why he holds the position in Africa that he does. He certainly has no affection for the place, complains about it constantly. Still, he is a typical German, conscientious and painstaking. He knows his business."

"How about his aide?"

"Othmar Untermeyer is also painstaking and conscientious. He is a polite and self-effacing young man." Again, we saw the duke smile. "My daughter is quite taken with him. Really, Mr. Holmes. Your brother and I know each other well, and I am both flattered and honored by your concern, but this particular negotiation is not the sort of thing that leads one to fear for his life."

"Perhaps the danger comes from other quarters. Have you any personal enemies?"

"Only political ones. We don't assassinate each other in the House of Lords, Mr. Holmes. Not for some time, at least. *Please*, what has happened to cause your concern?"

"Information received. It would be pointless to burden Your Grace with the matter, especially since nothing can be found to substantiate it at this time."

"I'm sure your informant is mistaken," said the duke.

"Still, it is best to be thorough. Have I your permission to question the servants and the other inmates of the house?"

The duke waved his hand. "You may have carte blanche, if it helps to resolve the matter. But before doing that, you must come and speak with Geitzling. Perhaps this will get a few more tons of magnesium ore per annum from him."

Holmes rarely agreed to socialize, but when he did he could be utterly charming, as he was on this occasion. This was perhaps helped by the fact that Herr Geitzling seemed to know every aspect of the detective's career, and be impressed by all of it.

"It is gratifying to know that my accounts are so well perused in such a faraway place," I said at one juncture to a compliment of Geitzling's about my writing.

"It helps keep me to Europe tied," said he. "I have a duty, and this I do, but I miss home. Even here, I have the things I have not for two years had at Christmas. The snow, the promise of a roast goose, the smell of the *tannenbaum*. His Grace also the custom follows, and though he tries to keep it from me a secret, I can hardly wait to see it."

"How did you know that, Geitzling?" demanded the duke.

"Because in the nose I can smell it when I come in. It the lower hall pervades, and makes me feel as if I am already home."

"I hope," said His Grace, "you will think of this as your home while you are here."

Geitzling said, "His Grace has been so kind as to invite Herr Untermeyer, and Frau Geitzling and myself, to Christmas Eve keep with him here. It was Lady Caroline's idea."

I gave an involuntary glance at Othmar Untermeyer and saw on his face a young man's pride in his attractiveness.

Holmes took a last sip of his brandy and soda, rose, and announced that we must be off on further business.

Geitzling was crestfallen; His Grace, seeing how upset his counterpart was, had a suggestion. "Mr. Holmes, Doctor, if you've no previous plans, why don't you keep Christmas Eve with us as well? Then you can regale us all even with your adventures. It will be just a small gathering, but I fancy we'll generate some holiday cheer."

"We shall be delighted," said Holmes. "No idea could suit me better." He was, it seemed, giving free rein to his sentimental side.

The butler was summoned to show us out, but Holmes told him we had permission to roam the house and talk to those around. The butler conceded that His Grace had given him some such instructions, and left us to our own devices.

"Holmes, have we nothing to ask the butler?"

The Adventure of the Christmas Tree

"Nothing. Come. Let me first retrieve my parcel in the hallway."

This done, we came to the locked door behind which stood the tree. I could now perceive that Geitzling had been right; there was a strong smell of pine even here, on the other side of a thick oak door. I remarked on this to Holmes.

"Yes, Watson, like the railway, you are frequently late, but you get there. Now, if you will just stand guard …"

From his pocket, he drew a skeleton key and put it in the lock.

"Holmes!" said I. "You're not —"

"His Grace gave us carte blanche, remember?"

"Yes, but —"

I was talking to the oak panels of the door. Holmes was already inside. The pine scent that had been drawn out of the room with the opening of the door was nearly overpowering. Carefully, I put my ear to the door in an effort to perhaps hear what my friend was up to.

What I did hear was a soft, feminine voice saying, "Dr. Watson?"

I turned to see a lovely young lady of about one–and–twenty. She had a large quantity of blonde curls, and large brown eyes that dominated her rather pleasant face.

"Forgive my forwardness. Father told me you were here. I am Caroline Bentley." She gave me her hand.

"Lady Caroline," I said with a slight bow.

"Are you feeling well, Doctor?"

"I'm quite all right, thank you."

"Forgive me. I only ask because you were leaning against the door, I thought you might feel faint."

"No, Lady Caroline," said I. "Not at all. I was, um, investigating the source of the pine odor that Herr Geitzling was so enthusiastic about."

She laughed like tinkling bells. "Then, Doctor, you have sniffed out the truth, for in that room is the great tree sent down to us from Scotland. I can hardly wait to see it."

"Haven't you?"

"None of us has. It's part of the fun of the holiday — we trust the judgment of our forester implicitly. Othmar — that is, Herr Untermeyer — thinks it a charming custom."

"As do I, Lady Caroline," I said. I spoke, I suppose, louder than need be, for I wanted to make sure that Holmes heard us through the heavy door, and did not create an embarrassing situation by emerging while Lady Caroline was there.

"Father tells me you and Mr. Holmes will be keeping Christmas with us. I am so pleased."

"You and your father are very kind," I said.

"Not at all. We enjoy spreading the spirit of the season."

"Where is Mr. Holmes?" she asked.

"I can hardly say," I told her truthfully. "He stepped away for a few moments, and asked me to remain here."

Lady Caroline said that as much as she'd like to, she could not remain, and that she looked forward to seeing us again tomorrow evening. I watched her safely down the corridor, then knocked on the door to let Holmes know he might emerge if he chose.

He did so in a few moments, bringing with him another strong breath of pine.

"Excellent, Watson," said he. "You are by little and little overcoming your inherent honesty and developing a positive skill for indirection."

I sniffed. "I hardly know if I should thank you for *that*. Were your efforts successful?"

"Eminently. I have changed the nature of the trap; it remains for tomorrow evening to see who shall fall into it."

After a brief visit with our clients, to tell them the situation was well in hand, we returned to Baker Street.

That evening, Holmes as usual was maddeningly unwilling to discuss the case at hand. Only once did my opportuning avail anything. "I'm sorry, Watson, but you know how I dislike to explicate a case before it is completed. I shall only say that you should have sniffed out the solution for yourself."

"Confound it, Holmes. Are you or are you not drawing my attention to the strong pine odor that suffused the lower part of the house?"

"I am, indeed, Watson."

"What can one infer simply from an odor? I am not, after all, a bloodhound."

Holmes pulled his lower lip. "More to the point, you are a city-bred man. My people, as you know, were country squires. I know how a tree is supposed to smell."

I felt some of the old excitement; perhaps we were getting to the meat of the nut at last. "What was wrong with the smell, Holmes?" I asked.

"Nothing, Watson. Absolutely nothing. That was an especially intense whiff of the unmistakable fragrance of Scotch pine."

Before I was done sputtering, Holmes had picked up his violin. "I feel the spirit of the season upon me," said he, and he began playing "God Rest Ye, Merry Gentlemen."

There was but one more allusion to the case before we left Baker Street for His Grace's residence. Just prior to leaving, Holmes said, "It would be as well, Watson, to slip your revolver in your pocket."

"Holmes!" I cried. "On Christmas Eve?"

"Evil takes no holidays, Watson. Therefore, neither can those who would stop it."

We were greeted heartily by His Grace and Lady Caroline upon our arrival. The hall was now open, the tree revealed in all its green magnificence, the Yule log roaring in the fireplace. Holly was hung liberally about, and the tree had already been garlanded and hung with some ornaments. The duke invited us to join in the work of decoration, which, to my surprise, Holmes did.

"It is good, Mr. Holmes, we haff you to help the ornaments hanging, you are tall like Othmar, and can reach up high." Herr Geitzling was in high holiday spirits, frequently remarking that this was just like home, and constant in his attentions to Frau Geitzling, a woman as red and plump as her husband.

"I will get the candles," said Othmar Untermeyer. I had wondered how the candles were fixed to the tree so they wouldn't fall over, and, watching Untermeyer, I learned. He lit one candle and carefully softened the bottoms of the others letting the wax conform to the irregularities in the bark as he put them on. With his reach (he was, in fact, even taller than Holmes) he had little trouble placing the candles at the top of the tree, and he worked his way down, blowing out the softening candle and putting it on a lower branch.

"Lovely," exclaimed the duke. "Just lovely. We will light the candles after a holiday toast."

A servant came in with a tray of hot toddies. These were passed around, and the scent of the warm, buttered rum brought back holiday memories for me. I could see on the faces of the others that I was not alone.

His Grace raised his cup. "To friendship and happiness. To family and memories. To Her Majesty and the kaiser and all their subjects. To Christmas."

"To Christmas," we echoed, and drank.

Just then, the butler entered. He spoke a word to His Grace, then went to Untermeyer, with whom I was discussing the aseptic theories of Dr. Lister of Vienna. The butler told him there was a German person outside who needed to see him; some sort of emergency. Untermeyer in his turn made his excuses to the duke, and followed the butler.

As soon as they were gone, Holmes materialized at my side. "This is it, Watson. He will return in a moment and say he has to leave the party. Mark what he says, and leave a minute after he does. You have your revolver?"

"At the ready."

"Good man."

With that, Holmes himself slipped out of the room. Typically, he did it unnoticed by all save myself. And true to Holmes's prediction, Untermeyer was back in seconds, making apologies to the duke, then to the party at large. "A family emergency," he said. "I must go."

"Othmar, can I of service be?" asked Mr. Geitzling.

"No, sir, no. I wouldn't dream of spoiling your Christmas. I insist you stay."

He left. Now I was supposed to go. Not being surreptitious, like Holmes, not having a ready–made excuse like Untermeyer, I simply told Lady Caroline that I had to leave the room and would be back in a few moments. She was already missing Untermeyer, and barely heard me.

The Adventure of the Christmas Tree

I headed for the front door and down the steps. Holmes was waiting, not quite invisible in the shrubbery.

"This way, Watson," he whispered. Following his finger with my gaze, I could see that two men were about halfway down the block. "Quickly now," he said.

"Do you recognize them?" he said as we closed the distance between us.

"The tall one is Untermeyer," I ventured.

"Indeed, and the other is Von Tepper, a notorious anarchist. Mycroft has suspected he has been secretly in London. He will be pleased to know we have captured him."

"We haven't done it yet, Holmes."

"Confidence, Watson, confidence."

We had now drawn quietly to within ten yards of our prey. Holmes drew his revolver; I followed his lead.

"Untermeyer! Von Tepper!" he barked. The men turned. "Your plot has failed," he went on. "There will be no explosion. The duke and Geitzling will not die. You will start no war between England and Germany. At least not *this* Christmas."

"You are wrong, Mr. Holmes," Untermeyer said. He sneered around a small black cigar. "Even now, His Grace is lighting the candles. When he gets to the last one I placed on the tree, he is doomed. They are all doomed. I am sorry about poor, foolish Lady Caroline. And I am sorry you will not be there to die with them."

"Sorry to disappoint you, *mein Herr*," said Holmes, reaching under his cape, "but I pulled the teeth of your little monster yesterday." He held up a parcel. "Quite an interesting device, the latest in high explosives."

"Herr von Tepper was responsible for procuring it. Well, you have spoiled our little plan. There will be other occasions."

"Not for you," said I.

"It does not matter. Others will rise until government and privilege have been done away with forever!"

"Indeed," said Holmes. "Your movement will need conspirators more intelligent than yourselves. Why did you select the very tree that Camber had marked for cutting?"

"Our allies in Scotland did that. It was done so that the tree would be acceptable to the duke when it arrived. We didn't know that the fool of a forester would come here to identify the thing." He took a puff of a cigar. "Or that he would consult you. He *did* consult you, did he not?"

Holmes gave a slight bow. "So you got hold of the tree, bored a hole through the back of the trunk and into a thick lower limb, packed that with explosive, and placed a sharp end of fuse through the remaining shell of wood for a candle to be placed on, a candle you would shorten by using it to soften the bottom of all the other candles. Did you think I wouldn't notice that the last candle stayed erect *without* having its bottom softened? I wasn't even forced to wait to see who made an excuse to leave the party early; I already knew you for the conspirator."

"How did you come to suspect the bomb?" Untermeyer had no air of a villain thwarted. He seemed honestly to wish to know where his errors had been.

"The tree was already suspect, thanks to Mr. Camber. The pine scent told me the rest. When you cut into a resinous wood like pine, you increase the intensity of the fragrance manyfold. I suspected something implanted in the tree even before I reached the duke's house. A breath of air within it, and the matter was settled. I had stopped at an ironmonger's shop and provided myself with an auger. A few seconds' work was enough to disarm your little toy. Here," Holmes said.

Then, to my astonishment, he tossed the parcel to Untermeyer.

The German mouth widened in a grin that was almost hideous. "Thank you, Mr. Holmes. I believe I know what you have in mind, and I shall avail myself of it." He puffed deeply on his cigar, causing the end to glow bright red. "However," said he, "I fear you underestimate the power of this new substance."

He took the cigar from his mouth.

Von Tepper screamed the only word I ever heard from him: *"Nein!"*

The Adventure of the Christmas Tree

Holmes brought me to the pavement with a rugby tackle just as Untermeyer said, "See you in hell, Mr. Holmes," and touched the coal of his cigar to the parcel.

The blast felt like the kick of a spirited horse, and made my ears ring for a moment, but I was otherwise unharmed. Of Untermeyer and Von Tepper, nothing remained but a stain on the pavement.

"He *was* a fool," said Holmes. "Had he not the wit to imagine I would adjust the amount of explosive in the parcel?" He shook his head, and helped me to my feet.

"Come, Watson. We must go and spoil everyone's Christmas with the sad news that Herr Untermeyer and his friend have been assassinated by anarchists."

On Christmas Day in our Baker Street rooms, with Mrs. Hudson's wonderful goose inside us, Holmes puffing on the new pipe I had given him and I placing early engagements for next year into the leather physician's pocket diary he had given me, Holmes finally deigned to discuss the events of the previous night.

"It takes but little imagination to see, Watson," said he, "that arresting Untermeyer and putting him on trial would be little better than letting his assassination plot succeed in the first place."

"In what way, pray?"

"The man wouldn't admit to being an anarchist; he was an employee of the German government. He would say he was following orders."

"But the Germans would deny it!" I protested.

"Which they would in any case. And our government no doubt, would believe them. But the suspicion would remain, poisoning relationships, and adding to the already dangerous international tension. Mark my words, Watson, if war comes, it will be caused by just such a trivial incident as the assassination of a duke."

"Hardly trivial to the duke," I ventured.

"Quite so, Watson."

"And so you offered yourself, and me, though I hesitate to mention it, as bait to make it worthwhile for Untermeyer to kill himself."

"If you wish to put it that way."

"Strictly for patriotic reasons."

"Indeed. Mycroft is beside himself with the joy of it, I'll wager. My Christmas gift to him."

"You had no thought of Lady Caroline? She was well on her way to falling in love with that evil young man. You let her remember him as a martyr, rather than as a scoundrel who used her trust in an effort to kill her father and her."

"Well, Watson," he said in mock surprise. "So I did." Then, more somberly, he said, "I am sorry I could not prevent Christmas from becoming a time of sad memories for her. But we cannot be expected to pass miracles, eh, Watson?"

"Not that kind," said I. "Happy Christmas, Holmes."

"And the same to you, my dear Watson."

Prince Charming

She opened her eyes to semidarkness, cuffed by one wrist to a pipe by the wall opposite the stairs. She could slide the other cuff up the pipe and stand up if she wanted to, or needed to use the bucket they'd provided for her. She had about six or seven feet of radial reach out from the pipe. Not much, but enough to keep from going totally insane in the week and a half or so she'd been in captivity.

She hoped. In this kind of situation, how could you really tell the state of your mind?

She never saw her captors. They never tortured her or anything. They changed her bucket and her food tray while she slept, a sleep so sound that she was sure on occasion they drugged the food. She had a kid's sleeping bag, occasional clean clothes, and as many towelettes as she needed to keep her body decently clean.

Nobody ever spoke to her.

In a way, that might have been the absolute worst of it. Rachel Hanver had a decent measure of both intelligence and imagination, and her father, Leo Hanver, could have been a lot less rich and powerful than he was and still have the Society press feel justified in saying that Rachel was "stunning" or "beautiful."

Rachel had grown more sophisticated than that in her nineteen years. In the real world, she would have been classed "Okay–pretty." Expert makeup and hairwork. Perhaps a little surgery for the fleshy bumps on the nose or jawline.

Rachel also realized she was rich enough not to have to worry about any surgery, and she was definitely not interested in any surgery.

She was, however, interested in being rich. So many of the girls from school never even seemed to give it a thought. Maybe it was because Leo Hanver had made the money during Rachel's own lifetime, and she had seen it grow, seen the kind of difference it made in her life, and in the last few (restful, at last) years of her mothers life.

So she thought about it, and she had come to realize that yes, there was a downside to it.

Leo Hanver had seen fit to refer to his daughter frequently as "my princess" — he was persistent rather than original — and that word undoubtedly helped her make the fairy tale connection. The beautiful, rich princess could frequently wind up as the focus of a diabolical plot of some wicked warlock or modern–day equivalent, someone against whom she could focus her own hatred and defiance. A person to match wits against. Something to fight, even if only emotionally, until she was rescued. Here, she saw and spoke to no one. There was nothing to focus on.

Of course, the person she was angry with right now was herself. There was no reason for her to be in this "dungeon," just as there had been no reason for her to have gone to the party they'd kidnapped her from.

She couldn't now even remember what had decided her to go along instead of staying home and reading a book. You can toss a book aside if it doesn't please you. If you went to one of Jennifer Clarke's impromptu parties, even knowing in advance that Jen was one was of the most boring people who had ever lived, and kept a coterie of similar personalities around for constant comparison, it wasn't that easy.

She sincerely hoped she hadn't gone because Daddy had nagged her about spending time with "more people of her own age." People of her own age seemed to be stodgier than practically anybody she knew, and besides, her father had promised to let the subject drop a long time ago.

In any case, all she remembered was that she had wanted to think and she wanted a cigarette. She didn't want anyone to tell her it would be bad for her health. She didn't want to be commended as a champion of libertarian rights. She just wanted to get away from the hive–society mind and enjoy what she considered a minor vice, to think for a couple of minutes, then decide how soon she could make her excuses and get the hell out of there.

She walked over the small rise among the oak saplings, a nice walk on a warm spring night.

It also provided a lot of cover for whatever person or group was waiting in ambush for her with the pungent-smelling rag that was clapped over her nose and mouth without Rachel's ever having had a chance to see a thing. She didn't remember being dragged to a car. She didn't even remember losing her feet.

She just remembered waking up with a headache who-knows-how-long-ago, chained to the same pipe she was chained to now.

And then came the crashing.

After her week of comparative silence, the sound came like an exploding bomb. All it was really was the prying open of the bolt outside the cellar door at the top of the stairs.

Suddenly, Rachel was speechless; she couldn't have made a sound if her life depended on it. She had room in her brain only to watch that doorway and to see what came through it.

It was a young man in jeans and a short-sleeved shirt. In one hand he had a crowbar; in the other, a remarkable bunch of keys, what looked to Rachel's inexpert eye like handcuff keys.

It was darker now than when she'd first woken, but there was enough dim light coming through the high window for her to form the impression that he was handsome.

He stopped on a platform and scouted the basement. "Rachel?" he said.

She tried to talk, but managed only to make a weak grunt. Still, that was enough for him to find her. He ran to the bottom of the cellar stairs, and across the concrete floor toward her.

"It's good," he said, "you're being quiet like this —"

He rolled her over to try to shine the small plastic flashlight he'd put in his mouth on the handcuffs, when the week of fear, of silence, of doubt broke inside Rachel, and she started to scream. She didn't want to; she just couldn't help it.

"Look," the young man said, "this isn't a good idea. They're not back yet, but they're never gone long, and if they hear us —"

Rachel screamed again.

"Oh, to hell with it," he said. A little awkwardly, he took the flashlight into the hand that held the crowbar.

Then he leaned forward and kissed her, firm but not rough. She stopped screaming.

When he finished, Rachel looked at him. He *was* handsome. She moved toward him, and they kissed again. It was reassuring. Rachel let him get the handcuffs off. It didn't take long at all. He helped her up the stairs, helping her weakened legs fight gravity. The house, she could see now, was one of those cottages they'd managed to fit in on the north shore before people like her father had decided that any real estate lapped by any clean bit of ocean had to be worth incredible amounts of money. She could hear the gentle waves not too far off.

Little by little he hurried her faster through the small house.

"There're three or four of them," the young man said. "I've already scared myself to death doing this much, so I'd really like to have you safely back to your father before I have to fight them or anything."

She was too breathless to speak at the moment. As soon as he strapped her in the passenger seat of the dusty little Nissan wagon, and ensconced himself safely into the driver's side, she said, "Don't be ridiculous." She looked at him. He really was handsome, small but strong, regular features under curly brown hair, and bright, tender eyes.

"You're a hero," she said.

PART TWO

"Your father's out at the country place," he told her. "I guess he wanted to be closer to the action."

"You guess? Don't you know?"

"Huh? Why would I know?"

"Didn't my father hire you? Aren't you a private eye or something?"

He laughed. There was a trace of bitterness in it that didn't suit him.

"I've been accused of that all week, of trying to profit in some way from your disappearance. I'm not. I'm just ... not, that's all.

"Okay, now I'm sure they've got a doctor inside for you, but believe me, when he's done they're going to have a lot of questions for you."

"I'll tell them whatever I know," she said.

"That's exactly the way to do it," he told her.

Rachel pointed up a private drive. "There it is," she said.

"I know," he said. "Look, things are going to get confusing around —"

She cut him off. "*Get* confusing! I don't —"

Now she was cut off as the car suddenly stopped just inside the first row of hedges. A group of security men, some uniformed, some not, all of them armed, ran out to meet the car.

"What's going *on*?" Rachel demanded. She was beginning to think she was less terrified back in the dungeon.

"Just routine," her rescuer said. "You'll even appreciate it once you understand why they're doing it."

"But I—"

The young man was already opening the car and stepping out very slowly with his hands up.

"Me again!" he called to the guards.

"It's the pest," said a gruff voice from among the guards.

"Better check and see who I've got with me this time," the young man suggested.

Rachel reached over and took a tight grasp on his wrist. "I don't even know your name!"

That brought a chuckle from Prince Charming.

"Richard," he said, "Richard Keating. Don't worry about it, you've never heard of me, either."

"I will," she promised.

"I'd like that," he said.

They brought Keating to a sitting room, a room he'd been in before, if only long enough to be threatened with the police and then thrown out of. This had led to a longer session down at the local station, which lasted until they'd convinced themselves that he was just a social–climbing crank who wanted to get his name in the papers.

It ended with a warning not to bother them anymore.

He suspected that what he had done tonight, delivering the victim alive and well (so far as a cursory examination would show) to her father's doorstep, would not be considered a bother.

The evidence of the sitting room seemed to bear him out on this. For one thing, they invited him actually to sit, in a very nice chair, at that. Jenkins, the houseman, who had shown the ability to make the syllables "Richard Keating" sound completely interchangeable with those in the phrase "pariah dog," had offered him a drink. Keating had just taken orange juice, but he was sitting in the chair.

They had even left him alone.

Keating was sure he was under surveillance, so he was very careful simply to sip his juice and enjoy his chair until Leo Hanver came back.

Keating rose to take the old man's hand, which enveloped his, and gave a squeeze of real appreciation.

"I owe you an apology, Mr. Keating," he said.

Actually, by Keating's rendering, it was more like six or seven apologies, but he let it go.

"You were distraught, sir," he said. "I can't imagine anything worse than having a child disappear."

Hanver took a seat of his own and called for Jenkins, who brought him something light brown on ice. Hanver took a sip, then let out a breath he seemed to have been holding for a long time. He leaned back with his eyes closed and nodded.

"Of course," Keating went on, "I had one great advantage."

"What was that?"

"I was the one person who was absolutely certain that Rachel had, in fact, been kidnapped."

Hanver began to get huffy. "I never for a second doubted that my daughter had been kidnapped!"

"I'm sure you didn't, sir. But you must have gotten an ear of Patty Hearst from the local police and from the FBI."

"The FBI," Hanver grumbled, and Keating expected there'd be some intense questioning for potential congressmen in this district from at least one powerful citizen before the next election.

"It had to have been a distraction. Sergeant Meggessy hit me pretty hard with it, did a pretty good job of implying I was in on it with Rachel somehow, even though I had never laid eyes on her before Jennifer's ridiculous party the night of the kidnapping."

"Yes," Hanver said. "Yes, you must tell me everything that happened."

Keating spoke quietly.

"I tried to, sir."

Hanver grimaced. "I know, I know — I should have listened to you at the time. I'm ready now, if you're ready to tell me."

Keating grinned apologetically and began to tell his story.

He'd only been at Jennifer's party in the first place because he was a part of the huge family to which they both belonged — very distant cousins, something like that.

Keating's role was something between hereditary black sheep (he was the third generation of his branch who had been tragically denied the gift for making money) and stray dog (he was insufficiently guilty about this).

The idea had been to ship him off to this part of the country for a while and see "if he would fit anywhere into Jen's circle."

He'd been there about two weeks before the party, and he'd already known he'd never fit into that circle.

"They're perfectly fine young people," Hanver insisted.

"I know they are, sir," Keating said. "But none of them has made or found his or her own place. The way you have, for instance. And I'm having a hell of a time finding mine. Maybe I don't have one."

Hanver leaned forward and ticked points off on his fingers.

"Nonsense, boy. What are you? Twenty–two years old? Considering what you did tonight … and we didn't make it any easier for you either. That kind of determination and guts is bound to make a place for itself. And for a total stranger, too."

"Well," Keating said, leaning back in his chair, "that's part of it. I didn't *feel* like a total stranger to Rachel, I felt like I knew her quite well."

Keating explained how standing near the bar, he'd been startled to hear someone else order straight orange juice. Usually at a gathering like this, the young folks made a game of drinking the stiffest (or in the case of the girls) most bizarre concoctions they could cajole the bartender into making.

He looked up to study his fellow juice-drinker and found himself looking into Rachel's eyes.

"It was the strangest experience," Keating said. "There was nothing you could call a physical resemblance, but it was like looking into my own eyes. Eyes that were looking for the same things, but finding them devilishly hard to find. Eyes that were much older than they ought to have been, and a lot less happy."

"I don't like," Hanver said, "the implication that my daughter is living a miserable life."

Keating shrugged. "You've asked me to explain what I did and why I did it. Well, part of the reason is that I felt — and still feel — as if your daughter and I are kindred spirits. She'd really be the one to talk to about this. I could be wrong."

Hanver rubbed his chin. "You're twenty-two?"

"Just."

"And Rachel's nineteen, almost twenty. Maybe you are kindred spirits. Go on. Want more juice?"

Keating said yes; refills were sent for.

"Anyway," Keating said when Jenkins was gone, "I decided I had to make an opportunity to talk to her, just to see if I was right. But I never managed to do it. Jen would ask me for a drink, or someone would want to know if I had played hockey for Dartmouth, and so on, and then when I got a moment I could never manage to find her."

Then Keating had seen her heading out a side door. This, he thought, was a great opportunity to catch up with her, and in the best circumstances to have an actual conversation as well, so he took off after her.

He didn't call out her name. They hadn't met, after all, and he didn't want to frighten her away. He got a little nervous when she passed in and out of the shrubbery — she seemed to know every twist and turn; he'd lived there for a couple of weeks but he hadn't made a point of exploring the place.

Anyway, he had a clear view of her when the man popped out from behind his own bush, grasped her around the neck, and clapped a rag over her face.

Rachel had a big head start on him. He knew there was no use in yelling; he saved his breath to run, and wound up chasing the man down the slope without, he was sure, the kidnappers' being even slightly aware of it.

Keating saw two other men hop out of a white panel truck (no writing on it that he could see) and stuff Rachel inside. They clambered in themselves, then drove off.

Keating, puffing by now, had run to the place where the truck had been parked. He tried to get the license-plate number, but distance and dim light kept it from him.

There was nothing to do now but to go back to the house and get some action started.

PART THREE

"They all thought you were crazy," Hanver said.

Keating shook his head with just a trace of bitterness. "They sure acted as if they thought I was crazy. I remember Jennifer pretending to be offended. 'I never thought I'd throw a party so dull that people would want to get themselves kidnapped away from it.'"

The rest of the guests seemed to think that was remarkably amusing, and they achieved even more hilarity when Keating insisted he'd seen a real kidnapping.

"Come off it, Richard," they'd say.

"What's this, your initiation?"

Keating, genuinely bewildered, demanded to know what they were talking about.

He learned that there were two primary theories. One: that Rachel was playing a joke on all of them, and two: that Rachel had somehow prevailed upon him to help with the hoax.

"Don't be ridiculous!" Keating said. "I never laid eyes on her before tonight. We've never said a word to each other."

A voice came around the rim of a Scotch glass. "So *you* say."

For a split second, Keating flirted with the notion of punching the glass down past the speaker's teeth, but he managed to control himself.

"So I say," he said grimly, "and so I'm going to tell the cops. Where's a phone?"

"The cops? Ha! Good luck."

Then they tried to keep him away from the phone. Finally, Keating had said to hell with it; he'd drive to the police station himself.

Jennifer looked up and surprised him. "That's probably the best idea. If you insist on going ahead with this."

"I insist, all right."

"Then the cops will probably need you there for descriptions and stuff."

She got to her feet. "All right, I'll drive you."

The Scotch drinker said, "Jen, you can't be serious."

"Oh, you people will think of something to do to keep the party going until I get back."

Another thirty seconds of verbal scuffling and they were out there on the road in Jen's Mercedes. When Keating tried to thank her, she said, "Don't. The cops will probably think you're just as crazy as I do. They've got a Sergeant Meggessy down there who thinks we're a bunch of spoiled nuisances. You might even be asking for a whole lot of trouble."

Leo Hanver snorted. "Think of something to keep the party going," he murmured. "I take it back, about their being fine young people. The little bastards were *arranging* for you to have trouble."

Keating frowned. "You mean they called Meggessy and told him some kind of drunken crank was on the way to tell them a wild story?"

"I wouldn't be at all surprised; you can bet I'm going to find out."

"But why would they do that? Rachel's friends?"

Hanver sighed.

"Because I've been selling my daughter's observations short all her life — haven't wanted to believe it, you know? It's like having worked myself and my family into this particular social status, I wanted everything to be perfect about it.

"But I wasn't fair to Rachel. There's more to her than to these other kids, a need to know things more deeply, and to get things done. I'd say like me, if it wouldn't sound so egotistical."

He leaned back with a rueful sigh. "I don't feel as if I have a lot to be egotistical about tonight, that's for sure.

"Anyway, Rachel says sometimes — 'Beware the mutant.' I'm not entirely sure what that means, but I think a big part of it is that everybody senses Rachel's being different somehow, and they all resent it. Rachel herself most of all, I think."

Keating sifted through his own list of rueful memories and could come up with only agreement.

"So I apologize, Keating."

"For what?"

"For my part in your difficulties. Rachel's so-called friends poisoned the police's minds; I allowed them to poison mine. I was so worried about her — and, since it seems to be the night for admitting things, so afraid she *might* have run away from me, I was not a thinking man.

"*You*, however, seem to have been thinking all week. What have you been doing while the rest of us have been sucking our thumbs?"

Keating shrugged. "I did whatever I could think of. I went to the library, through the old newspapers, finding out everything I could about Rachel. Why she should be picked for kidnapping, that sort of thing.

"The key thing I found out was that she couldn't have been. Picked for kidnapping, I mean. Just couldn't. Unless she'd been in on it herself, which I totally rejected from what I'd learned of her character." And, he admitted to himself, what he wanted to believe. "This led me to think there was no personal element in this."

The kidnappers, Keating told the old man, had found out that a bunch of rich kids were having a party at Jen's house. Surely nothing too hard to find out, what with catering and liquor orders and the like.

All they'd done is drive their white van on the grounds, then post a lookout to see if one of them came outside for a minute. Then they could snatch him — or her — confident in the knowledge that anyone they did grab would have healthy ransom potential.

It was like kids setting themselves up besides the outfield bleachers at the ballpark, hoping someone hits a home run out. A lot less wholesome, though.

"The next thing to do was to wait and see if you *got* a ransom demand. The cops seemed to have the town pretty well sewn up, but I figured *that* ought to make it to the newspaper."

"It's pretty well sewn up," Hanver agreed. "There were a couple of messages — stand by for ransom instructions, no interference from me personally. The cops and FBI to lie low. None of that got out."

"No, I've been following the paper."

"But a ransom demand came in today. Just the amount, no pickup instructions."

"How much?" Keating asked.

"A hundred thousand dollars."

"Mmmm," Keating said. "If anything absolutely clears Rachel — I mean, if she needed anything further — that does it."

"How?" Hanver demanded. "Where do you get all this expertise?"

"It's not expertise, it's just a lifetime of reading and a lot of concentration and …" and, Keating couldn't force himself to say, the start of the quenching of a lifelong thirst for adventure.

"Anyway, the amount of money is wrong if Rachel is the one who is asking for it. For someone like her to do something so to tally out of character (we agree on that, don't we?), she'd have to ask for at least five times as much to justify it to herself.

"On the other hand, a hundred thousand is the perfect amount for *potluck kidnappers to ask for. You could pay it relatively painlessly,* and after a week of anxiety — that's probably why they made you wait so long — it would seem a cheaper price with every day that went by. It also makes a convenient split for three or four men."

Keating shrugged. "The main thing I tried to do during the wait for the ransom demand was to learn things and to remember things." He had tried motor vehicles, but when all you can say is "medium-sized white van" you don't stand a chance of learning much. He visited the caterer and the liquor store, even applied for jobs, just to see if he could get hold of delivery records and learn something that way.

He did learn that the liquor store had a medium-sized van in pale, pale green that could well look white under a sodium vapor lamp.

That just depressed him.

One cheering note, though, was that even with the reaming out and dressing down Sergeant Meggessy had given him the night of the kidnapping, the cops seemed to pay no attention to him at all. He even got so brazen as to wander into headquarters and ask to look at mug shots, on the theory that he might see *something*.

Well, okay, that hadn't gotten him very far, except for a minor tongue-lashing from Meggessy to the effect that some people don't know when they're well off.

Keating had shrugged and left. It had been the longest of long shots, anyway.

Perhaps not quite.

"Because the other day," he told Rachel's father, "something occurred to me."

"You remembered something?"

"Let's say I *noticed* something. So I made a couple of unwarranted assumptions, linked them together, checked them out, and found out they worked. They led me to the little house on the shore and gave me a timetable for getting her out of there."

"Then you know who did this." Hanver said.

"I know who I followed," Keating said.

"Well?" the old man demanded.

Keating was silent.

"Don't get coy on me now."

"I've got to talk to Rachel about this."

"Why?"

"She was the one who was kidnapped. This is still about Rachel. I have to talk to her before I can talk to anyone else."

The old man chortled.

"I don't think you'll need to talk as long as you might have thought."

"Why's that?"

"Because if I know my daughter, she's found her way to the nearest intercom, and she's been listening to practically everything we say."

Keating smiled. "Now that you mention it, I'd be surprised if she weren't."

Rachel apparently knew a cue when she heard one. She scampered into the room, shot her father an exasperated look, took a few more quick steps toward Keating, and ...

And stood there, suddenly shy.

Leo Hanver got to his feet.

"All right, all right," he said. "Take my seat, Rachel. I'll go check with the doctor to see exactly how you are."

"I'm a little wobbly, but I'll be all right."

She was more than a little wobbly. She plunked into her father's chair with real gratitude.

"I'll still go check with the doctor," the old man said. "And I'll stay away from intercoms. But don't try to keep me in the dark too long on this."

"Of course not, Daddy. You're a dear."

"I'm something," her father conceded. "Keating, I owe you more than I can say."

With that, he left.

There was a long, awkward silence, the stuff of absolute cliché. They'd both start talking at once, or they'd insist the other go first until nobody went at all.

Finally (for the first of many times) Rachel settled it.

"Well," she said, "according to you, you've been wanting to talk to me for a week and a half. Start talking."

PART FOUR

Four days and a couple of good nights' sleep later, Keating and Rachel were driving toward town in a car somewhat bigger, cleaner, and more impressive than Keating's Nissan.

"I love you, Richard," Rachel said. Obviously the days had been filled with some intensive talking as well.

"You know how I feel," Keating told her. "At first sight. I never believed in it."

"I do. I always have. I saw you drinking orange juice, too, you know."

He smiled.

"So why do you seem worried?" Rachel demanded. "Everything is under control. We're in love, my dad is crazy about you, and you and I are about to find that place in the world we've always been looking for."

Keating smiled disbelievingly and shook his head. "Private eyes, for God's sake."

"Not private eyes, if you please. We will head up the Leo Hanver Foundation, and we will help crime victims and their families of whatever social or economic level as soon and as suitably as we can. The amount of personal involvement is up to us."

"Sounds ideal," Keating admitted. "The only thing is, we haven't wrapped up our first case yet, remember?"

"Oh, but that can be wrapped up any number of ways," Rachel said. "I insisted we do it this way for the personal satisfaction."

"You insisted?"

She looked at him. There was no banter in her eyes now, or fear. Just pure, righteous anger.

"I was chained to a pipe for a week and a half, and I'll never forget it. So let's finally go explain to Sergeant Meggessy how you found me, and get some arrests made."

The sun was bright on Main Street, and it seemed to follow them through the front door and past the venetian-blinded doors of police headquarters. They reminded the receptionist they had an appointment with Sergeant Meggessy, and were shown right in.

Meggessy's smile was something more than embarrassed as he rose to shake hands. At that, Keating thought, it was an improvement. The only other smiles he'd ever seen on that face were cold and mean.

He gestured them to seats. "Well, Keating, I guess I owe you an apology, to say the least."

"Forget me," Keating said. "What about Miss Hanver? She's the one with the bruised wrists."

"Of course, of course. I'm so sorry. We — I — took the wrong attitude. Police work isn't an exact science — well, Keating, you must realize that. Without luck, you could never have found Miss Hanver with a needle-in-a-haystack search the way you did."

Keating smiled.

"I won't deny I had luck," he said. "But it wasn't exactly that kind of search. I was following up a notion I had, and it paid off."

"Oh? What kind of notion?"

"That's what I've come here to tell you. You see, when I first came here with the news that Miss Hanver had been kidnapped, you were full of dire threats about what would happen to me if I 'kept sticking my nose in police business.'

"Now, I went ahead and did, anyway. I didn't even bother much to keep a low profile after the first day or so.

"Nothing happened. No boom got lowered. No additional warnings listed. I was left to go my way."

Keating leaned forward in his chair. "In fact, I didn't hear from you again until I put myself right in your face, asking to see mug shots. Even then it was hardly the wrath I'd been promised."

"What the hell, kid, I could see you were having a tough time with this …"

"So you *were* keeping track of me. And you knew I was working my tail off trying to get something like proof. But that wasn't enough to get you to listen to me, or to throw me out of town.

"You could have done either one of those two things, except for the fact that they *might* have gotten somebody to pay attention to me.

"So it seemed to be enough for you simply to know I wasn't making any progress — and to keep bad-mouthing me to Mr. Hanver and the local media.

"I began to ask myself questions about that."

Meggessy wasn't trying to look tough anymore, or friendly, or any particular way, and now, for the first time, he seemed frightening. "Go on," he said.

"At first, I started with useless questions like Who'd know better how to stage a crime than a cop? Or, Do they pay cops enough in this town that a quick, tax-free twenty-five or thirty grand in cash wouldn't be a help?"

Keating got to his feet and walked around behind his chair. "Then I asked myself something intelligent, like Did Meggessy have access to the right kind of van? You did.

"One night I followed you — you weren't in the van — and saw you bring some things out to the house near the shore. I knew you didn't live there. I staked out the place at random intervals and saw you go back a few times. So the other night, I made some preparations and went and got her."

Now Meggessy leaned back in his chair and laced his fingers behind his head.

"Yep," he said. "You've got her. But you don't have much else. It'd be your word against mine, and no one ever even sent any ransom instructions. So why don't you just call yourself a winner, and get on home and enjoy the rest of your life?"

"Yes, sir," Keating said. "As soon as we get the pro private eye in here to talk to Rachel's friends. So-called friends."

"Her friends?"

"Sure. The ones at the party. One of them had to be a lookout for you, to tell you if something'd gone wrong, if you'd been spotted. How long do you think it will take to break one of those wimps and get him or her to talk?"

Meggessy sighed. "I knew it." He drew his gun. "You're too smart for your own good, Keating. Come on, I've got a bag packed. We'll take your car. You're coming, too, Miss Hanver."

"No, we're not, Sergeant," Rachel said firmly.

Just then, the first-floor window behind him shattered. Rachel and Keating hit the floor as dark-uniformed state troopers climbed through the glass.

"Didn't you think, Sergeant," Rachel said, "that when we made the appointment to see you, my daddy helped us make the appointment for you to see the State Police, too?"

Keating went to her and kissed her as the troopers led Meggessy away.

EPILOGUE

Autumn leaves burned red and gold in the trellis as Richard Keating and Rachel Hanver were declared husband and wife. They couldn't have looked happier.

Nearby, Leo Hanver (who had personally chosen the guest list, making sure to leave the right names out) was talking to a business associate named Breen.

"Beautiful day, Leo," Breen said. "Beautiful day. Beautiful bride."

Leo Hanver beamed. "My princess," he said.

"But look," Breen said. "This foundation thing. It's great for publicity, and it's a good cause, but isn't it a handful for a couple of kids?"

"Don't you worry about those kids," Hanver pronounced. "The kids will be fine."

Actually, they did a lot better than that.

They lived happily — and adventurously — ever after.

Murder at the End of the World

Deep in a man–blasted cavern in the Colorado Rockies is the headquarters of the North American Air Defense Command. NORAD, ever–vigilant, even in these post–Cold War days, has the mission of safeguarding the United States and Canada from attack by aircraft or missile.

Tucked away in a corner of the cavern is a man who sits patiently at a small desk. On the desk is a machine; hanging before the man's eyes on hooks are three pieces of paper tape with coded messages punched into them.

Twice a week, at pre–determined times, the man takes one of the pieces of tape, and feeds it into the machine. The machine decodes the tape, and automatically channels it into the teletype news wire services that link every radio and TV station in the United States. The stations then read the message, log it, do what they're supposed to do, then go on with their business.

One day, though, in the early 1970's, in the days of Vietnam and protests, of the International Communist Conspiracy and the Military–Industrial Complex, the man at the desk made one little mistake ...

I got to the station at quarter after five. It was cold and drizzly, but then it's *always* cold and drizzly at quarter after five on a Saturday morning in Syracuse, New York. The station was WAER–FM, 88.3 on the dial, the student operated voice of Syracuse University.

I was there to open up the station and to do the Saturday morning news. I did the Saturday morning news for two reasons: one, no other college student was stupid enough to ruin both his Friday night *and* his Saturday just to be on the radio, and two, Saturday morning was the one time the freaks who ran the place let us squares do what we wanted to.

So, while during the rest of the week you might hear somebody oh so mellowly rhapsodizing about the Grateful Dead concert at Manley Field House last week, Bob Cessna, the DJ, Nick Drivas (the sports announcer) and I would be playing my own personal Neil Diamond records and doing five voices each in our weekly installment of "As the Worm Turns," a soap opera written by mutual consent when we all got together in the morning.

WAER in those days was housed in a quonset hut, a pre-fab erected in 1946 to deal with the influx of GI's returning to campus, and still in use over a quarter-century later. You could get into the place with a can opener, if you were determined enough, but I was one of the trusted few who had a key. I let myself in, and walked the length of the building, turning lights on as I went. In the newsroom, I grabbed a metal ruler and began to cut the copy from the UPI radio newswire into individual stories, so they could be mixed with local news into a newscast. If I had time, I'd rewrite the copy.

I was nearly finished when I heard a groan from the lounge.

The lounge was just past the newsroom. It was really just a room in the building that no one had found any use for since 1946. It was called the lounge because it had a coffee machine, a soda machine, and a ratty old couch in it.

There was another groan, then a curse.

I grabbed a bulk-eraser — a electromagnet inside a plastic case with a handle, about half the size of a steam iron, but twice as heavy, and went to check it out.

I threw the door of the lounge open, and punched the light on.

"Son of a bitch!" a voice yelled. I was looking back in the bleary blue eyes of Darrell Pembroke, our program director. Darrell had long, wavy red hair that he couldn't have been prouder of if he'd been a Renaissance beauty. The locks were a part of his anti-establishment image, but they weren't long for this world. Darrell was a senior, and everybody knew that the day after graduation, Darrell was going to show up in an office in his father's factory with his hair cut short and a tie in place. I had made the mistake of mentioning this to him, once.

His reply took the form of a Memo To The Station Staff stating that whether he fought the system from within or without, he would always remain true to the Revolution, and anybody who said otherwise was a fascist.

God, we were young in those days.

Half awake, Darrell produced a brush from somewhere, and started rearranging his hair.

"Good morning, Darrell," I said. "What are you doing here?"

"Samantha's roommate came back from Scarsdale a night early. Had some great shit with her. We smoked it, but then I had to go."

"Don't you have a room?" I asked.

"Yeah. I also have a roommate. I wouldn't give Harry the satisfaction of knowing I didn't spend the night with Sam. What the hell time is it?"

"Five thirty," I said. "Harry's going to be here later this morning, you know."

"He is?"

"Sure," I said. "Sam, too. After the morning show, we're broad-casting the women's rally from Hendricks Chapel. Sam is anchoring; Harry's going to do the audio."

"What kind of idiot makes assignments like that?"

"It was arranged ... before."

Darrell didn't ask me before what. Up until about three weeks ago, Samantha Becker and Harry Londo were an item. I didn't know about her, but Harry had it bad. Since, by some alchemy of personality I had become the Designated Sophomore all the seniors confided their innermost secrets to, I knew, even if nobody else did, that in those free-love, pre-AIDS, anything goes days, Harry was actually thinking marriage.

That might have been where Darrell got the idea to break it up. I didn't like him much, but when he wanted to be, he could be charming, he could be persuasive, and he knew how to fight dirty. He'd done a number on Bob Cessna last spring, acing him out of the Program Director spot that everyone thought Bob had had in the bag.

Anyway, Darrell had moved in on Sam, thereby, I suppose, curing his roommate of any middle-class notions like marriage.

"Oh, God," Darrell said. "Keep him away from me, all right? I don't need soap opera on Saturday morning. I just have to get some sleep."

"What if somebody wants a cup of coffee?"

Darrell pulled a twenty dollar bill out of his pocket and gave it to me. "Here. Order breakfast out for the whole staff. Just let me sleep. I wish there was a lock on the goddam door."

I took the twenty. I'd certainly offer to buy breakfast, but I wouldn't cry if nobody took me up on it. My father worked in a factory, he didn't own one. Darrell could take comfort in thinking of it as a redistribution of wealth.

"Fine," I said. "I'll get back to work now."

"Oh. DeAndrea. Before you go, make sure the monitor in here is turned off, okay? Being awakened is one thing, but being awakened by the tripe you bourgeois assholes put out over my radio station would be enough to kill yourself over."

I worked a knob. "It's off," I said. "Sweet dreams."

I went back to the newsroom, used the bulk eraser to get rid of yesterday's network audio feed, and recorded today's. Then I sat down to write the sign-on headlines for six a.m.

Bob Cessna arrived by the time I was finished. He was a stocky guy, a little shorter than I was, with curly sandy hair and a voice made for middle-of-the-road radio. Bob was from Buffalo; his father was on disability from an accident in the mill. Being program director at WAER would have been a big boost for him toward a good job come June, but it didn't happen. Darrell had decided Bob was too big a square to run the station, and taken steps to see he didn't.

"Morning, Bill," Bob said brightly. I looked at the stack of records he had under his arm. The one on top was Bert Kaempfert.

I grinned. "I should have left the monitor on." Bob asked me what I meant, and I explained.

"Oh, wonderful, wonderful," Bob said. "Maybe he'll throw me off the station entirely." He went into the announce booth and started warming up the transmitter.

I was in the news studio ready to go, about one minute to six, when Nick Drivas breezed in. You know Nick — of all of us, he's made it the biggest, with his network sports anchor slot, and his own talk show. Even then, we could tell he was special. Not the least of it was his ability to come into the station eleven minutes before he was due to go on the air (sports at ten after the hour) and prepare a flawless sportscast. I stuck my head out of the studio and told him about Sleeping Beauty. Nick shrugged. I wasn't sure he would have recognized Darrell if he'd seen him — the sports guys tended not to get involved in station politics, and lucky for them.

Despite the presence of our slumbering leader in the lounge, it was a normal Saturday morning. I did my newscasts on the hour and half hour, Nick did the sports, Bob spun records, we all shmoozed together. That week's episode of "As The Worm Turns" featured a man who slept through a fire, a flood and an invasion from outer space, but we knew we were safe. No one Darrell talked to listened to us.

Harry and Sam came in separately, but within a few minutes of each other, about ten minutes to nine. Harry was medium sized, round–faced guy who had to keep pushing his bangs off his face. Sam was a knockout. Jet black hair, smooth skin (smooth looking, anyway — I never touched it), bright brown eyes, wide, soft (looking) mouth, etc.

There was some bad dialogue ("Uh — hello, Harry." "Uh — hello, Sam.") then I took them to the newsroom to check out the audio equipment. I was in a bit of a hurry (I had a lot of the nine o'clock cast to write), and I forgot to be diplomatic. I told them to try to be quiet, and why. Harry turned white; Samantha looked guilty. There was more bad dialogue, and some wandering around the station. I packed them off to the Chapel to set up.

When I got back to the studio, Bob was grinning. "Opened your big mouth, didn't you? I saw their faces when they went out." I was going to explain, but the red light went on in front of me, and I was on the air.

An uneventful half hour later, I was in that same studio, doing my last full newscast of the day. After that, I'd go down to the newsroom, pull the Emergency Broadcast System test off the wire, do the test, do the ten o'clock headlines, throw it over to Sam at the women's conference, stagger back to the dorm, and go to bed.

The bell on the teletype was going crazy when I got back to the newsroom. Ten rings were the "flash" notification (PRESIDENT DEAD! — that kind of thing), and it always gave the flash notice for the EBS test. The test notice came down the wire at 9:33 a.m. Eastern time on Saturday, and at 9:33 p.m. Eastern time on Sunday. It had occurred to most of us at the station that if the Russians really wanted to take our butts by surprise, they would pick one of those times to attack.

Then I looked at the wire.

Jesus Christ in heaven, they had.

This wasn't the test notice. This thing, purple ink on thick yellow paper read:

HATEFULNESS   HATEFULNESS

THIS IS AN EMERGENCY ACTION NOTIFICATION ... THIS IS AN EMERGENCY ACTION NOTIFICATION ... THIS IS NOT A TEST. REPEAT: THIS IS <u>NOT</u> A TEST. ALL STATIONS WILL PROCEED AS INSTRUCTED IN THE MONTHLY CODE ENVELOPE.

HATEFULNESS   HATEFULNESS

The code envelope was stuck to the newsroom bulletin board with a map pin. I couldn't get the thing open. My fingers were sausages — to limp and too fat to do any good. I finally got it open using the metal ruler.

There were new code words for every day of the month, an activator to start the alert, and a terminator to end it. I found today's date. The activator was HATEFULNESS. The terminator was IMPISH. How appropriate, I thought.

I read the instructions as I ran back to the studios. Bob had just started a record.

"Put me on the air," I said.

He was amiable. "Right after the record."

"Right now, Bob," I pulled the EBS package from its hook in the engineering booth, and ran to the studio. The red light came on just as I got to my seat.

"This," I read, "is an Emergency Action Notification." I couldn't believe how steady my voice sounded, how professional. "This is an Emergency Action Notification. This is not a test. All stations will broadcast Message One, white card. Emergency Action Notification means that an actual emergency has been declared by the President of the United States, and that citizens should monitor authorized radio broadcasts for information and instructions."

This whole bit was repeated. Then I read on. "This station will now leave the air. Citizens are instructed to turn their radio dial until they find a station broadcasting news and emergency information for your area." Then I read the whole card again. I probably would have read the thing over and over until I believed it, but I looked up and saw Bob and Nick's faces staring at me through the glass. I turned off my own mike and left the studio.

"You've got to turn off the transmitter, Bob," I said. We walked, sort of holding each other up, back to the master studio.

"This would be a terrible joke, Bill," Nick said gravely. Without a word, I held up the notification and the list of code words.

"My God," he said. "Oh, my God."

I was only half listening. Facing the end of the world is not good for your manners. I was inside, paying attention to my own thoughts.

They've done it, I thought. The assholes have finally gone and done it. A million years of evolution, then one cloudy Saturday morning, and bam — right back to the caves.

I wanted to talk to my parents, my sisters. Be with my family when whatever was about to hit, hit. I thought of calling them on the phone, but then I thought, no, they might be asleep. Better to go out dreaming than in terror.

I said a silent prayer for them. For me. For everybody.

Then I thought about maybe surviving this mess. There were bound to be some, why not me? As far as I could tell, Syracuse wasn't likely to be a primary target. It was too small a city to be terror bombed, like, say, New York (I thought again of my family), and the nearest military base that I knew of (the Russians were undoubtedly better informed on this than I was, but I was going with what I had) was the missile base way the hell up in Plattsburgh. Closer to Montreal than to us.

All I had to do (all!) was to outlast the fallout to have a fighting chance. A week, two weeks?

WAER was right near the Physics Building, which happened to have three basements. There were vending machines down there, all kinds. Could I break into a bunch of vending machines with my bare hands? Damn right I could. The station was loaded with flashlights and batteries. I could drink the water from the toilets if I had to. At least it was a chance. What else did I need?

Oh, right.

A woman.

Where the hell was I going to get a woman at quarter ten on a Saturday morning with Russian missiles flying? Samantha Becker sprang to mind. At least she was awake. But I didn't want to start day 1, year 1 of the Apocalyptic Age fighting with two other guys over a woman. Besides, Sam thought I was a creep.

It didn't have to be a pretty woman — after today, there'd be a whole lot less competition, around, anyway. Just a good conversationalist and not a whiner.

I thought of a couple of candidates, and was on my way out of the station to try the ace pickup line of all time ("Hey, want to maybe live?") when Bob Cessna stopped me.

"We ought to go tell Darrell about this. After all, he is the program director," he said.

Darrell. I'd forgotten all about him. I sighed impatiently. "Yeah, okay," I said. "Let's make it quick."

Nick was already in the newsroom, looking at the UPI wire, seeing nothing but the third sports roundup. "Come on," he said. "Come on. Who started it? I want to know who to curse with my dying breath."

I smiled at Bob, who smiled back. We knew how Nick felt. I opened the door of the lounge. "Darrell?" Bob said.

"I told you assholes to leave me *alone!* Now shut that door!"

I'd had enough of him. The warheads were undoubtedly homing in by now. "Screw you very much," I told him, and shut the door.

"Shouldn't we —" Bob said.

"To hell with him," I said. "The station's off the air, what is he program director of? If we ever power up again, we can tell him.

"Now, excuse me, I've got something to do. Meet you in the sub-basement of the physics building. Find your own date. Tell Nick."

"What?"

My way was blocked again, this time by Sam and Harry. To see them clinging to each other, you would not have thought that Darrell Pembroke could ever have come between them. Right now, you couldn't have gotten a laundry ticket between them.

"We were monitoring the station over at the Chapel — we heard you go off the air, so we came back," Sam said.

"Was there much panic?"

"We didn't tell anybody," Harry said. "It never occurred to me." He looked guilty. I told him I wouldn't have known what to do either.

"There was hardly anybody there, anyway," Harry said.

"I told them not to have the women's conference on Saturday morning," Sam said.

"Yeah," I said. "Well, this ought to teach them."

Sam gave me a look that suggested "creep" was a flattering word for what she thought of me.

Nick Drivas said, "I've got an idea." Everyone looked at him. "We're citizens, right? Why don't we do what we're supposed to do, and turn the dial until we hear information and instructions?"

We all went down to the newsroom and turned on the radio there.

WSYR was on the air. WHEN was on the air. WNDR was on the air. WOLF was on the air.

"This is ridiculous," Bob Cessna said.

"Saturday morning," I said. "Just a combination DJ/engineer on duty. Even if they've heard the bells, they haven't looked at the wires, yet."

"The world is coming down around our ears, and we're the only ones who know," Harry said. "Who's the EBS station around here, anyway?"

"WFBL," Bob said. "Thirteen–ninety." Nick spun the dial. They were on the air, too.

"I can't believe this," I said. "Look, let's try to call these guys."

"Who?"

"FBL first, but all of them. Let's try to give the public a fighting chance."

Things got pretty confusing after that. Everybody was running from one end of the station to another, looking for phone books, stockpiling emergency supplies, of which there were quite a few. No one at the other stations would answer the phone. Harry, by far the best engineer among us, was trying to figure out if there was a way we could set up a remote and broadcast from shelter, when the worst came. He and Bob started running around the station looking for tools. It was easier not to be scared with something to do. Then came the scream. Then another one.

For a second, I was sure it was the missiles coming in. Then I thought, that's it? Just a scream? No shock wave? No light? No death?

Then another scream came, and I realized it was Samantha. I ran to down the other end of the building. Nick and Harry were already there, Bob was right behind me. Sam was standing in the doorway of the lounge, Harry moved her aside. The rest of us went in.

"I — I didn't know he was in here," Sam said. "I mean, I forgot. I just wanted a cup of coffee."

I remembered I still had Darrell's money in my pocket.

"I opened the door," Sam said, "and there he was."

And there he still was. It looked as if someone had poured a can of thin red paint all over his famous auburn hair. His eyes were closed, or just glued shut with blood, it was hard to tell. The bulk eraser sat in a red puddle on the floor. Even from a distance, it was possible to see the red hairs clinging to it.

So I, the life–long mystery fanatic, made a brilliant deduction. "Somebody *did* this!" I said, exactly as though I thought it possible for a man to smack himself seven or eight times in the head with a heavy weight.

Then I did something slightly more intelligent. I touched his neck. "I think he's still alive."

Bob Cessna said, "He doesn't look it."

Sam let out a little yelp. I ran to the newsroom phone. Behind me, WFBL was playing a Mamas and Papas record. I dialed 911.

I had to wait a good long time before somebody answered.

"I'm calling from the Hill," I said. The Hill was what the townies called the University.

"Where else?" a gruff voice replied.

"I need an ambulance and the police at pre–fab sixteen on campus. There's been an assault and a head injury."

Suddenly he was all business which suited me fine. He asked my name, and I told him.

"DeAndrea?"

"That's right."

"You calling from the radio station up there?"

"Yes, I am."

"You're the one who's got half the teenagers in this town convinced the world is coming to an end? And they're tying up the emergency lines to check?"

"I was just doing what I was supposed to do. I wasn't kidding about that, and I'm not kidding about the ambulance and the cop. A detective, even."

"You'll get 'em," the voice at 911 promised me. His tone implied I'd get a lot more, too.

The flash bell went off again. Instantly, there was a crowd around the teletype.

THIS ENDS THE EMERGENCY ACTION NOTIFICATION. REPEAT, THIS ENDS THE EMERGENCY ACTION NOTIFICATION. RESUME NORMAL BROADCAST ACTIVITIES. THE EAN WAS SENT IN ERROR, IN PLACE OF THE SCHEDULED TEST.

"Hallelujah!" Bob Cessna said. "I'll go sign us back on."

"I knew it had to be something like this," Nick Drivas said.

"Not so fast," I said.

Faces with expressions ranging from anger to nausea looked at me.

"No code word, I said. "The Emergency Action Notification is supposed to stay in effect until we get the official terminator code word."

"That could be just a mistake," Samantha said. "If we keep this up, there'll be panic, and we won't be able to get Darrell taken care of."

"It could also just be the Russians," Harry said. "Trying to confuse everything. And if it's for real, it won't make any difference what happens to Darrell."

"You're forgetting something else," Nick said. "One of us beat in Darrell's head."

There was silence while that sank in. I'd thought something to the same effect as soon as I'd seen the body, and I still had trouble accepting it. Once I did, I started to wonder who it might be. I could tell by the suddenly shifty eyes of my companions that they wondered about it, too.

Bob broke the ice. "Not me," he said brightly. "If I wanted to kill him, I would have done it last spring when he screwed me out of the Program Director's job."

Before anybody else could say anything, the ambulance got there.

A cop showed up right behind them. He bustled into the station all set to give us the stupid–college–kid–practical–joke lecture, but he stowed it when he saw the ambulance guys carrying Darrell's bloody form out of the station.

I took advantage of the silence to ask the paramedic if Darrell had any audio tape about his person.

"Tape? No. Are you crazy? We've got to get this kid to the hospital."

"Just an idle thought," I said, stepping out of the way. A very depressing idle thought.

Officer Conner, to put it mildly, was no genius, but he knew what he was supposed to do — detain the suspects and secure the crime scene for the detectives. Which he did. He used the phone to call for help, locked us all in the newsroom, and mounted a personal guard on the lounge.

We sat around looking at each other.

"Who would have thought," Bob Cessna said, "waiting to die would be so boring."

"He didn't even *believe* us," Sam said. "We showed him the code words and everything. We don't have a chance inside this shack."

More silence. Then Nick Drivas said, "Hey, Bill, why so sad? You're acting like it's the end of the world or something." He laughed alone.

"Do you think Darrell is going to make it?" Sam said.

I shrugged. "The paramedics seemed to think he had a chance."

"If anybody has a chance," Harry mumbled. He reached out and turned the radio back on. WFBL was still playing upbeat MOR. "It's sure going to take everybody by surprise."

"I almost wish it would," I said. I didn't mean it. I was almost amazed at how much I wanted to live, no matter what shape the world was in. What I didn't want to do was live through the next twenty minutes or so.

Then Harry forced the issue. "What was all that about Darrell having some tape on him, Bill?"

I took a deep breath. "I read mystery stories," I said. "I always look for complicated answers."

"What do you mean?" Bob said.

Harry pushed his bangs off his forehead. "Ahh, what difference does it make now?"

"It ought to make a difference," Nick said.

"It's better than sitting and waiting for something to go BOOM!" Bob said.

"If you think you know what happened to Darrell," Sam said, "I'd like to hear it."

"Fine," I said. "Why not. Okay, complicated answers. I suppose we've all been assuming that somebody attacked Darrell during the time we were all milling around, trying to get hold of one of the other stations."

"That's the only time it *could* have happened," Bob said. "Remember? He yelled at us when we tried to tell him the bombs were coming."

"Yeah," I said. "Has it ever occurred to you that it doesn't make any sense?"

"A bunch of idiots in Moscow or Washington or Peking are going to turn the world into a charcoal briquette, and you want *sense*?" Bob demanded.

"That's the *point*," I said. "Why kill somebody when we're all likely to be dead before the day is out, anyway?"

"What else could have happened, then?" Sam wanted to know.

"Darrell could have been brained with the bulk eraser — the only one we've got, remember — earlier. Someone could have set up a tape to chase people away, and rigged it up so that it would play when we opened the door. You're the technical whiz around here, Harry. Could someone have done that?"

Harry rubbed his chin. "I don't know. How could you get Darrell to record the words for you?"

"It was a sleepy growl," Bob said. "Anybody but Sam could have done the voice."

"Well, then, sure. I could have done it. Bob probably could have done it."

"Wouldn't have done Bob any good," I said.

"Why not?"

"It wouldn't give him an alibi. He was here in the station the whole time, including plenty of time *after* we heard the tape. The only one who could have rigged up a gimmick like that and expected to benefit by it was *you*, Harry. You were going to be gone all afternoon with Sam covering the women's conference."

Sam said, "You must be crazy."

"I wish I were," I said.

"What is this shit?" Harry said. "I thought you were my friend."

"I am Harry. I told you, I'm just thinking things through. That's why I asked the paramedics about the tape. Because if there was such a device, it's been dismantled by now, right? But the tape is somewhere in the station. That's why I'm going to suggest to the detectives when they get here that we play every bit of tape in the place. If we don't hear what Bob and I heard, then they have to check it all for blood."

"Blood?" Nick said. "Oh, right."

"Right," I said. "Because in this theory, the bulk eraser, the only quick way to wipe out a tape in this whole place, has been covered with blood since before Sam and Harry left for the chapel. There would have been no way to erase that tape without leaving *some* trace on the tape itself."

Harry was practically smirking. "What happens when they run your tests and don't find anything, wiseass?"

"Oh," I said. "I don't think they're going to find anything."

"You don't?"

"No. It's too complicated. Fun in a mystery story —"

"*Fun*!" Bob Cessna said.

"— but too complicated for real life. For real life, I think it's a much simpler question."

Sam was indignant. "It was rotten of you to put Harry on the spot like that. I don't know —"

"It's all right, Sam," Harry said. He took her hand. She didn't pull away. "What's your question, genius?"

"The question is," I said, "who has a motive that would last past the end of the world?"

Four pairs of eyes looked at me. "Bob? No more station, no more program director, no more jobs after graduation, no more grudge. Me? I didn't like Darrell, but not enough to try to kill him, and certainly not enough to do it when I was going crazy trying to figure out how to save my own life. Nick? If Nick has exchanged ten words with Darrell since he came to the station, I'd be surprised."

"What about Sam?" There was no malice in Nick's voice. He was just asking. Samantha didn't appreciate the distinction. She shot him a look that should have burned a hole through him.

"She has no motive. If she manages to survive, she'll be able to pick and choose even more than she can, now."

"You sexist bastard," she said.

"Guilty," I said. "At least today, I'm guilty. As soon as the idea of surviving this mess came to me, I admit one of the first things I thought about was finding a woman. And to tell you truth, it *still* doesn't sound like a bad idea, if I live. Civilization is likely to be *over* you know? I remember thinking before, one bad morning, and back to the caves."

I turned to Harry. Little beads of sweat had appeared on his forehead. "Is that the way you figured it, Harry?"

"Back to me, again, huh?"

"We never really left you. I wanted to find *some* woman, but you'd already found *the* woman. We've all seen you moping around since she left you and took up with Darrell. We all saw what's going on this morning as a catastrophe, but for you, it was an opportunity, too. Day 1, Year 1 of the post apocalyptic age. A fresh start. You'd save Sam, somehow, and she'd love you again, and everything would be rosy. And just to avoid complications, you'd make sure Darrell wouldn't survive, *whatever* happened."

The teletype jumped to life — the flash bell rang ten times. Bob was closest to it. He got up, tore it off, and brought it to the table. We read it.

IMPISH   IMPISH

THE EMERGENCY ACTION NOTIFICATION IS HEREBY CANCELLED. ALL STATIONS MAY RESUME NORMAL ACTIVITY. THE NOTICE WAS SENT IN ERROR.

IMPISH   IMPISH

"That's the right code word," I said.

Nick said to Harry, "Boy, you'd better hope he survives, now."

Harry was licking his lips. "Sam," he said. "Sam, I —"

"Don't talk to me," she said. She got up and walked away from the table.

"No," Harry said. "No, I won't. I — I guess I'll talk to the cop, instead." He got up and knocked on the door to be let out.

Over the next few minutes, we learned a lot of things. We learned how the guy in Colorado had simply grabbed the wrong tape to feed into the machine. We learned that ninety-nine percent of the radio and TV stations in the United States had failed to notice the Emergency Action Notification, or had ignored it. That included all the stations in Syracuse, New York but one, which was to earn us college kids a commendation. We learned, from a phone call made by Officer Connor, that Darrell would be all right.

I learned a lot of things personally, too. I learned I was brave enough to face the end of the world without going catatonic or running screaming into oblivion. I learned that a lot of people were, maybe most of them, since none of us at the station that day did anything like that.

I learned that civilization is thinner than an eggshell, and it doesn't take much to crack it. I'd felt it starting in myself, saw it happen in Harry.

We were still locked inside the station, and the people who'd shown up for the next shift were locked out. Still, we might as well go back on the air, we decided.

"What'll we say?" Bob asked.

"I'll think of something," I told him. I sat in the news studio and waited for the red light to come on.

"This has been a test," I said. "For the last ninety minutes, this station has been conducting an unintentional test of the Emergency Broadcast System. It needs a lot of work ..."

Bibliography

"Snowy Reception." *Alfred Hitchcock's Mystery Magazine*, June 1979.

"Killed Top to Bottom." *Syracuse University Magazine*, Fall 1989.

"Killed in Midstream." *Cat Crimes III*, ed. Martin Harry Greenberg and Ed Gorman, 1992.

"Killed in Good Company." *Private Eyes*, ed. Mickey Spillane and Max Allan Collins, 1998.

"Hero's Welcome." *San Jose Mercury News*, November 1985.

"Sabotage." *Solved*, ed. Ed Gorman and Martin Harry Greenberg, 1991.

"A Friend of Mine." *Frankenstein, The Monster Wakes*, ed. Martin Harry Greenberg, 1993.

"The Adventure of the Cripple Parade." *Resurrected Holmes*, ed. Marvin Kaye, 1996.

"The Adventure of the Christmas Tree." *Holmes for the Holidays*, ed. Martin Harry Greenberg, Jon L. Lellenberg, and Carol-Lynn Waugh, 1996.

"Prince Charming." *Once Upon a Crime*, ed. Ed Gorman and Martin Harry Greenberg, 1998.

"Murder at the End of the World." Previously unpublished.

Murder — All Kinds

Murder — All Kinds by William L. DeAndrea is set in 11-point Palatino Linotype font and printed on 60 pound natural shade opaque acid-free paper. The cover illustration is by Juha Lindroos, and the Lost Classics design is by Deborah Miller. *Murder — All Kinds* was published in November 2003 by Crippen & Landru, Publishers, Norfolk, Virginia.

CRIPPEN & LANDRU, PUBLISHERS
P. O. Box 9315
Norfolk, VA 23505
USA

Crippen & Landru publishes first editions of short-story collections by important detective and mystery writers. Most books in the regular series are issued both in trade softcover and in signed, limited clothbound with either a typescript page from the author's files or an additional story in a separate pamphlet. Among the authors whose short-story collections have been published by Crippen & Landru are Doug Allyn, Lawrence Block, P.M. Carlson, Hugh B. Cave, Liza Cody, Max Allan Collins, Michael Collins, Brendan DuBois, Susan Dunlap, Michael Gilbert, Joe Gores, Ed Gorman, Jeremiah Healy, Edward D. Hoch, Wendy Hornsby, Clark Howard, H.R.F. Keating, Michael Z. Lewin, Peter Lovesey, Ross Macdonald, Margaret Maron, Patricia Moyes, Marcia Muller, Bill Pronzini, Ellery Queen, Peter Robinson, Georges Simenon, Carolyn Wheat, Raoul Whitfield, Eric Wright, and James Yaffe.

> ☞This is the best edited, most attractively packaged line of mystery books introduced in this decade. The books are equally valuable to collectors and readers. [*Mystery Scene Magazine*]

> ☞The specialty publisher with the most star–studded list is Crippen & Landru, which has produced short story collections by some of the biggest names in contemporary crime fiction. [*Ellery Queen's Mystery Magazine*]

Crippen & Landru offers discounts to individuals and institutions who place Subscriptions for all of its forthcoming publications, either all the Regular Series or all the Lost Classics or (preferably) both. Collectors can thereby guarantee receiving limited editions, and readers won't miss any favorite stories. Subscribers receive a specially commissioned story in a deluxe edition as a gift at the end of the year. Please write or e-mail for more details.

E-mail: CrippenLandru@earthlnk.net
www.crippenlandru.com

CRIPPEN & LANDRU LOST CLASSICS

Crippen & Landru is proud to publish this series of short story collections by great authors who specialized in traditional mysteries. All first editions, each book collects stories from crumbling pulp, digest, and slick magazines, and from collectors and the estates of the authors. Each is published in cloth and trade softcover.

The following books are in print:

    Peter Godfrey, *The Newtonian Egg and Other Cases of Rolf le Roux*, introduction by Ronald Godfrey
    Craig Rice, *Murder, Mystery and Malone*, edited by Jeffrey A. Marks
    Charles B. Child, *The Sleuth of Baghdad: The Inspector Chafik Stories*
    Stuart Palmer, *Hildegarde Withers: Uncollected Riddles*, introduction by Mrs. Stuart Palmer
    Christianna Brand, *The Spotted Cat and Other Mysteries from the Casebook of Inspector Cockrill*, edited by Tony Medawar
    Gerald Kersh, *Karmesin: The World's Greatest Crook — Or Most Outrageous Liar*, edited by Paul Duncan
    C. Daly King, *The Complete Mr. Tarrant*, introduction by Edward D. Hoch
    Helen McCloy, *The Pleasant Assassin and Other Cases of Basil Willing*, introduction by B. A. Pike
    William L. DeAndrea, *Murder — All Kinds*, introduction by Jane Haddam

The following are in preparation:

    Anthony Berkeley, *The Avenging Chance: Roger Sheringham's Casebook*, edited by Tony Medawar and Arthur Robinson
    Joseph Commings, *Banner Deadlines*, edited by Robert Adey
    Gladys Mitchell, *Sleuth's Alchemy: Stories of Mrs. Bradley and Others*, edited by Nicholas Fuller
    Margaret Millar, *The Couple Next Door: Collected Short Mysteries*, edited by Tom Nolan
    T.S. Stribling, *Dr. Poggioli: Detective*, introduction by Arthur Vidro
    Michael Collins, *Slot-Machine Kelly: Early Private Eye Stories*
    Rafael Sabatini, *The Evidence of the Sword*, edited by Jesse Knight
    Philip S. Warne, *Who Was Guilty?: Three Dime Novels*, edited by Marlena Bremseth
    Julian Symons, *Francis Quarles: Detective*, edited by John Cooper
    Lloyd Biggle, Jr., *The Grandfather Rastin Mysteries*